My Second Chance

Middlemarch Shifters 10

Shelley Munro

My Second Chance

Copyright © 2022 by Shelley Munro

Print ISBN: 978-1-99-106310-6
Digital ISBN: 978-0-473-37047-3

Editor: Mary Moran

Cover: Kim Killion, Killion Group, Inc.

Munro Press, New Zealand.

First Munro Press electronic publication October 2016

First Munro Press print publication December 2022

For Paul.

Introduction

Lion shifter Leticia Huntingdon has FIV, the feline version of AIDS. For months she's been in remission, treated by Gavin Finley, the Middlemarch feline doctor. Now the disease has returned. Her feelings for Gavin can't go anywhere because of the FIV, so it shouldn't hurt when Gavin turns to Charlie, the new male cop.

Gavin can't believe how good sex is with Charlie, can't believe he's found a mate. The loving is amazing and hot, but Gavin can't forget Leticia. He wants her in his life. He wants Charlie too. Confusion and jealousy create torrid undercurrents for the trio.

Charlie McKenzie falls for Gavin quickly and can't understand why he's attracted to Leticia. A nightmare changes everything, drawing the three together and bringing new possibilities. A ménage a trois. Raw need and passion brings them closer. If only the disease threatening Leticia's life didn't loom on the horizon...

Chapter 1

Bad News

Leticia Huntingdon scrutinized the hair in her brush and knew the FIV or feline immunodeficiency virus was no longer dormant. A healthy feline shifter didn't lose this much hair during the grooming process. Fear, stark and frightening, kicked her in the gut and her legs trembled so much she thought she'd fall if she didn't sit. She sank onto the bed, the tremors speeding to her hands and her legs.

"Damn," she whispered.

A glance at her wristwatch confirmed she had little time before someone thumped on her bedroom door. The last thing she wanted was to socialize at a birthday party, but if she said she'd prefer to stay at home, her brother Lucas and his partner Saul Sinclair would worry. And she didn't want that. They'd both been so good to her—Lucas leaving the pride in South Africa to stay with her, and Saul and his leopard-shifter friends accepting her without hesitation.

Her gaze drifted to the tufts of blonde hair clinging to the black bristles of her brush and this time anger bloomed, hot and consuming. It wasn't fair. Nothing about this was fair. Her ex-lover, who had given her the disease by raping her and ripping open her shoulder, had never faced justice, his position as a lawyer keeping him safe.

His word against hers.

She'd thought she'd discovered a home in New Zealand, yet the disease, the feline equivalent of HIV in humans, would steal that from her.

No cure.

The two words echoed through her head. Mocking and final. Gavin Finley, the local vet and doctor to the shifters, had told her the prognosis was good, that they might not cure the disease but could manage it. According to him, although she had the disease, the symptoms were mild and only exacerbated by stress. So manage it they had, and pretty well. Thanks to Gavin, her health remained stable, apart from the latest sign. Not so good. Gavin had mentioned the symptoms to look for and losing hair sat at the top of the list along with weight loss and difficulty breathing. A harsh sigh whooshed up her throat, burning all the way.

AIDS. Such a little word. Such a big disease.

Tears obscured her excellent vision, making her reflection waver in the mirror.

A tap sounded on her bedroom door. "Leticia, sweetheart. Are you almost ready? We'll arrive late to Saber's party. We still have to drive to Middlemarch." Saul.

Leticia sucked in a deep breath, fighting anxiety and dredging up anger to hide her fear.

"Bite me. Don't you know you always have to wait on women?" she added, dragging the brush through her hair again and forcing humor into her voice despite the terror curling across her face. "Always in a hurry."

"Sweetheart, I'd love to bite you, but I don't want to upset your brother," Saul countered.

Leticia couldn't help the involuntary smirk when she heard a familiar masculine growl in the background. Lucas. It was all a front. Her brother and Saul were crazy about each other. Mates.

Unthinking, she drew the brush through her hair again. Her heart skipped a beat when she saw more loose strands glinting amongst the bristles. Setting it aside, she picked up a comb. It didn't stop the fall of hair. Apprehension lurched through her mind, her recent weight loss taking on a sinister meaning.

How could this happen almost overnight? Dammit, she'd followed Gavin's instructions, eating healthy foods, vegetables even. Cosseting herself and keeping stress to a minimum. True, things were difficult at work, the pressure of a big case making for long days. She'd thought she was coping.

By the time she finished, her long blonde curls appeared tidier and less. Thin. Too thin. A hat. She'd have to wear a hat. She'd get through tonight and after that...

Well, she didn't want to think about that now. Dying at a young age wasn't something she wanted to dwell on tonight. She shoved the thought aside and stood.

Leticia dressed rapidly, rejecting the black trousers she'd intended to wear in favor of a short red skirt. Tonight, she needed to distract, and bright colors and long legs would do the trick. Deftly, she twisted her hair into a loose knot at the back of her neck. A low-cut red-black-and-cream top covered her upper half and hid the scar on her shoulder from public view. With her makeup already done, all she needed to do was add dangling earrings and a jaunty black hat. She slipped her feet into black slides, the heels giving her three extra inches in height. After grabbing a black clutch and looping the long strap over her shoulder, she pasted on a smile to prepare for the best acting job of her life.

"About time," Lucas said when she strolled into their den. He and Saul stood close, and she knew she'd interrupted a romantic moment. Envy washed through her in a wave, followed by self-pity.

Gavin. Every time she saw him she wanted to jump him. They were compatible. Possible mates.

"Are you sure you don't want me to leave?" Leticia aimed for light and teasing. She surprised herself with her acting abilities, but then she'd had plenty of practice, pretending she cared nothing for Gavin Finley, the shifter doctor. "It looked as if you were having a private moment." She arched a brow, letting the ghost of a smile quiver her lips.

6

Yep, award-winning performance.

"Shut your mouth, brat," her brother drawled, the familiar South African accent bringing a yearning for home. She was home, she reminded herself. The savannah land of the veld was no longer her habitat.

"She needs to get her own man," Saul said, his green eyes glinting with mischief. "Gavin wants you. Why don't you stop running and let him catch you for a change?"

Lucas nodded agreement, and Leticia had to swallow to force back the building emotion. She would not cry. She would not. "There's no magic between us," she said, once again forcing out the lie without flinching or lowering her gaze.

If things had been different, she might have mated with Gavin by now. After meeting him, she'd realized the feelings she'd had for her ex were a pale imitation. *No*. No matter how much she craved the same closeness Saul and her brother experienced, she refused to put Gavin through the trauma of being with her and unable to bestow the mark. One taste of her blood and she'd pass on the FIV virus. Unthinkable to place Gavin under the same death sentence she struggled with on a daily basis.

When she realized both men still studied her she added, "Besides, I've seen how it is between you and Saul. Why would I settle for anything less? Why would Gavin settle for me when we all know he can't complete the mating process? It would be difficult for both of us because we couldn't have a proper feline relationship."

"She has a point," Saul said.

Any other day Leticia would have snapped back a witty rejoinder, thriving on teasing the two. Not today. She turned for the door.

"Emily said there are other single males attending," Lucas said. "Maybe you'll hit it off with one of them."

"Maybe." Leticia kept her reply noncommittal. Let her brother and Saul think there was hope.

She knew better.

Charlie McKenzie stepped outside onto the tiled courtyard in Emily and Saber Mitchell's garden, joining the partygoers who had spilled into the night air. He spotted Gavin Finley over on his left, his heart lurching and his feet heading in that direction almost before he'd decided to give in to his curiosity and the weird attraction he sported for the feline doctor.

Embarrassing. From the moment he'd spotted Gavin a few weeks ago he'd thought of him sexually, the yearning spilling over into explicit dreams that had him waking in a sweat and with a dick hard enough to cause damage. Initially, he'd fought his attraction to Gavin—to no avail. Something compelled him to seek the shifter male, and since Gavin seemed to welcome his company, Charlie had given up his fight. He liked Gavin, and the physical attraction didn't repulse him since he'd experimented in his late teens. Recently, fate had led him to date only women, and in small country town Middlemarch, he'd expected to continue in the same way.

Maybe not.

The shifter community had welcomed him and Laura Adams, the other Middlemarch cop, and he enjoyed the forward thinking of a species some would call beasts. Laura had hooked up with a shifter, so the thought of becoming romantically involved with one didn't perturb him. So far, the feline shifters he'd met were decent, and he was proud to call them friends.

"Charlie," Gavin said, sweeping him into a manly hug before he could speak or avoid the contact.

When their chests touched, Charlie's cock bucked and an electric current surged through his body. A soft groan sounded and, mortified, he realized it came from him.

"Damn," Charlie muttered, realizing this was more serious than he'd thought. He wasn't sure what to do next, where to look. His stomach roiled with nerves and mortification.

Gavin pulled away, his curly black hair falling over his forehead. His green eyes sparkled, crinkles of humor forming at the corners. Gradual heat replaced the amusement. He raised his right hand and brushed his fingers over Charlie's jaw, the rasp a soft sound in the night, barely discernable above the chatter of the other guests. "Good."

Charlie groaned again at the heat in Gavin's eyes, the weight of his fingers now resting on Charlie's shoulder, and moved out of the light into the shadows cast by a large oak. As he hoped, Gavin followed to the private spot.

"You knew?" He shook his head, still unsure of where to look. He ended up scowling at his feet. "That's embarrassing." Perplexed, he glanced at Gavin, apprehension a jumpy sensation hollowing his stomach. "Good?" he demanded, Gavin's words piercing his self-consciousness to make sense.

The dim light screened Gavin's expression, which gave Charlie hope. If he couldn't see Gavin, then the feline wouldn't witness the tinge of color creeping into his cheeks. Memories of an awkward first date came back to haunt him. He'd thought age and experience would get him past discomfort and give him confidence.

Not today. No, right now he possessed the self-assurance of a green kid, panicking about how to kiss without bumping noses.

"It's only embarrassing if I don't return the feelings," Gavin said, his voice a shade huskier than normal. He lifted his hand and stroked his fingers over Charlie's cheek again before letting his arm fall to his side. "And I do, so what are we going to do about it?"

Charlie's body pulled tight, awareness arcing between them, the silence throbbing with possibilities. He cleared his throat. "Damn it, man. Did you have to pick a public place to tell me?"

"I'll be happy to tell you later, in private."

"Are you flirting with me?" Bloody stupid question. The man teased with each sly caress.

"I must be out of practice." Gavin paused a beat. "Yeah, I'm flirting with you. You know how it was between Jonno and Laura?"

10

"Yes." Charlie stirred, shifting his weight from foot to foot, recollecting the atmosphere when the two were in the police station together—the way he'd felt like a voyeur. "You mean the mating thing?" He drew in a sharp breath when Gavin's meaning hit him. "You mean we're mates? That's why I've been jumping out of my skin each time I see you?"

"Yeah." No mistaking his tone for anything but satisfied. Gavin glanced over his shoulder. Charlie followed suit and saw no one was watching them. Gavin turned back to him and, after a slow grin, prowled closer, pushing into Charlie's personal space. Disquiet had Charlie edging back until the tree trunk at his back halted his retreat.

"You're not frightened of me?" Gavin whispered, his breath warm on Charlie's face. "I'm a real pussy cat."

Charlie's fingers curved into Gavin's muscular shoulders, neither holding him off nor drawing him closer. "That's reassuring. I've seen Jonno's teeth. I suspect yours are just as sharp."

"All the better to nibble with," Gavin said with a wolfish smirk.

"I suppose I should thank the gods you're not a wolf."

Gavin barked a laugh. "You fancy yourself in Little Red Riding Hood's shoes?"

"Yeah, must have a fetish of some sort." Amusement faded. "Seriously, what does this mean?" Charlie wanted to know even though he admitted deep down what other people thought wouldn't matter a damn. His desire for Gavin held more power than the thought of public condemnation.

He might worry about the speed of the attraction if he hadn't witnessed Jonno and Laura together along with the other feline couples. To hear them tell the story, the attraction was instantaneous and strengthened by sexual contact. It took a strong person to resist. "The mates' thing between men. How does the shifter community view same-sex relationships?"

"About the same as humans. Some think gays are an abomination while others don't mind. I'm hoping Saul Sinclair and Lucas Huntingdon will come tonight. Emily said she invited them. They're mates." A chorus of welcomes had Gavin glancing at the door. "Speak of the devil. Leticia's arrived."

The way Gavin's voice softened had Charlie frowning, glancing at the doorway.

A tall, slender woman stood with Emily and two men. One male looked like many of the locals—tall with dark hair—while the other man was a big blond. But the woman, she stole his breath. She seemed all legs in her short red skirt. Her low-cut blouse showcased a set of stunning breasts without tipping over into obvious and tacky. Her profile promised beauty, but he couldn't tell what color hair she had because she wore a black hat.

"That's them now. Come on. I'll introduce you. Charlie?"

"Yeah?" He couldn't take his eyes off the woman and wondered if she'd come with anybody. Probably. In his experience, men gravitated to women with her eye-candy appeal.

"Charlie?"

Fuck, what was up with him tonight? He'd just admitted his attraction to Gavin. He was genuinely interested in seeing what happened between them, but this woman...this woman drew him too.

Weird. Plain weird.

He couldn't blame it on alcohol because he hadn't had a single drink. Swallowing his unease, he dragged his attention off the stunner to give Gavin his total concentration. He hoped Gavin hadn't noticed his fascination with the new arrival.

Gavin wore an intense expression, a glitter of arousal darkening his eyes. "Don't bother looking at anyone else tonight. You're coming home with me."

"I'm not a pushover." While Charlie liked the idea, he didn't like orders.

"Not what I meant to imply. My bluntness is so you know where I stand. I want you." Gavin squeezed his forearm before stepping away.

And that was what Charlie wanted. His gaze swept over Gavin's face before darting over his upper body. Like the rest of the Middlemarch shifters, he stood over six feet, a couple of inches taller than he did. Muscle packed his body without making him bulky. Yeah, it wouldn't be a hardship being with Gavin. His cock twitched, reiterating the sentiment.

"How long do we have to stay?"

Gavin smirked. "Long enough to meet a few people and act polite. Sing happy birthday to Saber Mitchell. Two hours tops. Come and meet Saul and Lucas. You'll like them."

Charlie followed Gavin back into the house, taking pleasure in watching the other man move. He prowled yet didn't seem to dawdle, his tight buttocks flexing beneath his blue jeans. A man who knew what he wanted from life, and who bore confidence and charm. Oh yeah, Charlie looked forward to the coming night. At least now that he knew the attraction wasn't one-sided.

"Hey, Saul," Gavin said. "Great to see you. Lucas, how are things?"

Charlie bit back a protest when Gavin gave both men a quick hug. It seemed his...mate...liked touching.

Gavin stepped back. "This is Charlie. He's one of the new cops here in Middlemarch. Oh, and you can trust him. He knows about the feline thing."

"You might trust him," Lucas said. "But that doesn't mean we have to."

Charlie had to concentrate to interpret the South African drawl. They were all staring at him, including the woman. A blonde he saw now that she stood a few steps away from him. Nice. He'd always had a thing for blondes.

Charlie turned his attention back to Saul and Lucas. He thrust out his hand. "That's understandable. You don't know me. But for what it's worth, I like living and working in Middlemarch. For the first time, I've found a home, and I don't want to screw with that." He grinned at Gavin. "It's kinda of funny because neither Laura nor I wanted to transfer here and now neither of us wants to leave."

"Who's Laura?" the blonde woman asked.

Also South African, Charlie discovered.

"Laura is Jonno Campbell's mate. Have you met Jonno?" Gavin asked. "He's friends with Leo and Sly, Saber Mitchell's younger brothers. Charlie, this sexy lady is Leticia Huntingdon, Lucas's sister."

Was it his imagination or was there something between Leticia and Gavin? Charlie narrowed his eyes and decided his instincts were right. It was the way they took care not to look directly at each other. He needed to think about this. Damned if he wanted to catch Gavin on the rebound.

"Hi, Leticia," he said. "It's great to meet you. Would you like to dance?"

She accepted the hand he extended to her, and he managed not to flinch at the jolt of sensation that raced up his arm. What the fuck? That was weird. Taking a deep breath, he slipped his arm around her shoulders and urged her toward the makeshift dance floor in the lounge. The strange electrical current raced along his arm and down his body, coming to rest in his dick.

This time he kept his mouth shut and didn't react, either verbal or physically. He needed to talk to Gavin later tonight about this mate shit because color him confused about the entire situation. While he understood the concept, his body was having problems with the application, telling him to make a move on Leticia.

A slow song started just as they arrived on the dance floor. Charlie gritted his teeth and pulled Leticia into a loose embrace, one that wouldn't cause any offense to those watching but still way too close for his liking. Thank goodness the lighting was low in here because his cock was trying to exert a say about the situation.

"You can come closer. I won't bite," Leticia said with clear amusement.

"What the hell is it with you felines and biting," Charlie snapped. "That's the second time someone has threatened to bite me tonight."

She tipped back her face, and he glimpsed interest in her brown eyes. "Do tell."

"Not likely." He surrendered to his instincts, drawing her closer. It wasn't as if there was a heap of room for dancing. Charlie caught the humor on her face again.

"Something wrong?"

"Are you busy at work?"

Huh? "No more than usual. Why?" Charlie's brows rose in a subtle highlight to his question.

"Because judging by the state of you, you're not seeing much action. I wondered if you were all work and no play." Her downward glance left him in no doubt as to her meaning. In fact, his skin prickled, her gaze lighting a path down his body that led straight to his cock. Blood swished through his veins, pouring in the same direction until he swayed, lightheaded and off balance. Not how a tough cop should act in public.

"That's not polite," he said, fighting to keep his voice even. Not so easy with his ultra-awareness of the woman in his arms and his rampant reaction.

"What? I'm meant to pretend I'm comfortable with that spike digging into me?"

"We don't have to dance together," Charlie said, irritated now rather than embarrassed. With the high heels she wore, Leticia stood nose to nose with him. His gaze dipped a fraction. Mouth to mouth. When he caught himself leaning in, he knew he needed a distraction. "What do you do for a job?"

"I'm a lawyer," she said. "I work part-time at a law firm in Alexandra."

"A lawyer. That explains a lot."

"Oh no. He's gonna start on blonde lawyer jokes." The gentle wit made him shake his head. A woman with a sense of humor. Just the sort he liked. "And you're a cop. We could get a lot of mileage out of that," she added.

A snort of laughter escaped and, grinning, he shuffled her a few steps, coming to a halt when they ran out of floor space. His cock hadn't subsided much, but he figured that could be her punishment. He shouldn't have to suffer alone. Her fragrant perfume filled his lungs each time he breathed—something spicy rather than a floral scent. Sexy. Seductive.

Charlie wasn't sure what to make of Leticia. Gorgeous, yes. She attracted him—yes. But the haunted expression in her eyes,

17

the way her mouth curved into a smile that didn't echo in her eyes. It made him wonder, brought a surge of curiosity and a wave of tenderness.

No, not going there. Tonight he'd made a promise to Gavin—to pursue the attraction between them. He didn't need his head messed up by a woman with problems, not when Gavin filled his mind. Charlie had never thought about something permanent. A cop worked irregular hours and some of the things he'd witnessed made him wonder about ever finding a woman to fit into his life. He snorted. A woman. Just like him to be contrary and hook up with a man.

The thought should have worried him. It didn't. His family might have other ideas—his mother and three older sisters. Too bad. Life was too short to waste on unhappiness.

"You're deep in thought. Have I put you to sleep?"

"Never." He slid his hands down her back and drew her closer to prevent a crash with another couple. The slide of her soft breasts against his chest and her spicy scent sent another zap of pleasure south to his groin. What the fuck was he doing? He stumbled and cursed, glancing across the room in time to see a weird expression on Gavin's face. The man recovered quickly, winking at him. Not jealousy after all. He imagined stripping the man, and a gasp slipped free at the resultant surge of lust. Damn, this party couldn't pass fast enough.

"How do you like Middlemarch?"

"Honestly?" Charlie loosened his hold on her a fraction so they could see each other's faces.

Her brows rose. "I wouldn't have it any other way."

"And you a lawyer," he scoffed.

Her chin lifted in challenge and he couldn't restrain a chuckle.

"There is such a thing as an honest lawyer," she said, a tart note in her voice. "There are just as many rogue cops as there are crooked lawyers."

"Touché."

"Would you mind if we found something to drink instead of finishing this dance? I'm thirsty."

Charlie nodded, noting her paleness. "Why don't you grab a seat over there and I'll get drinks for both of us. What would you like?"

"A fruit juice or something without alcohol," she said.

Nodding Charlie headed for the kitchen.

He found Jonno in there with two men he hadn't met.

"Charlie, this disreputable pair are my friends Joe and Sly Mitchell." He pointed at each so Charlie could differentiate between the two. Charlie was glad of it and mentally added the color of their shirts to their names so he'd remember the correct identity for the rest of the night. Tomorrow all bets would be off because once the pair donned different clothes he wouldn't know one from the other. The brothers were identical as far as he could see, right down to the dimples when they grinned.

"Saber's brothers?"

"The same," Joe said. "We're the well-behaved brothers."

Jonno snorted and Charlie laughed. "Not what I've heard."

19

"Damn, have you been listening to Saber?" Sly asked.

"Nope. Emily," Charlie said.

Joe clutched his heart, his dimple deepening. "Emily? I'm fatally wounded."

"We can't threaten her," Sly said to Joe. "Saber would beat us up."

"We can think of something sneaky for payback," Joe said. "Something embarrassing for her next birthday. A sex toy or something like that. She goes an adorable shade of red."

Sly smirked. "I know just the thing."

Jonno shook his head. "Saber won't be happy if you upset Emily."

"Who said anything about upset?" Joe said. "We're talking embarrassed. There's a difference. Besides, Emily is used to us teasing her. She expects it."

"And it won't hurt to see the speechless expression on big brother's face either," Sly pointed out.

Charlie could tell the brothers loved Emily, even as they discussed various plans with Jonno. "Is there something nonalcoholic to drink for Leticia?" he asked Jonno.

"Emily keeps orange juice in the fridge." Sly reached past his brother and pulled out a carton of juice, handing it to Charlie. Jonno passed him a glass.

"Is Leticia involved with anyone?" Charlie asked, curious despite his agreement with Gavin. He shoved aside his discomfort at lusting after two people at the same time. Just curiosity, he told himself even as he acknowledged the lie. He could take either of them back to his house tonight with a sense of satisfaction. What the hell did that make him?

"No, Leticia hasn't been well," Joe said.

Charlie thought about her paleness. "What's wrong with her?"

Sly shrugged. "Some virus that shook her. I think she's okay now. In fact I thought I might ask her out."

"Back off," Charlie growled. "I have first claim."

Joe sniggered. "It's the quick and the dead around here."

The pair reminisced about the Middlemarch dance that had started them all on the path to matrimony while Charlie struggled to deal with the confusion rioting through his body. He didn't understand the weird feelings, the attraction to two different people at the same time.

Puzzling over the matter, he listened halfheartedly to the recollections. Saber had fallen first followed by Felix and Leo. Joe and Sly were the only single Mitchell brothers left. As much as Charlie would have liked to hear more, he grabbed a beer for himself, picked up the juice and headed back to Leticia.

When he arrived, he found her sitting with Emily. He handed over the glass of juice, noting the color had returned to Leticia's cheeks.

Emily patted Leticia's arm and stood. "It's time for the cake. I'll leave you two together while I find Saber."

Charlie glanced at his watch, surprised at how much time had passed since his arrival. He'd spent time with Jonno and Laura, chatted to Felix, discussed rugby with Leo and the stopping power of various weapons with Isabella. Then this emotional crap and struggling to find his balance with Gavin and Leticia had filled the rest of his evening.

Interesting times.

Emily Mitchell left Charlie and Leticia and wound through the crowded room in search of her mate. Initially, she'd planned on having a party at Storm in a Teacup, her café in the township of Middlemarch. Saber had pre-empted her and requested a family dinner at home for his thirtieth birthday.

She grinned, recalling his comment about the big birthday cake. "Was she trying to send them into a sugar coma?"

Her mate had sensed there was something afoot. The sneaky feline had thought he'd bested them, but after discussion with her sisters-in-law and the members of the Feline council, she'd adapted the plan and everyone had arrived after their family dinner.

She spotted Saber, speaking with Sid, one of the council members. Saber lifted his head, as if he sensed her presence, and a slow, heated smile curled across his lips. He winked and her heart did a little skip. She had a special present for her mate. A very special present.

Saber said something to Sid and strode across the room toward her. Their family and friends parted as if by magic, and he reached for her hand. Strong fingers, slightly callused, curled around hers. He tugged and she followed as he led her along the passage to their bedroom.

"Saber! What are you doing? We have guests. It's time to cut the cake."

"They won't miss us for a few minutes."

He opened the door and pulled her inside, closing the door behind them. Then his mouth was on hers, halting her next protest dead on her lips. His scent wound through her and her entire body softened at the sensual assault. She curled her arms around his neck and clung, so happy she didn't know if she could contain her joy.

When Saber pulled back, they were both breathing hard. He cupped her face and grinned down at her. "I love you, Emily Mitchell."

"Saber," she croaked. She coughed to clear her throat. "Are you mad about the surprise party?"

"Of course not, kitten. I've had a lovely time. Family. Friends. Presents. A big-arsed cake."

She giggled, then sobered, every particle of her knowing that this was the right time to give Saber her gift. "Saber, I have to tell you something."

"What?" His expression sharpened.

"No, it's nothing bad."

His features relaxed. "What then?"

"I'm certain we're pregnant."

He froze before delight spread across his face. "I think we are too."

"What? Wait, you knew? How?"

"Your scent has been different for the last week. I doubt if anyone else has noticed yet but they will. Make an appointment to see Gavin this week."

Emily wrinkled her nose, fighting the urge to pout. "I can't believe you knew."

"Hoped, kitten. Hoped. I'm so pleased."

She grinned her excitement, her happiness digging into her cheeks. "I am too. We'd better join our guests before they send out search parties."

"Wait, I wanted to give you a present," Saber said.

"It's not my birthday."

"The present is for my benefit too."

"Okay." Excitement bubbled through her. A baby. She and Saber were going to be parents.

"Remember that holiday you wanted. The week in Rotorua and one in Taupo."

"Yes."

"We leave next week for a month. We're flying to Auckland, hiring a car and making our way down to Wellington where we'll jump on a flight back to Dunedin."

"Saber! Are you sure? You don't like flying. And what about the café? Saber, it's too long. I can't leave for that long."

"London has agreed to take over cooking duties for a month. Isabella and Tomasine are taking care of staffing, and I believe Ramsey will be here to help London," Saber said, referring to the teenage leopard shifter who now lived with his brother Felix and his family. "Felix and Leo are in charge of the farm. And the council—well, they'll have to take care of themselves."

Emily smiled at him through happy tears, her heart aching with pleasure. He wasn't a happy flyer, yet he'd done this for her. "We're going on holiday."

"We're having a baby."

Emily threw her arms around his neck and kissed him again. They didn't surface until someone thumped on the door.

"Emily, Saber, it's time for the cake," Isabella said in a stern voice. "Don't make me come in there."

"Saber is blocking the door." The words emerged with a side of smug.

"If there weren't non-family members around, I'd prove to you I could get in there, even though your lug of a mate is leaning against the door." Now it was Isabella who sounded smug. "You know I can do it in the blink of an eye."

"We'll be there in one minute," Saber promised, and Isabella retreated with another threat if they didn't keep their promise.

Emily lifted her right hand to brush the tips of her fingers over his cheek. "Are you ready for off-key singing?"

They shared a grin and hand in hand, headed back to join the party.

Silence fell as Saber led Emily into the main lounge.

"Ah, there you are, lad," Sid said.

Agnes Paisley, one of the female members of the Feline council, stood at Sid's side. Instead of her normal prune expression, she wore a happy smile that echoed in her feline-green eyes. "Sid has something to say," she said, and even her querulous tone held more humor than normal.

Saber nodded, keeping his mate's hand in his.

"Friends and family," Sid began. "Some of us have known Saber Mitchell since he was a lad, a wee kitten with a mischievous bent and a nose for trouble. He—"

"Really?" one of his twin brothers shouted from the back. "Saber, you lied to us."

"He told us we were naughty and should follow his good example," his second twin brother called to a ripple of laughter.

Sid held up his hand. "Now, now. It's the nature of a feline male. We're all trouble until a good woman tames us."

"That's true, kitten," Saber whispered in Emily's ear while Sid entertained their guests with tales of his exploits. "I was waiting for you." An understatement. Emily had changed his life—changed all their lives—for better.

"Shush," Emily whispered, her breath warm against his ear. "I want to hear about you being naughty."

"I rapped his knuckles many a time," Agnes said. "It's no wonder Janie McGregor moved the instant she was old enough to leave. Saber terrorized her with frogs in her desk, bugs in her locker and the tip of her plait was pink for two months."

"What about when he was learning to drive," Ben, another council member, added. "I thought we'd have to send Herbert to therapy."

"Uncle Herbert said I was a good driver," Saber said, indignant. Although he had to own to terrorizing Janie. Her squeals were so loud. He and his friends had wagered on who could make her screech the loudest.

"He lied, lad." Sid lifted his hand and once the laughter died down, he continued. "While you were a naughty child, you came into your own after we lost Herbert. You're a credit to him, Saber, and I know he'll be watching over you and your brothers with misted eyes. You make us proud with all you do for our community."

Saber opened his mouth to speak, but nothing emerged. He pressed his lips together, so he didn't resemble his niece Sylvie's goldfish, and realized his eyes had misted. Must be a family trait.

"We had a whip around and would like to give you this to enjoy during your upcoming holiday."

Saber accepted a white envelope from Sid along with a quick embrace.

"Open it, lad. Tell everyone what is inside," Sid prompted.

Saber opened the flap and pulled out a single sheet of paper. Emily peered past him and gave a squeak. She bounced up and down on her toes, clutching his arm for balance.

"It's a voucher for a two-night stay at The Chateau in the Tongariro National Park. Thank you." Saber lifted his head and scanned the smiling happy faces.

"Oh, this is brilliant. I've never visited The Chateau. It's such an iconic hotel. Thank you for Saber's birthday present," Emily exclaimed.

"It's time to cut the cake," Tomasine, his brother Felix's mate, said. She pulled out a box of matches and expertly lit the thirty candles.

"Make a wish," someone shouted.

Saber frowned.

"What's wrong?" Emily asked.

"I don't know what to wish for. I have everything I want," Saber whispered.

Her beam widened, and his chest ached with the wave of love engulfing him in that instant.

"Wish for world peace. Go on. Blow."

His bossy mate. He grinned, wished that their friends and family experienced the same happiness and satisfaction in their lives that he did every day and blew out all thirty candles to an off-tune rendition of happy birthday.

"Happy birthday, dear Saber! Happy birthday to you!" everyone chorused.

Yep, no doubt about it, Saber thought. Something about the feline gene killed off singing talent, but he grinned as wide as everyone else.

This day was one to treasure.

After uncovering his aching ears—stilling ringing from the horrendous singing—Charlie's skin prickled with the weight of a stare and glanced up to intercept Gavin's intense gaze. With a jerk of his head, Gavin indicated it was time to leave. Charlie nodded, struck with the same excitement and lust he saw in Gavin's face.

He slipped through the crowd to speak with his hosts.

"Thanks, Emily. Saber." Charlie finished the last of his beer and set the bottle aside. "I need to leave since I have an early start in the morning. I told Laura I'd open up shop. It was a great party." He nodded to Leticia who stood beside Emily. "It was nice to meet you, Leticia, even if you are a lawyer."

Leticia smiled as he meant her to and watched him stride across the room, taking in his fit appearance and the muscular body beneath the clothes. He kept his blond hair short, shaped to his head. Pale blue eyes had alternately filled with teasing or radiated sharp intelligence during the time she'd spent dancing with him while the light covering of stubble on his cheeks had made her itch to touch. She sighed. Sexy blue eyes were a weakness, especially when coupled with a natural smile. Not even the small scar running from his eyebrow to the top of his cheekbone detracted from his appeal.

Imagination came into play as she mentally removed his clothes. First, she'd strip off the casual cotton shirt that picked up the blue of his eyes, unfastening the buttons one at a time to let the tension build. When the shirt hit the floor, she'd run her hands over his chest, exploring the dips and curves of his pecs with the pads of her fingers. Then she'd turn her attention to the dark-wash jeans he wore, unfastening them at the same slow pace until he was almost naked. That was assuming he wore something underneath his jeans. Hmm, a question to ponder.

"Nice arse," Emily said.

"Yes." Leticia started, realizing she was staring at said backside and that Emily shouldn't be. She turned back to her friend and fixed her with a mock glare. "I'm going to tell on you. Saber wouldn't like you ogling other males' butts."

Emily shot a quick glance in her mate's direction. "But it's so nice. Besides, I wasn't the only one looking."

"He's human," Leticia said, tapping her fingernail against the frosty surface of the juice glass.

"You shouldn't hold that against him. Some of the best people are human."

"Emily," Leticia said, embarrassment flooding her cheeks. "Sometimes I forget you're human rather than feline. You smell feline and act it too."

"I smell feline?"

"Yeah."

Emily's brows rose. "Should I switch my soap?"

"No." Leticia sniggered. "It's an attractive scent, sort of wild and green."

"That's a relief. For a while there I thought I might have a litter box scent."

A surprised laugh erupted from Leticia. "I'm sure someone would've told you before now. No, I think it must have something to do with your mark and because you associate with felines so much."

"Interesting. I know I heal better than I used to, and my eyesight has improved. I don't rely on my glasses as much. My instincts are better too, when I think about it. Have you met Laura? She's the other Middlemarch cop and is Jonno's mate."

"No, I haven't met either of them."

"Let's find them. I'll introduce you. Laura is human. I want to know if she smells different to you."

"Sure. I'd love to meet them." Leticia followed Emily through the crowded room. A human. Leticia considered Charlie. She'd thought Gavin was the one for her, but Charlie made her hormones stand up and salute. And the interesting thing was he'd experienced the same attraction.

A human. Was it possible?

Although the disease had taken a turn for the worse, maybe she could experience closeness and friendship again. For a long time the rape had made her loathe herself and she'd had to deal with the aftermath. But she'd talked to Saul. He'd made her realize she wasn't to blame. Saul had helped her recall the good times she'd spent with men, those she'd gone out with and the ones she'd slept with before the rape.

Gavin had tempted her, but she'd remained aloof because she hadn't wanted to infect him with FIV. A human couldn't catch FIV from her or any other cat. For the first time in

31

months, a flicker of hope rippled through her. Although part of her ached for Gavin, perhaps it was possible to experience emotional closeness again with Charlie before she succumbed to the disease.

Chapter 2

Seduction

When Charlie walked outside, he found Gavin leaning against his car, a shadowed figure barely discernable until he shifted his weight. Charlie glanced over his shoulder and couldn't see anyone else.

Alone. With no audience, he could give in to temptation, the urges that had his gut tied in a knot. Nothing to stop him stroking Gavin, touching the way he wanted to touch.

"What took you so long?" Gavin asked.

Without breaking stride, he walked up to Gavin, stopping close enough to feel the body heat coming from the feline male.

"I needed to say goodbye to Emily and Leticia." He studied Gavin, and with heart thudding, leaned in to steal a kiss. Their lips slid together, warm mouths caressing and exploring. Heat. Pleasure. Charlie sighed. The kiss surpassed his expectations. So right...not enough.

The need for intimacy, greater body contact pushed at him despite his earlier crisis of doubt. Damn, a car park wasn't the place to do what he wanted. He'd have to content himself with a kiss. Charlie nibbled Gavin's bottom lip in a silent request for him to open. When he did, Charlie took the kiss deeper, savoring the faint taste of beer and the seductive heat of Gavin's mouth. Their chests brushed and Gavin cupped his butt, drawing their hips together until their groins rubbed. Frissons of tension rippled through him, stealing his breath and making his heartbeat race.

Gavin gripped him in place, not that Charlie would have moved an inch if he could, and ground their cocks together.

"Damn, Gavin." A gasp whooshed up his throat as he lifted his head to stare. A grin bloomed on his face when Gavin chuckled. The friction of their bodies sliding together slayed him. So good, and yet it was only the beginning, the promise of more, of something better shimmering between them. The jolt settled in his balls with a faint sizzle. Spirals of smoke wouldn't have surprised him. Unable to resist, he rocked his hips against Gavin, savoring the rough resistance of denim against his groin.

"This would be so much better if we were at my house," Gavin said in a thick voice. "With privacy."

Charlie barked a laugh before brushing a kiss on Gavin's jaw. The rough sensation of stubble abraded his lips brought home the fact he was kissing a man. The reality didn't change his mind about going with Gavin. He wanted this. "Yeah, I'd hate someone to call the cops because of lewd behavior or indecent exposure."

"All the Middlemarch cops are at the party," Gavin said, his eyes twinkling and glowing in a weird manner, reminding him of cats. Funny that. "We might luck out."

"I'm not going to risk it." The idea of the head brass calling him on sexual misconduct was enough to make him agree to shift this party. "I'll follow you home."

Gavin nodded, his gaze watchful. Measuring his reaction. "You won't change your mind?"

Hell no. "No, I want this. I've been thinking about it since the first time I met you." Nothing less than the truth.

"No kidding?"

"No kidding," Charlie said, admitting the truth. Each meeting with Gavin had fueled his fascination, and that had morphed to desire. Need. "I'll see you soon. Actually, I might stop by my place and grab a uniform for tomorrow."

"You want to stay the night?"

"You have a problem with that?" Charlie countered, his eyes narrowing while he waited for Gavin's reply.

Gavin pressed a swift kiss to Charlie's lips before pushing him away. "No problem at all. I'll enjoy waking up with you. Sometimes it's lonely living by myself."

"I'll see you in about quarter of an hour."

"I'll leave the door unlocked," Gavin said before walking away.

Charlie watched until he blended with the night then circled his car and pulled his keys from his jeans pocket. For the first time in months excitement pulsed through him. This thing with Gavin seemed right.

He'd heard about the feline mating process from Laura and Jonno and observed the other feline couples. While the concept of belonging or surrendering to another person might upset some, to him it seemed secure and enviable. No way did he want to end up like his mother. She was on her third marriage, each one meant to last forever. They never did. After tears and tantrums, his mother moved on to another man. Another marriage. Growing up in an atmosphere like that had bred caution into Charlie, yet this time certainty replaced wariness. He hadn't even had sex with the man or taken part in many getting-to-know-you conversations. What should have been unnerving only intrigued him. For once, Charlie wanted to jump blindly and see where the interesting situation took him.

Despite his fascination with Leticia.

He stilled, thought about the blonde, then pushed her from his mind and climbed into his vehicle.

The drive to the police-owned house where he lived took ten minutes. Charlie gathered his shaving gear, a change of underwear and socks, his work boots and a clean uniform. He also grabbed a bottle of whiskey and headed back to his car, anticipation humming through him.

As promised, Gavin had left the door unlocked. Charlie stepped inside, carrying his uniform in a suit bag and the rest of his stuff including the whiskey bottle in a daypack. A pair of black boots stood by the door. Charlie removed his shoes and socks. He flicked the lock to discourage visitors from walking in without announcement before following the sultry notes of a saxophone.

Charlie found Gavin in a room off the kitchen. The light of two lamps pierced the darkness with a warm glow. Mismatched furniture—two brown leather chairs plus a green couch dressed the lounge room. Charlie could see Gavin kicking back with a beer to watch television. Magazines on farming and animal medicine littered the surface of a glass-topped coffee table. A large screen television hung on one wall while a stereo system filled another corner. Several plants—Charlie wasn't up on green things and didn't know their names—perched on a shelf. Unlike many bachelor pads he'd visited, the plants here were green and healthy, the room clean.

"Do you fancy a whiskey?" Charlie slung the suit bag over the back of a scuffed leather chair and set the daypack beside it.

"My mind is made up. I don't need liquid courage."

"What do you want?" Charlie asked, his gaze intent as he searched Gavin's face. The desire he saw there seared straight to his cock. He took half a step toward Gavin before halting. Maybe he'd wait for an answer before he attacked the other man and ripped off his clothes.

"I want hot, naked sex. I want you." Gavin regarded him steadily, the beginnings of a smile curving the corners of his mouth. "If that scares you—"

"It doesn't scare me." Charlie interrupted him midsentence. "But I'd like to know one thing. How can you be so sure I'm the one for you? How do you know?"

Gavin stood and unfastened his shirt, one button at a time. He watched Charlie the entire time, his green eyes glowing, the color deepening. "It's a gut instinct. I've spoken with other shifters and asked how it was for them. Experiences differ but most said the minute they saw their mate, they knew. There's a driving instinct to touch and a high state of sexual arousal when you're around the other person." He undid the last button and shrugged his shoulders so the cotton shirt slid down his arms. "It's difficult to resist the lure, although some felines do for reasons known only to themselves."

"People walk away from this?" Why would anyone want to resist? Charlie stared at Gavin. Sensations and emotions bombarded him from every direction. And need... So much need.

A compulsion inside screamed at him to act. He trembled, transfixed by the light hitting Gavin's muscular chest. It was almost hair-free. Charlie's fingers tingled with the urge to touch, to trace his fingers over the smooth muscles and flat nipples. He'd stroke and tongue them until they pebbled and soft, needy sounds escaped from Gavin. He wanted to give in to the *thing* building between them. Urgency simmered through him, demanding action. Instead, he forced himself to wait, knowing the delayed gratification would make for spectacular lovemaking. For both of them.

"Yeah, it's happened. And from what I hear, when you're making love the urge to mark your partner can be overwhelming."

"That right?" Charlie's gut lurched and the fleshy spot between neck and shoulder on his right side itched. Memories crowded his mind, dampening some of his driving sexual desire for Gavin. "When Jonno marked Laura it was painful."

Gavin shrugged. "The marking process normally takes place during lovemaking. It's not painful then. Jonno had no choice. It was either that or lose Laura."

Yeah. Charlie remembered vividly with Laura's pained screams fresh in his memory. But Jonno loved Laura, and honestly, Charlie would've made the same choice to save someone he cared about. He scrutinized Gavin, measuring his words for truth. A breath eased out when Gavin never flinched. Tense muscles relaxed, and he realized he trusted the feline.

Even with pain involved, he'd face it without hesitation. "And you think we're mates?"

"I know we are. Can't you feel the compulsion? All I can think about is fucking you."

"Fucking implies lust." Charlie enjoyed lust and quick, hard fucks as much as the next man, except this thing with Gavin seemed different. *More*.

He raked an agitated hand through his hair. Hell, was he buying into the mates thing or not? Charlie didn't know what to think. Maybe he should give in to the driving need? Go with the flow? Unsure, he concentrated on Gavin, mesmerized by

39

the sensual, confident manner as he unbuckled his belt and unbuttoned his jeans. Doubts didn't plague him.

The whine as the zipper teeth released sounded extra loud to Charlie's ears, drawing his attention again while the bronzed flesh displayed by the parted jeans left him breathless. Wanting. The discernable bulge was also an attractive proposition. His tongue stroked over his bottom lip.

"Fucking also implies hunger and desperation. Charlie, the first time might be quicker than I'd like but my heart *is* involved here. Never doubt it. I haven't stopped thinking about you since I first saw you." Gavin studied Charlie. "I've had weeks to think about this. I hesitated because I wasn't sure. Until I noticed you watching me." Satisfaction throbbed in his husky voice.

He meant it. Gavin wanted *him*.

Charlie sucked in a hasty breath and held it when Gavin slid his jeans over his hips to reveal a pair of tight black boxer briefs. His erection strained the fabric in a noticeable bulge.

Charlie found the strength to wrest his gaze away from Gavin's groin to look him in the face. The blue shirt Charlie wore stuck to his clammy skin while his jeans did a real restraining number on his expanding cock. "I'm overdressed here. Not to mention constrained." He unfastened the first button of his shirt but Gavin stayed him with a few words.

"Wait. I'd like to undress you. Last night I dreamed about dancing with you."

Charlie nodded, the mischief lurking in Gavin's eyes telling him there was more to the story.

"You looked very sexy in your police uniform while I wore nothing but a smile."

A snort escaped Charlie. "If you think I'll mess up my one clean uniform, you have rocks in your head."

"My fantasies are flexible." The strains of a ballad replaced the saxophone, the singer asking his lady friend about gettin' it on. A dimple flashed beside Gavin's mouth when his smile widened to a dangerous smirk. "Perfect background music for what I have in mind."

"You're not naked," Charlie pointed out.

"We have all night. Let's try to keep things slow. It will be better if we can." He stepped close and Charlie's arms wrapped around him. They were of a similar height, and for Charlie, it was like two pieces of a jigsaw puzzle slotting together. Perfect. The only thing that might be better was if they were skin to skin.

"I've never danced with another man before," Gavin added.

"You have had sex with another man?"

"Yeah. I went through a wild stage at university when I experimented."

"How wild?" Charlie asked.

"Let's just say I had plenty of friends. Felines don't catch sexually transmitted diseases, but I always practiced safe sex, so I didn't stand out as weird."

"You don't think gays are weird?"

Gavin chuckled, the sound rich and full of amusement. "Nah, it's bisexuals who are the strange ones."

"That would be me then." Charlie shuffled a few steps, the brush of their limbs sending urgent messages to his groin. Right about now he would've loved to remove his jeans. "I haven't slept with anyone, male or female, for a while. Safe is my middle name."

"How long is a while?"

The warmth of Gavin's lips against his neck made it difficult to think. How long had it been? "About four months," Charlie murmured. Damn, the heat of Gavin's body and his scent—something citrusy and underlying man—was doing a number on his restraint.

All he could think of was the next step. The pleasure of intimate contact. Instead of following his instincts to rip off his clothes and jump Gavin, Charlie focused on driving him crazy instead. More than one way to tease a cat. He ran his hands down his broad back, finally dropping them to cup Gavin's buttocks. At the same time, he ground his groin into Gavin, closing his eyes at the jolt of pleasure. The tension between them exploded, masculine groans and harsh breathing interspersing the lyrics of the song.

Charlie's balls drew tight, and he thrust Gavin away, desperate to regain control of his unruly body yet running low on self-discipline. "I can't do this."

Gavin paled.

"Aw, shit. No! I mean I want you desperately but I can't go slow." Charlie ripped off his shirt and scrambled out of his jeans. He yanked down his boxers and almost groaned with relief.

Naked, he prowled up to Gavin and stopped a foot away. His brows rose in silent question. "I'm out of patience."

"And willpower by the looks." Laughing, Gavin held out his hand, and when Charlie took it, he led him from the lounge, tugging him down a dark passage. He pushed open a door and drew Charlie after him.

Charlie went without fighting, anticipation throbbing through every inch of his body. A sharp yank on his arm had Charlie flying through the air. A lamp flicked on. He landed on the bed with a soft grunt, bouncing once before Gavin grabbed him. Although Charlie had imagined them skin against skin, his mind hadn't done justice to the sensation. His groin throbbed as he ground his erection against Gavin's warm thigh. Already pre-cum leaked from his tip and a heady sense of anticipation filled him. Gavin's hands swept across his back and downward to rest on his rump. Charlie clenched his butt muscles, tensing at the thought of the coming pleasure.

One moment Charlie sprawled on top of Gavin and the next, he viewed the world from a different perspective. Gavin moved without warning, his feline strength giving him an advantage. With his arms he caged Charlie, holding him prisoner. For a second Charlie thought about protesting before deciding he couldn't lose. Instead, he waited for Gavin's next move with heightened awareness skittering between them.

Charlie licked dry lips and grinned at Gavin's soft curse.

"You're not making this easy on me." Gavin nuzzled his neck, warm lips lingering against his skin.

"I'm a desperate man. Why should I make it easy when I know there's pleasure ahead for both of us?" Charlie relaxed into the mattress, turning his head in silent permission for Gavin to explore further. Charlie's heart drummed against his ribs when Gavin's lips and a hint of teeth nibbled down his neck and headed for his shoulder.

"You have no idea of the payback I could exact from you," Gavin warned, the twinkle in his green eyes belying the forewarning in the words.

A sharp jolt of pleasure shook Charlie when Gavin bit a fraction harder. His groan was a dark sound. A plea for more. It had never been like this...an avalanche spinning out of control. Hell, they'd barely started and his balls ached as if they'd explode at the smallest amount of stimulation.

"Is that the marking site?" he asked, panting against the urge to beg Gavin to bite. Gavin had implied restraint was necessary and instinct could take over if a couple wasn't careful. Now he believed. He understood the driving need to claim because the dark wanting swirled through him, driving him to tease and seduce. To take Gavin as his mate. Awe filled him at the magical bond flowing between them.

"Yeah. Damn, I didn't realize how difficult it would be to stop or I'd have steered clear." Gavin lifted his head, his breathing coming hard and his eyes shining in the eerie glow Charlie had noted before. "I want to bite you so bad."

"We haven't even started with the good stuff yet," Charlie said.

"I know." Gavin seemed to force himself to move away from Charlie's shoulders. He trailed kisses down his chest, taking small bites from his pecs. "There are lots of things I'd like to do to you, ways I crave you." He nipped. Charlie hissed, enjoying the attention, the combination of pleasure and pain. He slipped his hands over Gavin's back. Muscle packed the man's body. Working as a vet and feline doctor kept him in great shape.

With each touch hunger bounced between them, razor-sharp. Charlie arched his body against Gavin in blatant invitation. He craved release, to beg Gavin to hurry yet contrarily he wanted to relax and enjoy every kiss and touch because instinct told him the loving between them would be way beyond anything he'd experienced before.

Gavin continued to tease, dipping his tongue into the indentation of his bellybutton. In silence thick with sensual tension, Charlie dug his fingers into Gavin's dark hair and tried to control his breathing. Then Gavin moved lower. He ran a finger down Charlie's shaft from tip to root. Charlie fought a girlie whimper. His dick jerked. When Gavin repeated the move along the prominent vein on his underside, his breathing went shallow and Charlie realized he gripped tufts of Gavin's hair in his fists. Hell, if he pulled any harder, he'd make the other man bald. He clenched his thighs together and loosened his hold on Gavin's hair, trying to relax and ignore the ache in his balls.

"You like that."

"I'm fighting the need to grab your head and direct your mouth straight to my cock." The hoarse note in Charlie's voice made him sound like the crazed criminal he remembered investigating in Wellington. He cleared his throat, relieved to hear Gavin's soft laugh.

"I'm trying to go slow, to make it good."

"Already know it's gonna be good," Charlie said. "I need you to handle the goods. Action. No more talk."

Gavin's hand moved past his groin to rest on one of Charlie's thighs. "Part your legs for me."

Charlie followed the order without hesitation despite a preference for the dominant role in his sexual relationships. He spread his legs, canting his hips upward at the same time in silent entreaty. Gavin glanced at him and their gazes connected. Held. Silent messages and promises passed between. Then Gavin dipped his head, and he took the tip of Charlie's cock into his mouth. Heat flared out of control in Charlie. He panted and his hips jerked, pushing his shaft deeper into Gavin's mouth.

Gavin lifted off him and Charlie couldn't help the groan of complaint. Gavin smiled. "Just a little teasing. Don't come. I want you to wait until I'm inside you."

"Bastard," Charlie said even though he grinned. "Do you have lube? Condoms?"

"I have both, although we don't have to use condoms. I told you I can't catch anything."

"Or pass anything on to me?" Charlie asked, even though he'd already decided to bareback. From what he'd learned about felines from Laura and Gavin, he knew he could trust what they said.

Gavin moved up the bed to lean over Charlie. "I swear you'll never pick up any sexually transmitted diseases from me." Once again, his green eyes shone with truth.

"Okay. How do you want to take me?"

"I'll take you from behind."

Not his favorite position. He liked to see his lover's face, see the raw emotions when they were in the grip of passion. "I'll choose next time."

"Deal." Gavin bent to kiss him, his tongue slipping into Charlie's mouth and stroking back and forth while their engorged cocks, trapped between their bodies, brushed together with enough friction to make him want to hurry. His cock wept, and judging by the dampness on his stomach, Gavin's was doing the same thing. Charlie trembled and the sharp pleasure in his balls told him he wouldn't last much longer. Talk about embarrassing.

"Now. Please. Damn, it's never been like this before. I'm so bloody desperate."

"It's the mate thing."

Charlie snorted, shivering at the stroke of Gavin's finger down his throat. The trembles intensified when the finger smoothed lazily over the marking spot. "If it's like this all the time, you're gonna kill me."

"It's intense," Gavin whispered, replacing his finger with his mouth. The sensation of his warm mouth pushed at Charlie's control. He swallowed, shivering in the aftermath, every nerve lit up like the lights of a Christmas tree.

"Dammit, Gavin." Charlie's heart beat in a sharp staccato, and for a moment, he wondered if it might leap up his throat.

With a soft laugh and a final nibble across the mating site, Gavin pushed to a sitting position. Almost instantly, Charlie's senses reacted to the lack of contact and craved Gavin's touch. A protest formed on his lips but he bit it back, instead waiting impatiently for Gavin. He never dallied on purpose, found it a new experience. Not one he enjoyed.

One hand dipped to stroke his erection, the flash of pleasure something to focus on instead of the intense craving he experienced when the feline shifter touched the fleshy spot at the juncture of his neck and shoulder.

Gavin bent over to open a drawer and pulled out a bottle of lube. He turned back to Charlie and popped the lid. The bottle made a wheezing sound when Gavin squeezed it, and a jolt of anticipation shot through Charlie.

He cleared his throat. "I hope you're warming that."

"Of course," Gavin said, but his eyes glinted with mischief. He slapped Charlie's hand away from his cock. "Spread."

"Oh man," Charlie murmured. His eyes fluttered closed, and he sank into pure sensation. Gavin blew warm air along his straining shaft but otherwise ignored his cock to tease him in different ways. He took small nibbles from Charlie's inner thighs, the nips becoming increasingly harder. The pinches of pain ran together until he ached and throbbed in one big mass of craving. Gavin moved back to his taut shaft, nuzzled his balls, licking and stroking him with mouth and fingers. A croak emerged, but thankfully, Charlie kept the begging words on the tip of his tongue trapped inside. Sensual tension coiled into a tight ball and his breathing deepened to harsh. He thrilled at the firm footsteps of a finger along his perineum, tingled at the warm massage of a finger eased by lube.

Charlie tensed, remembering the burn of pain that sometimes accompanied the initial intrusion of a finger.

"Relax," Gavin said. "This is gonna be good between us. So good, you won't ever want to be with another man."

"Promises, promises." Charlie barely recognized his own voice. The sharp prod of a finger fought the ring of muscles at his entrance. He panted, his body straining to accept the intrusion. Gavin slipped his finger deeper and worked his hole until the inward and outward glide was smooth and easy. A second finger and the scissoring action prepared him, the faint bite of pain keeping Charlie grounded. Did he want this? Hell yeah. His entire body jerked with pleasure when Gavin angled his fingers and skimmed over his prostrate. A moan escaped and when Charlie opened his eyes, he caught the satisfied smirk on his lover's face.

"You haven't done this for a while."

"No, not with a male."

"Lack of opportunity or desire?"

"A bit of both. Dammit, Gavin. No more torture. Please."

But Gavin didn't listen. He thrust his fingers into Charlie, nailing his gland only now and then, just giving him enough to keep him on edge. Finally, Gavin slipped his fingers from him and reached for the lube again. Their gazes connected when Gavin stood, peeled off his underwear and squeezed the transparent liquid into the middle of his palm. He set the bottle aside, smiling while he greased his cock.

"On your hands and knees."

Charlie's cock pulsed and somehow thickened even more as he turned and pushed to his hands and knees. Nerves jumped in his gut then. Damn, this was like being a virgin all over again. Nervous and excited at the same time.

Gavin moved behind him, his slick hands urging Charlie to widen his stance. The mattress shifted as Gavin lined up his cock. Instinct made Charlie tighten against the intrusion, and he had to force himself to relax, to push back against the invasion.

"That's it," Gavin murmured, his breath warm against his back. "We'll take it slow." One of his hands reached around Charlie's legs and clamped down on his cock. Charlie started at the firm touch even though it was what he preferred. Most women were way too tentative in handling his cock. This was better, much better.

Gavin pumped his cock and took his time embedding his own shaft inside Charlie. The burning discomfort gave way to intense pleasure and a sense of rightness, as if he'd arrived home. Muscles flexed and rippled while Gavin rocked his pelvis and drove deeper. He glided in to the root and, fully embedded, Gavin leaned over him, his warmth scorching Charlie's back.

"Damn that is addictive." Gavin's teeth scored the marking site and pure lust and desperation grabbed hold of Charlie. He groaned and moved insistently, urging Gavin to cooperate.

He expected Gavin to tease and nibble but his teeth clamped down without warning. White-hot pain roared through Charlie, exploding into a pleasure so vast and deep Charlie didn't think he'd survive the shock of it. Climax ripped through him, semen splashing across his stomach and Gavin's hand. He kept coming, spasms shooting from his cock, pleasure scorching across his arms and legs, stealing his breath. A shout filled the bedroom as his channel clenched tight on Gavin's cock, then a tongue rasped across the place where Gavin had bitten him. Charlie shuddered through another round of pleasurable vibrations.

"Charlie," Gavin said in a harsh, strained voice. His hips pistoned with unrelenting strokes while his teeth still grasped Charlie's shoulder, the lash of Gavin's tongue soothing the biting sting. Gavin groaned and wet heat filled Charlie.

Gavin panted, leaning most of his weight on Charlie. "Damn, I didn't mean to do that." He pulled free and climbed to his feet. The next second Charlie heard the rush of water and light slid through the dark room. He dropped to the bed, lying in a sprawled heap on top of the green quilt cover. His fingers fumbled at his shoulder, producing a spike of pleasure that shot straight through his gut to his cock. When he removed his fingers, they were a little bloody.

Gavin returned with a damp cloth.

"My shoulder's bleeding."

"I'll fix that for you." Gavin gave him a searching look. "You okay?"

After cataloging the aches and twinges in his body, Charlie nodded. "Fine."

"Good." Gavin wiped away the sticky cum coating Charlie's stomach and groin, and after he'd cleaned to his satisfaction, he stood to toss the cloth into a cane hamper in the corner of the bedroom.

"What about my shoulder?"

"I said I'd fix it," Gavin snapped.

Charlie blinked at the flash of temper. Okay. It wasn't as if he was Mr. Sunshine all the time. Some days he needed coffee in the mornings before he managed a civil word.

"Sorry," Gavin said, striding across the room to sit on the bed at his side. "I'm angry at myself for marking you."

"I thought it was what you wanted."

"It is, but I didn't give you a choice. We scarcely know each other. I wanted to give you time to know me before I pounced."

Charlie couldn't find it in himself to care about maybes and should haves. Or the fact Gavin had taken away his choices. Instead, he savored his closeness to the other man, the rightness. A bond. Now that he'd experienced the marking, he understood Laura's explanations about her reactions, except in his case he didn't have an ounce of confusion. He knew this was right.

"Let me fix the bleeding." Gavin pushed him against the pillows. He'd expected antiseptic and perhaps a sticking plaster.

Gavin rasped his tongue across the site, lapping away the blood and cleaning his wound. Charlie opened his mouth to protest, thinking about all the germs in a bite. One of his colleagues had suffered a bite while trying to control a group of drunken partygoers. It had turned septic.

Charlie's cock bucked, coming to life when he thought he'd done his dash for the night. He gasped as Gavin continued to lap at his shoulder. "Is it meant to turn me on all over again?"

"So I hear. This spot will always be sensitive now."

Charlie rolled toward Gavin. He gripped his lover's cock and grasped his own in the same hand, pumping them both together. "I don't get to mark you, do I?"

"It's not necessary—no—but if you want to bite, I won't stop you. I heal fast so you won't hurt me. Damn, how did you know what I'd like?" His lids fluttered closed, making Charlie smile.

His lover. If anyone had told him the previous evening he wouldn't have believed it. But now...now his feelings about Gavin were certain. They encompassed him and in a weird way made him whole. The attraction he'd harbored had solidified to something more, stronger and powerful. He'd fight to keep this thing with Gavin, even if it made him seem possessive.

Charlie continued to work their cocks, using the beads of pre-cum as lubrication. Instinct told him to nuzzle Gavin's neck, and when his teeth grazed the marking site, Gavin shifted position to give Charlie better access.

Gavin's mouth worked on the wound he'd left on the fleshy part of Charlie's neck, and the tension ramped up inside the bedroom. This time Charlie knew what to expect. The searing, intense wave picked him up and hurled him into pleasure so deep he wasn't sure he'd survive. Semen spurted from his cock in thundering waves and Gavin came too, with a wet spurt on his belly and chest. It was rough and hot and raw. So damn right. Charlie wanted to repeat this again and again.

The metallic blast of blood across his senses made him realize he'd sunk his teeth deep into Gavin's shoulder, but the other man didn't complain. If anything, he seemed as stunned as Charlie by the sheer power and heat pulsing between the two of them. Charlie released their softening cocks and lifted his head to study the mess he'd made of Gavin's neck.

"Should I lick it?"

"Yeah." Gavin's eyes were a deep green, and they held heat and longing. Trust. He bared his neck, giving Charlie access.

Charlie gulped, awed by Gavin's easy acceptance of him. A rush of belonging and complicated emotions bombarding him.

A mate.

He'd thought he'd marry one day. This was bigger than anything he'd ever imagined. He lapped across the bite mark. Gavin's groan vibrated inside his chest. He clasped Charlie tight, obviously enjoying his attentions. The faint flavor of blood faded, and when he lifted his head, he noticed the wound appeared less angry.

"It's healing," he said in surprise.

"Yeah. I didn't realize how sensitive it would be, how much a mere touch would affect me. I didn't know a human's bite would drive me so hard."

A flash of humor shot through Charlie as they both regarded awakening erections. "Hand me that lube. It's my turn this time."

Morning came all too soon. They shared a quick shower with only mild groping before they both dressed for work.

"Will you come and stay tonight?" Gavin asked.

Charlie tossed his damp towel aside and strode the two steps needed to reach Gavin. "Not being with you hadn't occurred to me." He dragged Gavin into his arms and kissed him, not roughly but slow and gentle, pouring every writhing emotion inside into his kiss. When he lifted his head, they were both breathing hard.

"Damn, I wish I didn't need to go to work," Gavin said with a glance at his wristwatch.

"I know the feeling. Do you have time for a coffee at the café?"

"No, I have a patient arriving in half an hour and have to prepare the surgery." Gavin glanced toward the surgery with a frown. His shoulders tensed beneath Charlie's hands. "Fuck."

"You okay?"

"Yeah." Gavin didn't sound certain.

Charlie heard the tap-tap of shoes and turned to the door. "Your patients come to your bedroom? Is there another door I should have locked last night?"

"The one to the surgery waiting room," Gavin muttered. "I forgot to check it. I had other things on my mind."

"Gavin, I thought I'd—" A feminine form skidded to a halt in the doorway.

Leticia—the woman from last night. Today she wore tight jeans and a formfitting T-shirt in pale blue. She wore a cap on her head, her blonde hair poking through the back in a long ponytail. What little color she had in her face flooded away when she took in both Gavin and Charlie. They both wore trousers but neither had donned shirts and they stood way too close to try the casual friends ploy. The piquant scent of sex hung on the air and the rumpled bed gave more than a hint of how they'd spent their night.

Leticia's brown eyes swept over Charlie, coming to rest on the mark. His skin prickled as if she'd trailed her fingers over the spot, and he covered the raised site with his fingers.

"You marked him?" The pain in her voice had Charlie wanting to comfort her. He noted it had the same effect on Gavin. Collectively they took a step toward her.

Leticia slapped her hand over her mouth and backed up, her eyes wide with panic and betrayal.

"Leticia, it's not what it looks like," Gavin said.

"Oh yeah?" Bitterness filled her words. Her eyes swept over both of them, skimming their bare chests and the obvious marks on their shoulders. "He bit you too. You can't—I thought we...oh hell." Leticia turned and fled.

Chapter 3

Beyond Her Reach

I t wasn't fair. Pain lanced through Leticia as mortified color flooded her cheeks. She'd rejected Gavin's advances time and time again, citing the FIV as her excuse, even though she'd known they could be mates.

Could be. Should be.

Her gaze slid to the raised mark on Charlie's neck. *Too late now.*

Escape. She needed to get out of here.

After a last glance at the matching mark on Gavin's neck, Leticia fled down the passage, each breath a hoarse fight for air. Gavin had mated with another. He was beyond her reach now.

Beyond her reach.

The words echoed inside her head in a cruel replay. Leticia ran outside, wrenched open the door of her car and climbed inside, slumping against the wheel. Tears smarted her eyes, and she bit her bottom lip to keep it from trembling.

Betrayal.

Again.

Her hands rose to grasp the steering wheel in a white-knuckle grip. Even though he'd wanted her, and she'd refused, not once but several times, the knowledge he'd mated with someone else was a kick in the gut. Unexpected. Painful. As if the disease wasn't enough…

Leticia fumbled with her car keys, trying to force them into the ignition. Her hands shook. Tears flooded her eyes and she couldn't seem to manage the coordination to start her car. All she could think of was the loneliness. Gavin had mated with another and the bloody disease had come back.

She would die alone.

Charlie grabbed his shirt and thrust his arms into the sleeves, buttoning it before looking at Gavin. "Are you going to tell me what the fuck is going on? There is something between you and her. I sensed the ties between the two of you." He shook his head, yet didn't reject his certainty.

Gavin hesitated, his expression torn as he glanced down the passage. "I intended to talk to you about Leticia. Look…I…hell! I can't talk now." Gavin hurried from the bedroom.

Charlie scooped up his clean socks and followed, ending up in the kitchen. He prowled to the window and peered outside. "Damn, she's outside, bawling her eyes out. What's going on?" There was a connection between his mate and Leticia. Weird but true. He understood none of this magic shit, but he sensed—knew—there were ties between the two. "Have you marked her?"

"No. No, of course not." Gavin didn't sound defensive or embarrassed. Just tired and pained.

Charlie continued to stare at the woman because not only had he detected ties between her and Gavin, he'd experienced a forceful return of last night's attraction. Yearning. That correlation kept him from communicating his anger and frustration. He kept recalling the pain on her pale face. She'd reminded him of a whipped puppy, cowering in pain. His stomach flipped in sympathy.

"Leticia is my first patient this morning. I need to go to her."

A flash of jealousy flooded Charlie at the thought of Gavin touching her. His hand fisted at his side and he didn't trust himself to speak, his mind battling with the contradiction of his thoughts. Shit, what kind of man was he? The woman was in obvious pain. He gave a clipped nod instead, beating back the surge of possessiveness.

"Charlie, I truly meant to talk to you before Leticia arrived, to explain things." Gavin swallowed and Charlie could see—sense—his distress. His heart softened, and he moved toward the other man, taking him into his arms and hugging him tight.

"It's okay." Yet despite his reassurance to Gavin, worst-case scenarios filled his thoughts. Suspicions accompanied his churning stomach, and he wondered if he'd made a huge mistake by spending the night with the town vet.

"We'll talk tonight," Gavin said. "I promise. Right now I need to see Leticia. She...she's not well."

Charlie frowned, wanting to ask questions and remembering what Jonno and the twins had said about a virus. Gavin's expression told him he wouldn't get any answers, not now at any rate. Coming to a decision, he gave Gavin another quick kiss and stepped back. "Tonight. I should finish work around six, all going well. If I'm going to be late, I'll ring you."

"Okay. If I get a call-out, I'll phone you at the station," he said.

Charlie went back to the bedroom and grabbed his bag. He thrust the clothes he'd worn the previous night inside and after zipping it closed, headed for the front door. Gavin already crouched by the driver's door, talking to Leticia. Charlie wanted to say hello but forced the instinct aside and walked over to his car. Driving away was one of the hardest things he'd done since his sixth sense screamed at him to fix things. Bloody difficult when he didn't understand what the problem involved.

Hell, what a bloody mess. Charlie wasn't happy—Gavin could detect the waves of frustration and disapproval emanating from him as he drove away—and Leticia was weeping as if she'd lost her last friend in the world.

Gavin opened the car door and reached for her, drawing her into his arms and holding her while she buried her face against his chest and sobbed. The peak of her cap dug into his shoulder, and he jerked it off her head, barely restraining a gasp. Her hair...

A tight sensation gripped his throat and no amount of swallowing removed it. No wonder she'd wanted to see him. It looked like the FIV had become more aggressive.

Gavin dug deep for his doctor persona even though he wanted to scream at the unfairness of the disease. If it weren't for the FIV, he and Leticia would be mates by now. He'd wanted to spend time with her, show his love to everyone. She'd refused, and he'd gone through the past few months off balance with a part of him missing. Leticia.

"Leticia, let's get you into the surgery."

She lifted her head at the husky note in his voice.

"You don't want me anymore. I've lost you."

The forlorn expression on her face almost did him in. "No. No, you haven't lost me," he stated. "Do Lucas and Saul know where you are?"

"No. I haven't told them."

Gavin nodded, guessing she meant the advancing disease rather than her location. He scooped her out of the driver's seat and strode to his front door, shocked at how little she weighed. He'd seen her only last month for a checkup. The disease shouldn't have progressed this fast.

"Are you staying with Saber and Emily while you're in Middlemarch?"

Leticia nodded, still looking so vulnerable he wanted to hit something. Someone. It was a good thing Charlie had left. His emotions ran too close to the surface right now and it wouldn't take much to set off his temper. "It was easier than doing the two-hour drive home to Alexandra after the party."

"I'll ring and let them know you're with me."

Leticia grabbed his shoulders, her sharp nails digging in cruelly. "You won't tell them?"

"I won't tell them." Gavin ignored the twinge of pain in his mark, disgusted by the shot of pleasure darting through his body when Leticia was in such a bad way. He set her on a chair in the surgery and crossed the gleaming white tiles to reach the phone. The number was on speed dial and connected almost straightaway. To his relief Saber answered. One fictitious breakfast excuse later, Gavin hung up and turned to Leticia.

He owed her an explanation. He owed Charlie an explanation. Gavin sucked in a huge breath, acknowledging he'd made a right royal mess of the entire matter. In his defense, he hadn't realized how powerful the mating urge would be. With Leticia his willpower hadn't been tested since they'd never slept together, but with Charlie instinct had roared out of control. Hell, what a fuckin' mess.

"You and Charlie are mates." Leticia's brown eyes still glittered with tears.

"Yes." It was nothing less than the truth. They were mates. They didn't know each other well but the sense of rightness—he couldn't deny it. He'd wanted Charlie from the moment he'd first seen the other man.

"I thought we were mates."

"Possible mates." Gavin sighed. "You refused to have anything to do with me." He turned away, unable to face the silent condemnation. He deserved this. Honesty would have worked... Now it was too late.

"That's true." Leticia seemed to pick herself up. She stood and grabbed a tissue from the box he kept on his desk. After dabbing her eyes and throwing the used tissue in the bin, she turned to him. "I guess you've seen my hair. It's started to fall out by the handful. I've lost weight. I'm not sleeping well."

Gavin's heart sank at the list of symptoms. He'd read magazines and textbooks, spent hours searching the internet. In domestic cats, once they reached this stage, the result was inevitable.

Death.

"Have you done anything different?"

"No." She stopped and bit her lip. "Work is stressful, but I thought I was coping okay. I've tried to eat properly, get plenty of exercise. I go running with Saul and Lucas whenever I can. My energy levels are always better after shifting, although I'm not as fast as I used to be."

Gavin patted her hand, the contact of skin to skin jolting him. His hand jerked free, and he backed away. He kept in close contact with Saul and knew Leticia tried to manage her health. Huge amounts of stress weren't good for anyone. With a normal shifter or human, short-term stress didn't matter. In extreme circumstances a person might lose weight and suffer from insomnia, yet it wouldn't hurt them. With Leticia's lowered immunity, the added stress was a killer.

"You'll have to stop working, Leticia."

"I can't." Panic filled her gaze. "It's the only thing that keeps me sane. I need to *feel* normal." Her eyes sparkled with more unshed tears and it tore at his gut the way she tried so hard to hold back her grief. Always so brave. He loved her—he'd loved her since he'd first set eyes on her—but all the love in the world couldn't make her better.

And now there was Charlie.

"Stay here with me. Help me in the surgery."

"So you can keep an eye on me? Watch me die?"

"No! I love you, dammit. I want to help." Gavin closed his eyes, seeking control. If ever there was a time to keep his mouth shut, it was now. Did he do that? No!

"Won't your mate have something to say about that?" The mocking tilt of her luscious mouth told him she thought she knew the answer.

"Come to dinner tonight, as a friend. Ask Charlie if he wants you around." Gavin held his breath, waiting for her answer. If she said no, he'd have to rope in Saul and request his help. Maybe even Lucas. Hell, he'd use blackmail and every weapon at his disposal to get Leticia to move in with him. Selfishly he wanted to spend time with her before she died.

"I'll be in the way. I know what Lucas and Saul were like when they first mated."

"And yet you stayed with them."

"Lucas is my brother. Where else would I go?" Leticia jumped to her feet and strode two steps. Without warning, she crumpled.

Gavin sprang, catching her before she hit the floor and swept her into his arms.

"Put me down. I'm okay."

"You're not," Gavin snapped. "You've lost muscle and you look as if you need a week of sleep." He hurried down the passage to his bedroom, belatedly remembering he hadn't taken the time to make the bed.

"I love your scent. Charlie smells good too. He seems nice." Leticia's mouth curled into a sleepy grin, bringing a frown in Gavin. He didn't like her docile like this. It wasn't Leticia. He preferred her spiting and fighting, hearing her sassy comebacks. That was the woman he wanted. Gavin set Leticia on a chair and straightened the bed. He would have changed the sheets but Leticia needed to sleep now.

With the bed made, he crossed to Leticia, grasping her shoulder and shaking her gently.

"I'm just resting my eyes," she murmured. "I'm awake."

"Did you get much sleep last night?"

"No. My mind was too busy."

A sleeping pill, Gavin decided. She had to sleep or she'd never get through this. They'd lose her, and he didn't think he could cope with that.

He crouched in front of her to slip off her shoes. "Come on. Let's get you into bed."

"If I sleep now, I won't sleep later tonight."

"Sleep or you're never gonna kick FIV butt."

Her brown eyes widened before her lashes lowered to screen her expression. "It's too late."

"You follow my advice and we'll beat this, Leticia. I have a few ideas to try yet. Don't give up. You hear me?"

Gavin unfastened the button on her jeans and tugged them down her legs. This wasn't how he imagined Leticia in his bedroom. He swallowed, shoving aside the surge of lust. That wasn't what she needed right now. Seconds later, he tucked her into his bed. After a quick trip to the surgery, he returned with a glass of water and a sleeping pill that was safe for her to take. He made sure she swallowed the pill and sat with her until she dropped off to sleep before leaving the bedroom, pulling the door closed after him.

He had a lot to do in the next couple of hours.

As he'd expected Saul and Lucas arrived soon after he rang them.

"Where's Leticia?" Lucas prowled into Gavin's surgery, anger and worry vibrating in his rough voice. "Is she okay?"

Saul walked over to Lucas and squeezed his shoulder, his touch calming the lion shifter.

There was no point giving them half-truths so Gavin spoke bluntly. "The disease is advancing. Leticia is experiencing some alarming symptoms. I've told her she needs to give up her job and relax or she will die."

Lucas growled, fury flaring in his brown eyes. Gavin tensed, understanding the shifter's anger. He waited, giving both Lucas and Saul time to assimilate everything he'd told them.

"Can't you do something?" Lucas demanded.

"Why didn't she tell us she wasn't well?" Saul asked.

"I don't think she wanted to worry you."

Gavin watched Lucas warily, knowing the shifter hadn't realized he'd mated yet. A glance at Saul told Gavin he'd scented Charlie on him and recognized what it meant. Without a doubt, all hell would break loose once Lucas realized because he was so protective of his sister. Gavin understood and even admired the shifter for his strong family ties, his loyalty to his sister and Saul.

"I have a few things I'm going to try with Leticia. It's difficult because the incidence of FIV in feline shifters is rare and confined to Africa. I'd like Leticia to stay here with me so I can monitor her."

"What about your mate?" Saul asked.

"What mate? I thought Leticia—" Lucas's nostrils flared as he broke off to glare at Gavin. "I can smell her on you. The only way the scent would imprint like that is if you've mated. *Bastard*…" He moved with preternatural speed, his fist slamming into Gavin's face.

Pain rioted through Gavin. The force of the blow sent him flying, crashing into the wall. He hit with a dull thump, stunned for a second, although the entire time he kept his gaze on Lucas, his feline straining for release. A growl rumbled deep in his chest, his feline taking exception to the attack. Gavin batted the cat down, forcing himself not to act. Control. He'd allow one free shot. After that all bets were off—he'd strike back and bugger the consequences. Without haste he stood, muscles tensed to spring.

Lucas leaped at Gavin with a loud roar that echoed through the room. Gavin ducked to the side, attempting to avoid another blow. It didn't happen. Saul jumped between them with a snarl, shoving his mate hard enough to pierce the red rage thrumming though him. Lucas crashed into a chair, his muscular bulk scooting it across the floor.

"Back off, Lucas. Gavin is a valuable member of the shifter community. We need him."

"That doesn't give him the right to fuck with Leticia," Lucas snarled, picking himself up and shaking his head. His blond hair lifted with the movement, looking like a mane.

Gavin prodded his chin with his fingers, decided he'd live and rolled fully upright without taking his eyes off Lucas. Oh he'd like to fuck with Leticia, not that he intended to voice the desire. That would be like poking the big bad kitty with a sharp stick. Time for stating intentions later. And it wouldn't be Lucas and

Saul he stated them to—Charlie and Leticia were the involved parties and they'd know first.

"Gavin is trying to help, numbskull." Saul shoved Lucas in the middle of his chest, ignoring the lion's testy growl. "Back off."

"What's Leticia meant to do now?" Lucas demanded.

"Gavin will keep treating her as a patient." Saul strode across the room, pausing to return the chair to its proper place before coming to a halt by Lucas. He squeezed his mate's shoulder, leaving his hand resting there. The pair glanced at each other and Lucas relaxed. "Gavin?" Saul asked, returning his attention to him.

"Of course I'll continue Leticia's treatment. I'm a doctor, not a bloody child intent on revenge."

"How is your mate going to feel about another woman in the background?" Lucas glared at him, and the tightening of his face told Gavin he'd like nothing better than to pound him into the floor. The low growl rattling in his throat supported Gavin's theory.

Gavin took the precaution of moving back a few steps so both the chair and the couch were between them. While he wasn't afraid of a fight, he wanted to remain in top physical shape for the coming night.

"That's between us." Gavin didn't explain. No use adding to the strain pulsing through the room.

"Who is your mate?" Saul asked, his eyes narrowing in a catlike manner, intelligence settling on his face. Gavin could see his mind working while he attempted to match scent with faces.

"Charlie McKenzie." Gavin waited for the explosion and it didn't take long.

"You're a fuckin' queer?" Lucas asked in a tone of disbelief.

Gavin scowled. "Takes one to know one."

"I think I'm insulted," Saul said. Gavin noticed his thoughtful frown. "Was Charlie at the party last night?"

"Yes."

"A queer! Fuckin' hell. I could have sworn you were Leticia's mate."

Gavin ran out of patience. "I am Leticia's mate," he growled. "I'm gonna say this once then you're both heading home. Leticia is my mate. She refused me. Several times."

"But what about Charlie?"

"Shut the fuck up and listen, Lucas. I'm trying to tell you. Charlie is my mate. I have two."

"No one has two mates," Lucas snapped, his muscles bunching in preparation to spring at Gavin again.

Saul grabbed him by the scruff of the neck and exerted enough pressure to gain his mate's attention. "Didn't you listen? Leticia refused to mate with him. You know she refused to go out with Gavin and only saw him for treatment. What the hell would you have done? Think about it, man. You know what it's like when you see your mate. You want to fuck and you want to mark. In that order. It's hard to control."

"So what will happen with Leticia now? How long does she have?" Lucas's large frame slumped in defeat.

"That's what I'm trying to tell you," Gavin said with a touch of impatience. "I want Leticia to stay here with me because I suspect Charlie is her mate too. I'm hoping that between the two of us we can help her." Emotion grabbed at his gut, his throat and crushed the words he wanted to say. He swallowed, knowing he had to give them honesty. "Leticia is sick. I don't know if I can help her, but I want—need—to spend time with her."

Saul gave a clipped nod. "All right, but either Lucas or I or both of us will drop in every couple of days. You will keep us up-to-date with progress reports."

"Every day," Lucas said, looking as if he wanted to argue the point, but a quick glance at Saul changed his mind.

"Of course." Gavin dragged in a deep breath. It did nothing to settle the fear gathering in his gut. Losing her... The pain and sympathy on Saul's and Lucas's features told him he didn't need to explain any further. They understood the days with Leticia could be the last.

"I'll keep in close touch," he said. "Leticia is asleep in my room. I didn't have time to make the bed in the spare room. You're welcome to stay until she wakes, although it might take a while since she took a sleeping pill."

"We'll stay," Lucas said.

Gavin nodded, having expected it. "I have to go out to the Miller farm to check on their prize ram and make a couple of other stops."

"We'll wait here until you get back," Saul said.

"Thanks," Lucas said, his voice gruff with tamped-down emotion.

Gavin knew it was as close as he'd come to an apology. Brother and sister were a lot alike. Stubborn. Short-tempered. Strong. Loyal to those they loved. He prayed Leticia had enough strength left to fight the FIV so those personality traits came into play. He hoped so for all their sakes.

Chapter 4

The Truth

S aul's and Lucas's presence at his house posed a problem. Gavin hurried through his farm rounds. Four hours later, he pulled up outside the police station. He switched off the ignition, hesitating before climbing from his SUV.

No escaping the problem.

Charlie might not understand. They'd probably fight. Gavin sucked in a deep breath, struggling for calm. It did nothing to slow his rapid pulse rate.

Coward.

Gavin strode up the three steps leading into the police station and pushed through the door. To his relief Charlie was alone.

"Hey." Giving in to impulse and the driving need to touch and reassure himself, he rounded the large wooden desk. Grabbing Charlie, he kissed him. It wasn't an easy kiss. Noses collided and their teeth clacked together before Gavin managed the right angle. His hands curled into the blue cotton of Charlie's uniform, acting like an anchor. Passion ignited along with satisfaction at the unrestrained response from his mate. Mouths opened and tongues tangled together, the panic leeching from the kiss to leave need tinged with lust. When they pulled apart, they were both breathing hard.

"You missed me." Charlie's grin lightened his blue eyes, and his lips curved upward in a smug manner. "Hell, what is that stink? And what happened to your face?"

Gavin's nose twitched. He frowned, glanced down at his boots and shuffled from foot to foot. The telltale scent of cow manure rose to float through the police station. "My last stop was to check on a cow. She cut her leg on some wire. Guess I brought a souvenir home with me. She was a feisty thing. Got in a lick or two while I was checking her leg," he added in a creditable lie. Charlie didn't need to know Lucas had hit him.

Humor still sparkled in Charlie. "Is this what I have to look forward to?"

"Probably." Cautious hope filled him at the thought of a future. Despite bestowing the mating mark on Charlie, he knew Leticia and his feelings for the lion shifter would make things difficult. Even with his inner anxiety, being with Charlie soothed his worse fears. Maybe they could work through this dilemma.

"I can deal. I thought we were meeting at your place."

A reminder of the problem. Shit. Gavin's smile faded, replaced by fear. He couldn't lose Charlie too. He prayed he'd find the right words because everything depended on it.

"I have visitors."

A flash of hurt crossed Charlie's face, coming and going so fast Gavin would have missed it if he hadn't watched so closely. "I'll go home then. No problem."

"No, that's not what I meant. I need to talk to you about the visitors before you arrive. There's stuff I want to tell you. I thought I'd have plenty of time..." He trailed off, knowing that no matter how much time he'd had, nothing would've prepared him for this moment. Maybe if he explained. "We're mates. I want you with me. I want to spend my days and nights with you. All day I've been off-kilter, craving your presence, your touch."

"Hell, I've had a jittery feeling in my gut. It's a vague sensation of something missing or out of place." Charlie stared at him and it was like a physical touch. Gavin barely resisted a shudder. Damn, having a mate was turning him into a wimp—all soft and mushy. He backed up two steps and yanked an upright chair closer to Charlie's desk. Straddling it and leaning on the back with his arms, he wondered how to start, how to bring the Leticia subject up without alienating his mate.

"Gavin?"

"Huh?" Gavin slid from his fears to face reality. *Charlie...*

"Will it be like this all the time?"

"Yeah, from what I've seen with other mates. You'll want to touch and imprint your scent on me. It's instinct." A snort of amusement emerged, a release of silent tension. "Like a dog pissing on everything to mark its territory."

Charlie's lips quivered, humor flashing in his eyes. "And you'll want to do the same?"

"I'll try not to piss on you, but touch. Yeah."

Charlie slipped into his chair, grimacing before he leaned back, his weight making the springs protest. "Don't sound so happy about it."

"I'm trying to work out how to tell you something."

"Tell me straight out. I prefer honesty."

Gavin took him at his word. "I've known for a while that Leticia is my mate. Possible mate," he amended, trying to be as factual as possible. "She knows it too, although she's too damn stubborn to admit it and act."

"Leticia's your mate?" Charlie straightened, his gaze intent. "Where does that leave me?"

The flash of pain with its underlying fear and unease arced between them even though a desk separated their bodies. "I'm not explaining this properly. You're my mate too. For some reason I have two mates. Until I met you I had no idea double-mating was possible. Don't get me wrong—I'm happy we're together, but there is a hole in my gut because Leticia keeps refusing to consider anything except friendship."

"Why? You said she was sick. Isn't it built into your genes to mate?" Charlie picked up a pen, twirled it once in his right hand before tossing it aside with a grunt. "Hell, I don't like this. You should have told me. Before."

Guilt heightened in Gavin, a slash of heat filling his cheeks. Shame. Nothing like kicking a downed man. He inhaled. It didn't make a difference, didn't steady him or help him think of a way to explain.

Blurt it out, man. Just do it. "Leticia has FIV, the feline version of HIV. She was doing okay, but she's under stress at work. It has exacerbated the illness, amplified the symptoms and pushed her to the next level."

Charlie picked up his pen again, his expression cautious. Watchful. Dissecting. "She's worse?"

Gavin nodded, unable to speak straightaway. He blinked, struggling for composure. The thought of her dying...leaving... A sharp cough blew the emotional obstruction from his throat. "She's staying with me while I try to work out how to treat her. Will that be a problem?"

"I don't know. Will it?"

Charlie wasn't letting him off lightly, and why should he? He'd lied to him by omission, dragging him into this mess. "Her brother Lucas will be a regular visitor. Probably Saul as well. It might make things tricky for you. They know we're mates. They also know Leticia and I are mates."

"Prospective mates since you haven't marked her." The taut note in Charlie's voice spoke of jealousy. Fear. Worry about the unknown.

"Yes." Gavin faltered before going with brutal honesty. He owed Charlie that much. "I don't know if I can stop thinking about Leticia—sexually, I mean. It's funny because I haven't slept with her even though we're mates. Not even a kiss." He sighed and dragged his hands across his face before glancing at Charlie to see how he'd taken the confession.

Bad.

All expression left Charlie's face, and Gavin couldn't tell what he was thinking. Not even an inkling. At least Charlie hadn't bashed him into next week. *Yet.* Gavin wasn't sure he'd remain so calm in Charlie's position.

"If Leticia is your mate, why haven't you taken things further?"

"Because she's impossible. Stubborn and bullheaded." Frustration colored the words he spit out like bullets. They hovered between the two men, powerful and smelling of truth. "She won't take a chance on me catching the FIV virus from her."

"Because of the biting," Charlie guessed. "Gutsy lady. You could have sex though. Use condoms and stick to a no-biting rule."

A self-deprecating snort escaped Gavin. "You saw how successful I was with you. I don't think I could make love to Leticia without marking her. It's all I've thought about and is why I marked you. I shouldn't have, not straightaway. Saber will be pissed with me if he finds out. I...I didn't want to risk losing you."

"I'm still here, Gavin. How are you going to cope with Leticia living in the same house?"

"I don't know. All I know is that I can't turn my back on her, not when she's sick. I have to do everything in my power to give her a good quality of life."

Charlie nodded. "You don't need me hanging around. I'll head home to my place tonight."

"No, dammit. Don't do this. I need you." Gavin jumped to his feet and rounded the desk, grabbing him with a low growl. Charlie's chair flew backward, and he staggered off balance. Gavin shoved harder, his feline strength forcing Charlie toward the nearest wall. He hit with a startled *oomph*.

They stared at each other.

"Fuck off," Charlie growled.

"Make me."

Charlie snarled and pushed him. Gavin didn't budge. Instead, he kissed Charlie, pouring every bit of his frustration and anger into the kiss. Charlie continued to fight until Gavin played dirty, grabbing him around the shoulders and letting his fingers press on the mating mark. Charlie turned his head, pulling his mouth away from Gavin's and breathing hard. When Gavin's fingers moved, he shuddered, his body relaxing in defeat.

"Kissing me isn't gonna make this go away."

Gavin's breath came in harsh pants, his pulse rate slowly returning to normal. "It's all I have. I want you in my life. It's selfish. I know it, but I can't do this alone." He took a deep breath and admitted the truth—one he'd never verbalize to anyone else. "I'm scared, dammit." The rough sound of his voice echoed between them. He met Charlie's gaze, frightened of what he might see in the other man's eyes. Derision. Disgust.

"Everyone is scared at some time in their life. Admitting it doesn't make you any less a man."

Gavin blinked and knew in that moment what Charlie feared. Losing him. Losing a mate. It put them on level ground and steadied him. Marking Charlie and acknowledging the mate's bond came with responsibilities. Charlie needed him, and he owed his mate loyalty. He could do this—give it his best shot. He couldn't do anything less. "Will you help me?"

"I want to say no," Charlie murmured. "You don't know how bad I want to tell you to go to hell." His sigh tickled across Gavin's cheek. "Yeah, I'll help."

"Good. I need you in my bed."

A quick grin flashed across Charlie's face. "Sex? Is that all I am to you? A sex toy?"

"No, you're a fuck buddy too. Kiss me." It was an order, and Charlie obeyed without hesitation.

This time they took their time, leaning into each other, chests touching, groins brushing. Gavin licked across Charlie's bottom lip, breathing in his scent and luxuriating in the firm arms holding him. He sighed, soft as a whisper, when their lips moved together, the lazy stroke of tongues, the taste and scent of Charlie sending urgent signals to his cock. With a subtle twist of his hips, he rubbed against Charlie, the jolt of pleasure making them both groan.

Skin. Damn, he needed to touch Charlie's chest. Breathing hard, he pulled away enough to jerk open Charlie's shirt or at least the top three buttons. He slipped his hand beneath the fabric and downward until his fingers moved over one flat nipple. Charlie hissed, so he repeated the move, scraping his fingernails back and forth. He lowered his head again, seeking Charlie's lips.

Behind them, the station door flew open. Charlie made a low sound of protest when he lifted his head and turned.

"Um…" Laura, the other Middlemarch police officer, stood frozen in the open doorway. "Should I come back later?"

Under different circumstances, Gavin would've laughed at the shock on Laura's face and the dismay and desperate arousal on Charlie's.

Charlie shoved him away and fastened his shirt with jerky movements. Color crept into his cheeks. "No. Of course not."

Laura didn't look so sure. She edged through the doorway and shut the door with a firm click. "I…um…just came to…um…"

"I was kissing Gavin," Charlie snapped. "Get over it." He dragged his chair back to his desk and dropped into it, the chair squeaking as his weight settled.

"I didn't know…" Laura trailed off, her gaze jumping to him before settling back on Charlie. "I didn't know you were gay." Her blue eyes narrowed to slits. "I'd better not catch you eying up Jonno."

Charlie chortled, the bark of sound unexpected in the taut silence. "Jonno? I don't think so. The man is infatuated with you. Besides, I have my own mate." He pulled back his shirt collar to reveal a scar on the fleshy part between shoulder and neck. "I'm not interested in Jonno."

"Who?" Laura turned her attention on Gavin. "You're mates? You're both gay?"

"Neither of us is gay," Charlie said. "If you want to assign labels, we're bisexual." He glared. "I don't like labels."

Her nose wrinkled, and Gavin could practically hear her thoughts. They sure looked gay to her—two men kissing with obvious passion. "Okay. Right. Um...if you're gonna um...kiss and stuff, you'd better lock the door next time."

Charlie's brows rose. "Like you do, Laura?"

Gavin bit back a laugh, enjoying the bluster between the two cops.

Laura glared at him before turning back to Charlie. "All right. All right. You've made your point. Rules. We'll have rules."

"No hanky-panky in the police station? That sounds rough," Gavin said. "We could hang a pair of handcuffs on the doorknob to signify action inside."

"Shut up," Charlie growled.

"Shut up," Laura snapped at the same time.

"Wow, they agree." Gavin sauntered over to Charlie and bent over to brush a kiss against his mate's lips, despite the audience. Charlie made a soft growling sound but didn't avoid him, merely accepting the kiss. "See you later at my place."

"Later," Charlie acknowledged, his voice husky.

Gavin nodded and after a quick wave at Laura, he strode from the station and down the steps to his dusty SUV.

The main street of Middlemarch bustled with after-school traffic. Parents stood in groups while waiting for children to join them. A cream-and-maroon bus sat outside the school, the driver waiting for children on the school run to board. Gavin waved at several parents and climbed into his SUV, doing a U-turn, heading for his house and Leticia. Somehow, he had to make this work.

Charlie watched Gavin until the man disappeared from sight. His butt actually. The man had a fine rear end, and he couldn't wait to get his hands on it again. Yeah, despite the awkward kink in his new relationship. He had said nothing to Gavin because he wanted to be sure. He experienced the same attraction to Leticia he did to Gavin. Last night it had confused him. Today it still bewildered him. He tore his gaze away from the door to find Laura staring at him, her eyes full of curiosity.

"Men *and* women? How does that work?"

A chuckle burst free and Charlie relaxed, lighter despite the potential problems in his future. Gavin made him happy. Satisfied. "Use your imagination or ask Jonno when he arrives to file his report about that idiot driving through his fence."

"See that's where I'm having problems. You're gonna have to fill in the dots or connect them or something."

"Ask Jonno."

"Two at the same time?"

Charlie rolled his eyes. "I liked you better at the start when we didn't know personal stuff about each other."

"But two at the same time."

"Ask Jonno." A ménage a trois. Something to keep in mind if Leticia—no, when she improved.

The door flew open. "Ask Jonno what?"

"She wants to talk about sex," Charlie muttered.

"I walked in on him and Gavin kissing." Laura grinned at her mate. "He said he's not gay. Gavin said the same thing."

"You swing both ways?" Jonno asked, his brows cocking with distinct interest. "That's more exciting than the insurance claim for my fence."

"Do we have to discuss my personal life?" Charlie wondered if he should do a coffee run. Right now something stronger wouldn't go amiss.

"He's mated with Gavin."

"That was quick," Jonno said in clear surprise.

"Too quick?" That was what worried Charlie most. The invisible ties. What if Gavin had made a mistake? He knew Jonno hadn't marked Laura when they'd first hooked up together. The marking had come later.

Jonno sat on the corner of Laura's desk. "I knew Laura was my mate as soon as I met her. Gavin would've experienced the same with you. I suppose I moved quickly once I met Laura."

Charlie nodded, relieved by Jonno's words. Good to know. But what happened if Leticia died? Where did that leave him? Part of him wanted to ask questions. He held back, deciding he'd wait. Gavin would know more soon. He could ask questions later if he still needed answers. "That's what Gavin said."

"You okay with it?" Jonno studied him, his manner thoughtful, piercing the outer layers, as if he wanted to make sure Charlie understood the implications.

They shared a long look before Charlie nodded again. "Yeah."

"If you have questions, you can ask me or go to Saber."

"Thanks," Charlie said. "I appreciate the offer." He pulled a folder from the pile on the corner of his desk in a silent hint he'd finished discussing personal stuff. The phone rang, and he reached for it, taking the call from the local school principal about an upcoming road safety talk. Jonno completed his paperwork for the insurance company and left while Laura dealt with a complaint about tourists riding their bikes on private property instead of the rail trail. An hour and a half later Charlie stood.

"I'm off for the day." He checked for his cell phone and made a note to charge it before he drove around to Gavin's. "Do you want me to switch over the phones to my cell now?"

"Switch it over to mine if you like," Laura said. "I know what it's like at first. The out-of-control sensation, I mean."

"No, it's my turn. The phone probably won't even ring."

"If you're sure."

"I'm sure," Charlie said. "Thanks."

After switching over the phones, he grabbed his car keys and drove to his house. Once inside, he stripped off his uniform and jumped in the shower, both nerves and anticipation zinging the length of his body. He pulled the shower curtain into place, enclosing him in the steamy warmth of the cubicle. His cock filled as soon as he thought about Gavin, about the coming evening.

Groaning, Charlie wrapped his fingers around his shaft and flexed his hips. The surge of pleasure slid another groan up his throat. His body still hungered after their aborted kiss at the police station. Charlie barked a laugh. Just as well Laura had turned up then because no telling what she might have seen a mere five minutes later. Water poured over his head, flattening his short hair to his scalp.

He pumped his hand once before releasing his dick and grabbing the soap. Temptation nipped at him. No, he decided. Not now. Later with Gavin. The anticipation would make it all the sweeter. Unbidden, the fingers of one hand rubbed across the scar on his shoulder. The mark abraded the pads of his fingers, slightly raised to the touch but healed. And tender. The whisper of touch sent lust surging through him. His knees buckled and with a loud groan, he leaned against the cool tile wall of the shower, panting, his dick jutting outward.

"Damn." The hoarse whisper made him realize he wouldn't be going anywhere unless he jerked off first. Not with any comfort that was for sure. He grasped his cock with one hand and let his mind wander to Gavin, the abrasive skim of his lover's hands as they'd stroked over his shoulders and pulled him closer. The searing heat of Gavin's mouth when it surrounded the head of his cock. The pull of his lips, the lap of his tongue delicately prodding his slit. His hand tightened, gripping almost brutally as he pumped faster, sliding his fist over the crown and across the sensitive underside. His breath came in pants, almost louder than the splatter of water from overhead. With his mouth dry, heart thudding and body on fire he continued to fist his cock. A shudder worked through him when the pressure in his balls intensified and they drew up close to his body.

"Gavin," he muttered seconds before his orgasm ripped through him like a flash flood, swift and violent. Semen spurted against the cream tiles, and he shook so much he was glad no one was present to witness his weakness.

The water ran cold by the time he pushed away from the wall and grabbed the soap. With brisk movements, he spread lather across his chest, cleansed under his arms and his groin. Even brushing his cock started a low-level hum of pleasure. Damn, he had it bad. Charlie acknowledged in that moment that no matter what happened with Leticia, there was no way he could turn his back and walk away. Despite the rapid events, he wanted Gavin, even if it meant possible flak and adversity from others.

After grabbing more clothes plus his shaving gear, Charlie drove to Gavin's. He tapped his knuckles on the door once before opening it and stepping inside. Soft voices came from the kitchen along with a meaty scent. His stomach grumbled, and he realized how hungry he was.

He stepped into the kitchen, expecting Gavin. The smile on his face died when he found Saul and Lucas. "Is Gavin not home yet?" Damn, this was awkward.

"He's with Leticia," Lucas said, his voice not much more than a growl. Civilization at its lowest form.

Charlie hovered in the doorway, instinct telling him to flee. Instead, he drew himself up tall and pretended nonchalance. "Are you staying for dinner?"

Saul smirked, seeming to read his unease without effort. "Yeah. That a problem?"

"Of course it's a problem." Lucas scowled and gestured at him impatiently. "Come in. We don't bite."

"Not true," Charlie said, not moving. "I know you guys bite."

Saul snorted, his grin flashing to show a healthy set of teeth. Sharp teeth. "That's true." He slid a glance at Lucas before continuing. "Biting can be very sensual."

An arm slid around Charlie's shoulders, making him start. He'd concentrated on Saul and Lucas so hard he hadn't heard Gavin walking up behind him.

"Steady." Gavin nuzzled his neck and brushed a quick kiss over his mouth before stepping past him. "Stop trying to frighten Charlie. They're both leaving after dinner. Unfortunately we'll see quite a bit of them since they'll come back to visit Leticia."

Charlie couldn't get over the casual way Gavin touched him. He didn't seem to worry about the other two men seeing their kiss. That sort of openness with his friends and family back in

Wellington sent shudders of horror through him. Not gonna happen.

"They were telling me about biting," Charlie said. No point pussyfooting around. Huh! Amusement curled his lips. Good cat analogy. "Said it's sensual."

Gavin's eyes twinkled, the jewel-green color snaring Charlie and drawing him in like a patch of catnip. "And what do you think about biting?" Gavin purred. Heat seeped through Charlie's clothes and raced from the point of contact to the tips of his toes. Places in between tingled with distinct interest.

"Don't look, Lucas," Saul said, stepping up beside the big man and covering his eyes. "It's sex rearin' out of the closet."

"Quit foolin' around," Lucas growled, batting Saul's hands away. His lips curled up into a snarl, and Charlie got a good look at his teeth too. Then the man grinned—a full-out smile that smoked Charlie's insides. Suddenly he could see the attraction even though he didn't want it for himself. Not when he had Gavin.

"Enough about biting," Gavin said. "How long is dinner? I'm starving."

"About half an hour," Lucas said. "Is Leticia coming down?"

Gavin shook his head. "She woke up for a while but drifted off again. At this stage she's better catching up on her rest. She said she hadn't slept well for weeks."

"Damn, I wish she'd said something." Lucas turned back to stir something in a pot on top of the stove, but Charlie could see his distress.

"She's scared, Lucas," Gavin said. "Not thinking clearly. Now that I know there's a problem I can monitor her closer. I can't tell you she'll be okay, but I'll do my best."

The empathy and sorrow in Gavin's voice tore at Charlie, hitting him in the gut. A flicker of jealousy layered on top. Gavin seemed to sense Charlie's disquiet because he moved close and gave him a partial hug. Charlie took solace from the touch, and feeling shitty about his envy when Leticia was so sick, he attempted to tamp down his resentment.

Gavin had marked him and he knew feline shifters didn't take marking lightly. When they marked their mate, they were in the relationship for life. He had to remember that. The jealousy was his problem. He'd have to work on it because the felines seemed to have good instincts, sensing things he or other humans didn't. Yeah, he'd shove the animosity aside because he wanted to make the relationship a success.

"Can I do anything to help with dinner?" Gavin gave his arm a final squeeze before walking over to the table.

Charlie couldn't help but follow with his gaze, his body tightening to the point of pain. Like all the shifters, the male had a great physique, and Charlie's hands trembled with the need to touch. When he looked up he saw Lucas watching him, and he flushed, breaking the contact almost immediately. He didn't need that man knowing what he was thinking. Not that it would be difficult for Lucas to guess his mind dwelled in the bedroom. His bloody cock had become like an unruly teenager, rising to the occasion with little stimulus.

"Grab us a beer, will ya?" Gavin said.

Pleased to have something to do, Charlie strode around the table, covered with a black-and-white-check cloth, and opened the fridge. "You guys want a beer?" he asked Saul and Lucas.

"I put a bottle of wine in there earlier," Saul said. "Take that out and open it as well."

Dinner turned out better than Charlie thought it would. Saul seemed to act as a calming influence on Lucas and Charlie relaxed, the concern that Lucas would jump him fading under the effect of a full stomach and a few drinks.

"I'll check in every day," Lucas said.

"No problem," Gavin answered. "And you're both welcome to visit any time. Leticia isn't under house arrest."

Saul stood and removed all the dirty dishes from the table. "Should she be sleeping for so long?"

"I'll keep a close eye on her. If she's still sleeping tomorrow morning, I'll start worrying." Gavin picked up his wineglass and an empty beer can. "I'll check on her now."

Lucas sighed, concern flickering in his expression. Charlie watched him as he stood, noting the anxiety on the shifter's face. "I'll come up with you. Saul and I need to get home to Alexandra. Our farmhands are good but they need supervision."

Saul cleaned up and Charlie stood to help. They worked in silence for a while before Saul glanced at him. "You're good for Gavin."

"Yeah?"

"He seems more settled and determined. I know it was difficult when Leticia rejected him. It was a blessing we decided to move to Alexandra instead of buying a farm closer to Middlemarch where they would meet all the time. It was a fresh start for all of us and better work prospects for Leticia. The council okayed us staying, but I thought a bit of distance from my father was best." Saul pulled the plug and the water gurgled out of the sink. "Hell, if Lucas had rejected me, I don't know what I'd have done. He tried to push me away when I found out about the FIV because that's what all their friends and family did. It took a while to persuade him that it made no difference to me. Leticia is great. She's like the sister I never had."

"Gavin pushed none of you away." Charlie knew it without asking.

"No, he didn't, and he and Saber spoke up on our behalf. The shifter community is lucky to have Gavin, and he's a damn fine vet."

"This has all happened so fast," Charlie said. It was a relief to talk to someone who had gone through the mating process and understood the compulsion to touch, to have sex. "Does the need fade?"

"Nope," Saul said cheerfully. "The sex is bloody good, and the desire to fuck doesn't recede with time."

"I guess that's okay."

They smirked at each other before finishing up and taking a seat to wait for Gavin and Lucas.

93

"Of course it's not going to be easy for you, not with Gavin and Leticia having a link. If you need to talk, ring me."

"Thanks." Charlie liked the other man. In fact, he liked all the shifters he'd met in Middlemarch.

Lucas and Gavin arrived in the kitchen, putting a halt to the conversation. Lucas and Saul left soon after that and the tension in the room ramped upward.

"Fancy an early night?" Gavin's husky voice right next to his ear made his pulse leap. Good idea.

Charlie turned to face Gavin. "I'm guessing there won't be much sleeping."

"Is that a problem?"

"Hell no." Charlie headed for the bedroom but Gavin stopped him before he opened the door.

"Leticia's in there, and I don't want to wake her. We'll sleep in the spare room. I cleared it out and made the bed earlier."

Charlie pushed open the door to the spare bedroom and snapped on the light. He came to an abrupt halt. "A single bed?"

"It's not as if we're gonna sleep much," Gavin said. "And we're not arguing, so up close and personal isn't a problem." He yanked off his socks and unbuttoned his shirt without taking his gaze off Charlie. The dark green shirt slipped off his shoulders and dropped to the floor. Gavin's eyes glowed and held a hint of challenge.

"Don't let me stop you," Charlie said, his gaze skimming across Gavin's chest. The shifter was a man comfortable in his own skin, a man who knew what he wanted, and it was an incredible turn-on. Even now, Charlie's skin tingled beneath his clothing and his cock pulsed, pushing against his jeans. "Carry on with the striptease."

"The way I feel at the moment there's not gonna be much teasing," Gavin muttered. Deft hands unfastened his belt and the button at the top of his jeans fly. He pushed the denim down his hips, taking his boxer briefs with them. Seconds later, he posed in front of Charlie, proudly naked and aroused.

"Can I touch?"

"Hell yeah."

Charlie closed the distance between them and ran his hands over Gavin's shoulders. He pinched one nipple to a place just shy of pain. Gavin grunted, spreading his stance and silently daring Charlie to go further. Not a problem. Charlie had ached to touch Gavin intimately all day, had craved it. Trailing his fingers across the muscles of Gavin's chest, he dipped his head to take nibbles. Sometimes just a gentle scoring and at other times a sharp nip. Each sigh he dragged from Gavin, each moan of pleasure sent blood crowding into Charlie's cock. Hunger pulsed through him, a need, a desire to be slaked. He licked a nipple then sucked hard before pulling back to observe the string of red marks on Gavin's chest. His marks. A sense of possessiveness swept through him, contentment.

His marks.

His man.

Charlie ran his hands over Gavin's rib cage and smiled at the subtle shiver beneath his fingertips. His mate wanted this as much as he did. He licked across the faint indentations, tasting saltiness. He lifted his head to study Gavin's face. "My goal is to drive you crazy with wanting."

"It's working." Gavin's fingers threaded through his hair, tugging until Charlie experienced a smarting ache. Pleasure sang through him at the way his touch drove Gavin. Taking his time, he explored the muscular belly, bypassing the hard ridge of his cock to take a bite from the delicate flesh of Gavin's inner thigh. He stroked both thighs, enjoying the flex of muscles as Gavin shifted his weight. The musky scent of his mate filled his nostrils with each breath, and unable to resist, he breathed warm air over the tender skin, moving closer and closer to his testicles. Aroused male with a hint of soap. Nothing better.

Charlie licked his lips and nuzzled Gavin's balls with his lips, barely touching at first.

"No more teasing. Please. I need you now."

Good idea because, damn, he needed now too. Gradually his lips became firmer, more aggressive without causing pain, taking a ball in his mouth and licking. When he released it, saliva glistened on the taut surface. He traced the seam between with his tongue, glorying in Gavin's harsh intake of air, the sting caused by the grip Gavin had on his hair.

"I can't wait to fuck you," Gavin said, his voice thick with pleasure.

Charlie glanced up with a grin, noting the arousal glittering in his mate's eyes. "And do I get a turn?"

"Yeah." Promise shone on Gavin's face along with lust. "I'd like that, although you're gonna have to take it easy on me."

Charlie understood. "It had been a while for me too. Sitting was difficult today."

Gavin caressed his jaw, the slight rasp reminding Charlie he hadn't shaved. He'd meant to.

"Are you okay for another round?" Concern shaded Gavin's voice when he stared down at him.

"I'm fine. I'd tell you if I wasn't."

"Good. You gonna carry on? It's drafty standing here with no clothes."

"And yet you couldn't wait to take them off." Charlie stroked him, ran a finger the length of his shaft. Gavin ground into his touch, desperate for release. "Easy."

"Where you're concerned. Yeah, I'm easy. Probably won't change anytime soon."

Gavin's acknowledgment filled Charlie with satisfaction. He didn't voice it but showed his approval with touch, his mouth and fingers. Closer and closer they moved, up strong thighs until he cupped Gavin's taut balls and kissed them again. His heart pounded, heat swirling through him. His own jeans were uncomfortable now, but Charlie didn't stop. The urge to drive Gavin into climax filled him. Pleasure. For the first time he wanted to give. Waiting for his own pleasure didn't bother him in the slightest. He licked along the crease of Gavin's thigh and strayed onto the root of his erect penis.

Gavin's growl of pleasure echoed in the small room. "Are you trying to kill me?"

Charlie grinned. "No, I'm torturing myself, seeing how much pressure my jeans can take."

"Let me help you undress."

"Not yet." Charlie halted the conversation by running his tongue from the tip of Gavin's cock to the base. He rubbed his cheek against the hard shaft, inhaling deep. "I want to taste you."

"What's stopping you?"

"I'd like to enjoy every step rather than rushing."

Gavin shifted his weight from one foot to the other. "You realize I'm stronger than you? My feline genes give me extra power. I could jump you, toss you on the bed and have my wicked way before you even blinked."

Charlie rocked back on his heels so he could see Gavin's face. "Is that a warning or a promise?"

A frown creased Gavin's brow. "I'd never brutalize you. Never. Shit, that didn't come out right. I meant to tease you not to scare you into thinking our relationship will be anything but a partnership." Gavin dragged a hand through his hair, and by the time he'd finished, it stood up in dark tufts. "Anything we'll do will be consensual, Charlie."

"I'm a fair judge of character. It comes with the cop territory. Do I looked worried?"

Gavin shook his head, the tenseness leaving his shoulders. "Good. Can we get back to where we left off? You were about to take my cock into your mouth."

Charlie sniggered before grasping Gavin's cock and taking the tip into his mouth. Saltiness sprang across his taste buds and he moaned when seconds later another bead of pre-cum flowed free. He rasped his tongue over the crown and started moving, taking Gavin deeper and doing everything he liked, everything that turned him inside out, to his mate. Gavin's hands tightened in his hair, but apart from that, he remained still, letting Charlie work at his own pace.

A sense of power filled him while he pleasured Gavin. His head moved in a steady rhythm while his hands kneaded the globes of Gavin's ass and his tongue explored every inch.

"Damn I like that." Gavin's hips jerked when Charlie swirled his tongue across the head of his cock and used a little suction. Back and forth he swept his tongue, dragging a harsh groan from Gavin. Charlie ran a finger down Gavin's perineum and drifted it across his puckered entrance. Gavin moaned again and Charlie upped the pace, greedily sucking and making loud appreciative noises. He hummed, knowing how much he liked the sensations combined with the heat of a willing mouth.

Gavin's hips moved again, sliding his cock over Charlie's tongue. Together they moved in a down-and-dirty dance, pleasure soaring with each choked sound and teasing stroke.

Gavin's cock swelled, his balls drawing up tight. His hands tightened to a painful grip on Charlie's head, and he thrust. A second thrust brushed Gavin's cock over the flat of his tongue, and with a feral growl, his mate climaxed, large body shuddering while pleasure poured through him. Charlie swallowed, a little semen escaping to run down his chin. When Gavin stilled and released Charlie's head, he wavered on his feet, making Charlie laugh. Gavin sank onto the single bed, breathing hard.

Another snicker attracted Gavin's full attention. His eyes glowed and his pupils seemed more catlike than Charlie had noticed previously. "Isn't it about time you took off your clothes? We could have fun."

"Oh yeah?"

"I think it sounds like a plan," Gavin said. "Come here. Let me undress you."

Charlie didn't have to be told twice. But Gavin didn't undress him. He stroked and petted, drawing out the pleasure and the unveiling of his body. Shoes. Socks. His T-shirt came loose from his jeans and warm hands slid across his stomach. Gavin tugged until Charlie stood between his straddled legs. A smile that seemed a touch predatory curled across Gavin's mouth.

"Just the right height."

Charlie smiled down at Gavin, loving the teasing in him. But it was the intent shadowing the humor that made the heat roar through Charlie. "The right height for what?" Oh he knew. He just wanted to hear Gavin verbalize it.

"I want to taste you."

"No one's stopping you." He let Gavin see his challenge.

"I'll have you purring in no time."

"I'm not feline."

Gavin smirked at him. "Doesn't matter. You'll purr." Nimble fingers dealt with the button and zipper of his jeans. He peeled them down, the tip of his tongue poking through his lips while he concentrated on the task.

The rest of his clothes disappeared, ending up tossed on the floor.

Satisfaction glowed on Gavin's face. "That's more like it."

A stream of warm air teased Charlie's cock when Gavin spoke. Charlie sighed, shifting his weight, the prickle of awareness throbbing through his groin while he waited for Gavin's next move. Although he should have suffered impatience, instead he enjoyed the attention, of being the focus of his lover. And as he'd already learned tonight, giving was almost as good as receiving pleasure.

"On the bed," Gavin barked.

"Huh?"

"Bed. Now."

Understanding and acceptance came and Charlie nodded, obeying the order. His cock jerked with a surge of lust. He settled in the middle of the bed and sprawled out in comfort. While he stared up at Gavin, his hand went to his cock and he stroked himself. "Am I breaking any rules?"

Gavin stood and snorted. "You want me to spank you?"

"I don't know if I want to go that far, although I had a girlfriend who liked me to spank her. Really got off on it."

"We should try it some time."

A sizzle of white-hot heat shot to his groin. Charlie's eyes narrowed, and he slid his hand up and back down his dick. Perhaps he wouldn't discount the idea. "Maybe. Nothing wrong with experimenting."

"I have a toy collection."

"You're full of surprises," Charlie said, his heart beating a little faster. Who would have guessed?

"I've had girlfriends. Experimented." His eyes glittered and his brows rose in a silent challenge. "You want me to do that for you? My patients tell me I have good hands."

"Sounds like a plan, that's if we're talking about you handling my cock. Might have to work up to kink, even though it sounds interesting." Charlie let his hands drop to his sides, waiting for Gavin to make his move.

"Taste first." The bed dipped under his additional weight. Gavin's lips curled up in a sensual smile that promised pleasure. Charlie's heart stuttered, especially when he saw Gavin's sharp teeth.

"You're not gonna bite with those teeth?"

"I did last night."

And the pleasure had been incredible, better than he'd ever experienced before. "My shoulder is one thing. If you bite my dick, it will put me out of action for a while."

"Never fear." Gavin swooped, and an instant later wet heat surrounded the tip of Charlie's cock. A rough tongue rasped across his sensitive skin, more abrasive and stimulating than he'd felt before. His head lolled back on the pillow and his eyes flickered closed to savor the attentions of his lover. The build of pleasure was slow, gradual. A sigh escaped when the pressure in his balls increased. Gavin took his cock deep, with a faint scrape of teeth. The contrast of hard and soft shoved him higher. He groaned, his hips jerking upward, pushing his cock deeper into the warmth of Gavin's mouth. His heart thudded in sharp staccato beats, bolts of pleasure dancing the length of his body. The hot, wet slide of Gavin's mouth...

"Damn, more. Please." The ball of heat grew, expanding until he trembled and bells rang in his ears.

Gavin's tongue slid along the underside of his cock, drew back. The bells sounded louder, and he trembled on the cusp of climax. Gavin drew back. Right back.

"Fuck. The phone. I've gotta get it." Gavin stood and groped around the floor, finally extracting his cell phone from the pocket of his jeans. "Hello."

Charlie groaned, fisting his aching cock. After three short, hard strokes he climaxed, hissing at the pleasure that made him tremble.

Gavin hung up and started to dress. "I'm really sorry. Call-out. It's a mare having trouble foaling. I'll be out for most of the night." He hesitated while buttoning his shirt, frowning at Charlie. "I'm sorry." A faint trace of worry colored his voice as if he'd had problems in this area before.

Charlie didn't hesitate. "It's okay. No need to apologize. I'm a cop. I get late-night call-outs. Go. You can make it up to me later."

Sheer relief flickered across Gavin's face on hearing his words. He bent to kiss Charlie, and after a quick brush of lips, hurried from the room. A few minutes later Charlie heard the garage door and the roar of an engine. He sighed. So much for a night of hot sex. Bending over, he grabbed his T-shirt and swiped it across his wet stomach. He pulled back the sheets and climbed into the bed. Maybe Gavin would wake him when he returned. He should have suggested it. Charlie switched off the light and closed his eyes, willing sleep.

Dreams filled his head. Black leopards. Sex. A loud scream.

Charlie jerked upright, his heart beating erratically. Another scream sounded. Feminine. Cursing, Charlie pulled on his jeans and went to investigate.

Chapter 5

A Very Pretty Kitty

A nightmare. God, where was she?

With fear spurting through her veins, Leticia sat bolt upright, peering around the room and trying to figure out where she was. She took a deep breath and Gavin's scent came to the fore. The tension seeped from her body although tears took over when details of her dream floated through her mind.

Death. The grim reaper.

They'd stalked her through a forest, giggling yet menacing, never letting her get too far ahead or to rest.

Relentless. Taunting. Letting her know there was no escape.

The door squeaked open. Her heart practically sprang into her throat and she found her back pressed against the headboard, her hands clutching the sheet to her chest.

"Leticia? Are you okay? It's Charlie."

Leticia swallowed. Great. Another reminder of what the disease had taken from her. The chance of a mate. Her nose twitched, her stomach twisting and turning like a washing machine when she caught Gavin's scent on him. *Sex.*

Damn, it wasn't fair. All along she'd tried not to dwell on the injustice of the situation, of being sick. It wasn't easy. Sometimes resentment coated her every thought. Bitterness tasted sour. Nasty. No amount of toothpaste or mouthwash removed the sharp acidity. Nothing...

A tear slipped down her face, rapidly followed by another.

Charlie remained in the doorway. Hovering. Instinct told her he wouldn't leave until she answered. Summoning every bit of control, she forced herself to smile and hoped like hell the deception didn't show in her voice. "I'm fine. I woke up and wasn't sure where I was for a moment." She skirted the nightmare, shivering inside at the memory. Death was one ugly son of a bitch.

"Do you need anything?"

"No." No wonder Gavin liked him. He was nice to look at and it seemed his nature matched. Leticia dragged in a breath and batted away the jealousy. It returned like a lobbed tennis ball, the unexpectedness of it striking her in the heart. Unfair. *Unfair.* "No, I don't need anything."

"Well, if you're sure."

"I am." The hard note in her voice said bitch. True—she could be hell on wheels and didn't suffer fools. But she had compassion and the capacity to love, or so Saul said. Leticia thought a lot of Saul. Top man and perfect for her brother. Saul had pulled them into a family unit. A new pride. She liked being part of a pride.

Charlie still hesitated, so she scooted down the bed and pulled the duvet over her sweaty body. Surely he'd take the hint and leave her to wallow in her misery?

"Good night." Charlie pulled the door shut. Almost-silent footsteps padded away until she could no longer hear them.

Alone at last.

Another tear tracked down her cheek. She sniffed, swiped her right hand over her face. The tears kept coming. It was as if now that she'd let the first ones free other tears would follow whether she liked it or not. Crying was for sissies, and she was no sissy. She buried her face in the pillows that smelled of Gavin and...and Charlie. Misery weighted her down at the thought of what she'd lost, and anguish peaked, the last shreds of her control shattering. Sobs tore from her throat, hot tears flowing down her face in a never-ending stream to soak the pillowcase.

"Damn, I knew there was something wrong." The mattress sank beside her and she lifted her head, knowing he wouldn't see the extent of her torment in the dark room. All she needed was to get rid of him.

"Nothing's wrong. Go away."

He moved and the light flicked on, bathing the room in a golden glow.

Leticia attempted a glare. A single tear dripped down her cheek, contradicting every denial she tried to project. "I'm crying, all right? Just go away and leave me in peace."

"You're hurting." Charlie cocked his head, studying her way too close.

Leticia turned her face back into the pillow and tried desperately to stem the tears. It didn't happen. If anything, the sobs intensified. Powerful and noisy, they vibrated through her chest and tore at her throat. Surely he'd go away now and leave her to wallow?

He didn't.

He stretched out on the bed alongside her, hauling her into his arms before she could even think a protest let alone voice it. She stiffened, but he wouldn't release her, instead pulling her flush with his body and holding her tight. Leticia sucked in a hasty breath and his musky scent filled her lungs. Nice. Another time she might have enjoyed his closeness. Not today. Then, something else registered, overcoming her vulnerability at being this close to him.

He was naked.

She groaned a protest, arching away from him.

"Steady. I won't hurt you."

"Where are your clothes?" she asked in a low croak.

"Don't panic. I'm wearing jeans."

"Oh." Her voice still sounded full of tears, although at least her eyes had stopped leaking. "You shouldn't be in here. Gavin wouldn't like it." She tried to add a dose of anger and bitchiness to her words and failed. Would nothing go right in her life?

"Why are you crying?"

No way could she tell him the truth. She didn't want his sympathy. "I had a nightmare." The truth as far as it went.

"Scary?"

"Yeah." He had *no* idea.

"It's okay now." Charlie drew her back against his chest, and this time she didn't move away. With a soft sigh she relaxed, curling into the comfort he offered. His scent surrounded her. The steady beat of his heart reassured her and softened the edges of her loneliness.

"You're Gavin's mate. You shouldn't be in here with me. It's not right." But it seemed right, and that was the weird thing. It shouldn't. She shouldn't want to cuddle closer or explore with her hands. Yes! Explore. That was exactly what she craved.

"It's not awkward for me." Charlie's warm breath feathered across her cheek and she had to fight hard to prevent a shiver. He pressed his lips to her temple and smoothed his hands over her back. The heat of his body seeped through the oversized T-shirt she wore and her thoughts turned to sex. An image of Charlie and Gavin together flashed through her mind. Naked...

Leticia tensed again. There was something wrong with her. Yeah, a small inner voice taunted. She hadn't had sex for almost a year, not since a one-night stand with a human in Australia that had left her with a sense of dirtiness. She hadn't bothered to repeat the experience.

"What's wrong?"

"Nothing!" Damn, was she that transparent? She twisted her head to glare at him and a second kiss grazed her lips.

They both froze, Leticia in total shock. She'd liked Charlie when she'd met him at the party and had even considered, just for a fleeting moment, taking the attraction further. This...this...

"Well damn," Charlie whispered. A scowl furrowed his brow. His gaze swept her face, and he lifted a hand to smooth the hair from her cheek.

Another shiver whispered through her. Bother. She had to move. *Now.* This wasn't right. Before she had a chance to act, Charlie lowered his head and kissed her for real. Their lips slid together, a tentative touch that gradually became more confident. He traced the seam of her lips, and when she gasped, he took advantage, slipping his tongue inside.

Leticia growled deep in her throat, her feline flexing, reminding her of its presence and the way it...she...both of them loved touch. Apart from hugs from Saul and Lucas, no one touched her these days. Not willingly.

Greedily, she soaked up the sensations. The slide of his hands down her back. The musky scent of him and the lingering traces of sex. The softness of his lips as they caressed hers.

Charlie lifted his head, their lips clinging before parting. They stared at each other, the silence bringing home the intensity of the moment. Leticia closed her eyes and drew in a sharp breath. Charlie's scent and the underlying aroma of Gavin twirled

110

together into something very attractive. She cataloged what her senses were telling her and cursed on coming to a conclusion.

Mates.

Her feline stirred, pushing hard against her control. Every sense trembled with jubilation—the idea of love and belonging, even if it were only for a short time. *Mates*. The word tickled the tip of her tongue. Leticia clamped her lips shut. It would never happen.

Charlie and Gavin were mates. Marked mates. She had no right to come between mates.

"Stop thinking so hard," Charlie chided.

"But you kissed me."

"You're a very pretty kitty."

Leticia spluttered a little, trying to formulate an objection. "Don't call me kitty."

"I'm sure your brother called you worse when you were children. It's a brother's duty."

"You're with Gavin." She didn't need to pretend confusion. This human befuddled her without breaking a sweat.

"Yes, I am, but right now I'm with you. Wanna snuggle?" Charlie didn't give her a chance to refuse. He reached up to switch off the bedside lamp, plunging the room into darkness again. Leticia froze when he moved away from her. A zipper whined and clothing rustled.

"What are you doing?" Clear alarm sounded in her voice and her pulse rate jumped into choppy. "You...you're..."

"I'm not going to rape you or do anything nasty, not that I'm not tempted because you're a beautiful kitty. I need sleep and you need comfort. Figured we could help each other." Charlie slipped under the sheets, reaching for her. He tucked her against his body, his chest to her back, and then...nothing.

His even breathing told her he'd dropped off to sleep. Just like that.

Heck.

For long moments, she hesitated. They were just sleeping, she told herself, and it felt so good having someone hold her, someone who knew about the virus and yet didn't seem to care. At least she thought Charlie would know about the FIV. Gavin would have told his mate. Surely?

"Stopping thinking so hard. It's keeping me awake."

Air hissed from between her lips and she barely restrained a sharp squeak of fear. "I thought you were asleep."

"I keep thinking about kissing you, and all that thinking is interfering with my blood flow."

"Huh?"

"I have a hard-on," he said in a matter-of-fact voice.

"But you're with Gavin!"

"I'm a male, babe. We get erections. That's what males do."

Leticia snorted and turned in his arms so she faced him. Her T-shirt rode up a fraction and her outer thigh connected with something hard.

"I told you I had a hard-on. Now you've made it worse."

"This is not my fault." Leticia's nipples puckered against the soft fabric of the T-shirt she wore, and a tight ball of tension swelled between her legs. Charlie wasn't the only one who suffered from arousal.

Charlie's hands clenched her shoulders "Yes, it is your fault for being so sexy, but we're not gonna do anything. This is a bad idea. I'll go back to the other bedroom."

"No, please. Don't go." Being alone scared her. She was tired of being alone.

"Are you sure?"

"Yes. Stay." Gavin was a lucky man to have a mate like Charlie. Leticia turned back on her side and closed her eyes. Envy chased her into sleep. Gavin was so lucky. He'd never be alone.

Gavin trudged from his vehicle and into the house, dragging a muddy black bag containing emergency supplies with him. His eyes smarted, gritty and sore, and every muscle in his body ached. Even worse, the mare had died, although he'd saved the foal. He hoped it pulled through. He'd grab a quick shower and sleep before he returned to check on its progress. The only good thing about this was that he could cuddle up to Charlie. His mate's solid presence would help drive away some of the chill lingering inside, the sense of helplessness because he couldn't save the mare.

After removing his boots and socks at the front door, he stepped inside and padded down the passage, pushing open the door to the bathroom. Gavin took a quick shower and hurried to the spare bedroom. He'd finished shedding the towel around his waist before he realized the bed was empty.

Immediately fear thumped him in the gut. Charlie had left. Gavin was halfway to his bedroom to interrogate Leticia before he realized full-out panic mode was verging into overreaction territory. Charlie might have had a call-out for work. They both worked challenging jobs where overtime was inevitable. And if that were the case, he'd missed the note Charlie had left for him, which wouldn't be surprising given his state of exhaustion.

Sighing, he decided he might as well check on Leticia before he crawled into a lonely bed. He pushed open the bedroom door and came to an abrupt halt. Despite the dim lighting in the room, his night vision told him two people were in the bed. Jealousy crashed through him in a wave, stealing his breath and control. It ripped through his chest, anger tumbling in the undertow. He wanted to strike out, to loose the snarl building in his chest.

"Gavin?" Charlie's drowsy voice snared his attention.

"Yes," he snarled, his feline agitated and alarmed.

"Good. I was worried about you. Come to bed. There's room for all of us." Charlie threw back the covers in invitation. "Leticia was crying. I couldn't leave her alone."

Breathe, Gavin told himself. His lungs screamed for air and he sucked in a huge breath, immediately calmer. Comfort. Charlie had offered comfort. That was all. He realized he'd searched for signs of sex lingering in the air. Thankfully, he hadn't found a scent out of place.

"Gavin?"

Shaking himself, he took the two steps necessary to cross the room and slid into the bed next to Charlie.

"Damn, your feet are cold," Charlie complained. "Payback is a bitch, ya know."

Gavin grinned, releasing the final vestiges of jealousy and panic, the sensation of skin against skin soothing him as nothing else. Skin privileges. He hadn't realized how much he'd needed a mate's touch, how much his feline had cried out for soothing.

On the other side of Charlie, Leticia breathed slow and even, occasionally drifting close to snoring. The small imperfection brought a smile. Their combined scents wound through Gavin and some of the night's stress faded. He relaxed against Charlie, savoring the other man's strength and the glide of hands over his chilled flesh.

"I kissed her," Charlie confessed into the darkness.

Gavin stiffened in shock, a sliver of jealousy returning to add to the tense muscles in his shoulders.

"I wanted to do more."

Charlie's husky confession hung between them for a long moment while Gavin battled with the emotions pounding through him. He exhaled, searching for calm. Charlie didn't have to tell him this. "Is confession good for the soul?" he asked, his tone just short of snide.

Charlie chuckled, pulled him closer and pressed a kiss to his collarbone. He nibbled a little, laving the sting with the tip of his tongue.

"Why are you telling me?" Gavin persisted, uncertainty taking its toll and adding another layer to the destructive jealousy whirling around in his gut.

"Because I believe in honesty," Charlie said. "And because I thought we were mates. I don't understand how I could want to kiss her and enjoy it. Not when I have you."

Charlie's words finally pierced Gavin's befuddled, sleep-deprived brain. "You shouldn't," he said, wonder and sudden hope filling him. Maybe...just maybe there might be a way to help Leticia and in the process calm the angst roiling through him all the time.

"What's going on, Gavin? You said Leticia was your mate. Is she mine as well?"

"It's possible." Gavin kept his tone cautious while inside the possibilities rioted like a group of excited tumblers, whirling, jumping and doing handsprings through his tired mind. He'd told Lucas and Saul of his suspicions earlier but hadn't had a chance to do much thinking with everything happening so quickly.

"Did Leticia kiss you back?"

"Yes. Are you okay?"

"Perhaps the three of us are meant to be together."

"Three of us? The three...and you're okay with that?" Charlie's voice held shock along with astonishment.

"I...I was jealous when I saw you together." Charlie's honesty inspired Gavin to extend the same courtesy. They wouldn't work this out if they weren't upfront. Besides, he liked the fact his mate didn't lie, despite knowing falsehoods were the easier path.

"And now?"

Gavin sighed. "I'm tired."

"Fuck!"

No mistaking Charlie's curse for anything but upset.

Gavin spoke hurriedly. "No, I want to talk about this, but I want a clear head. It didn't go well tonight and I have to go back in a few hours."

Leticia moaned and thrashed in her sleep.

"I think she's having nightmares," Charlie said, letting go of his anger for a need to comfort. "A scream woke me before and that's when I heard her crying. Why don't you climb in on the other side of the bed and we'll keep her between us?"

"She won't be happy when she wakes up," Gavin said, quite liking the idea.

Charlie yawned and gave him a sleepy kiss, missing Gavin's mouth to hit his stubble-covered jaw. "Hmm, sexy." He rubbed his cheek against Gavin, his sigh of satisfaction sounding like a rough purr.

Gavin chuckled and aimed better than Charlie. Their mouths clung and the rightness of being with this human rippled through Gavin. He knew in that moment he'd started to fall in love with the other man. Ideally, love should come before mating, but he thought he'd lucked out. Love would give them added strength, and they'd need it to stand shoulder-to-shoulder and deal with Leticia.

She cried out again, thumping Charlie in the ribs. He winced and Gavin brushed another quick kiss on his mate's mouth before crawling out of the bed.

"Shift over," he told Charlie. "And take Leticia with you." Gavin rounded the bed and slipped in the other side, tugging the duvet over his shoulders. Leticia moaned again, a pained sound that raised a raft of goose bumps on his arms. Damn, he hated seeing her like this. He preferred it when she was arguing, spitting defiance, golden-brown eyes darkened with temper. Sort of the way he imagined her while making love. Hot and tousled.

Gavin drew closer and made contact with Charlie's hand.

"Pity she's wearing the T-shirt," Charlie whispered. "She's gonna be odd man out when she wakes up and finds herself in bed with two naked males."

Gavin yawned. "Knowing Leticia, she'll be pissed and wake up swinging her fists."

Charlie chuckled. "Now that's a sight I'd like to see."

Chapter 6

Mates and Other Problems

Leticia woke to warmth searing her from both sides. With eyes still closed, she yawned, savoring the coziness and the fact that after her nightmare she'd slept. Every sense sang a stronger tune with more alertness—better than the last few days for sure.

She turned and something hard prodded her on the hip. Her eyes blinked open, and she came face-to-face with Charlie. His eyes sparkled with vitality. The morning bristly look suited him. She stirred and something prodded her again. Comprehension dawned. *All of him was alert.*

"What will Gavin think if this is how you react on waking in bed with someone who isn't your mate?" she blurted. Oh boy. None of this showed her in a favorable light either—waking up draped all over another feline's mate.

A grin spread across Charlie's face and her heart raced a little faster. *Be still my heart.* The man was seriously sexy. His mouth drew her gaze, and she stared, wondering about sneaking a kiss or guiding his mouth to one of her nipples. She imagined suction and the reverberation to her sex. A ragged sigh spilled free and wetness pooled between her thighs.

"Why don't you turn over and ask him?"

It took an instant for Charlie's words to register. She blinked, then gasped and rolled over, coming face-to-face with Gavin. "You've got an erection as well!"

"Morning, sweetheart." Seconds later, he was kissing her in the way she'd always imagined and fantasized about but never let happen. Their lips brushed with bold strokes, the heat of his touch rampaging through her. She was vaguely aware of Charlie sliding closer and curving his hand over her hipbone. This was wrong. Wrong in so many ways, but she couldn't have stopped if she tried, so starved was she for touch and comfort on a physical level.

When Gavin licked her lips in a silent demand for her to open, she didn't hesitate. He explored her mouth, licking, stroking and nipping, moving at a languorous pace as if this weren't something bad. Because Charlie seemed happy with Gavin kissing her, she sank into the sensations, greedily grabbing memories to drag out later when she was alone.

Charlie's hand slipped between them to cup one breast. She stiffened and Charlie's hand stilled while Gavin continued kissing her, as if he had nothing else more important to do with his time.

When she relaxed again, Charlie caught her nipple between his fingers, rolling and tugging until desire flared out of control. She moaned and pulled away to stare into Gavin's beautiful green eyes. The man had eyelashes that were entirely too long and sexy. Her pulse thundered—a *bang, bang, bang* in her brain—and she swallowed, unsure of what to say, how to act.

Leticia was positive her mother hadn't included this in the courtship rules she'd spouted from time to time. Yep, this was uncharted territory. Her pussy hadn't bloomed like this for...for months. Hell, sex had been the last thing on her mind.

"Are you okay, babe?" Charlie's hot breath against her ear sent a ripple of awareness shooting straight to her clit. He seemed to know how his touch affected her because he tugged on her nipple again—a short, sharp yank that sent a hungry ache through her sex.

"What are you doing?" The words grew higher toward the end of her sentence and panic beat at her mind, yet she couldn't seem to get her traitorous body to move. Charlie...Charlie was driving her crazy, making her want more. Much more.

Gavin laughed, drawing her attention. When she studied him closely, she saw the bruises beneath his eyes. "We're taking advantage of the fact we both woke up with a beautiful woman in our bed."

Charlie said nothing but his fingers strummed and plucked at her nipple like a master musician. She could hardly think, let alone plan a smart-ass answer.

"Damn, I've got to check on the foal. I'd rather stay right here."

"It's early, Gavin," Charlie said.

Leticia decided she liked it better when they both ignored her, except Charlie hadn't released her nipple and it made her ultra-aware of her body. She concentrated on breathing, part of her wanting to shriek blue murder and kick their manly butts while the other needy part of her told her to enjoy the physical intimacy. Soon she'd lose the rest of her hair, and no one would want to look or touch then.

Gavin sighed. "I know."

"But you need to do this," Charlie said, his eyes intent while he studied his mate.

If she tilted her head a fraction, Leticia could see the two men and the way they looked at each other, almost hear the silent communication. Hunger clenched through her, squeezing the needy child she harbored inside her. Jealousy whispered, *She could have had Gavin for her mate if it wasn't for the disease.*

"I couldn't save the mother but I'd like to save the foal if I can."

Charlie nodded. "We'll be here waiting for you. Laura is opening up shop today. If Leticia wants, I might take her to Storm in a Teacup for breakfast. You want to meet us there?"

"I'll ring if I can't make it." Gavin turned his attention on her, smiling gently. With his thumb he traced the lower curve of her lip before dipping his head to follow the same path with his tongue.

Leticia gasped, and he took advantage, slipping his tongue into her mouth and taking the kiss deeper. The coil of energy in her lower body shifted, pulsed. Her feline stretched when she had been unresponsive for days.

Then Gavin lifted his head, breaking the kiss. "We'll continue this later."

Leticia swallowed, an audible sound so loud it made her wince. She raised her gaze and fought to inject attitude. "A warning?"

"No, sweetheart. A promise." With that he climbed from the bed, flipping the covers back over Leticia before the cool air attacked her bare legs. Naked. He was naked. Oh, she'd noticed while they were in bed together, tried not to think about it too hard. Seeing him in daylight, his long limbs, tight ass and broad shoulders, his calm smile, as if leaving his mate in bed with her wasn't a big deal. His unapologetic erection. "Charlie will look after you."

The door closed behind him, leaving shocked silence—on her part, anyway.

"What did he say?"

"I think he meant that you and I should continue our little adventure."

Leticia backed away, a sharp pull on her nipple a reminder of Charlie's proximity. "I don't think that's a good idea. I...you're mates." She peeled Charlie's hand away from her breast and immediately regret chased her.

"You could at least let me kiss you." Charlie closed the distance between them and brushed a lock of hair from her face. "Gavin got a kiss." He puckered his lips and waited.

"You'll stay that way if the wind changes." She wanted to laugh. With his tousled blond hair he looked cute and boyish, but his cock snuggling against her legs indicated a mature man. "Oh all right. If you insist." She gave his lips a quick peck before attempting to slide across the bed.

"Nah, we can do better than that," he whispered. "I want a kiss like you gave Gavin."

"But this is wrong."

"Not to either Gavin or me. We both want this."

"But you didn't discuss it. I was here the whole time."

"Shows what you know, babe. Just a kiss, okay?"

Leticia chewed on her bottom lip, struggling with indecision.

"Would it make it easier if I made you kiss me?" Charlie moved without warning and leaned over her, pinning Leticia to the mattress.

Leticia knew the right thing to do—shove him off and kick him out of the bedroom. A knee in the balls wouldn't go astray either, so he'd think twice about putting the moves on her again.

Didn't happen.

Instead, she sucked in a hasty breath, which made things worse. His masculine scent, musk and a trace of citrus filled her lungs, enticing her to step into danger. She stared up at him—his jaw shaded with blond stubble, his sensual lips, the challenging glint in his pale blue eyes—and admitted to herself she wanted this. Desperately.

She wanted to live a little—while she still could.

Her eyes fluttered closed, and she relaxed, tilting her head toward him.

"No, sweetheart," Charlie said in a stern voice. "Open your eyes. I want you aware of what's happening. No hiding. No pretending."

When she opened her eyes he smiled—a slow curl of his lips that lit up his features. Her heart kick-started with a solid thud, scampering like an excited kitten. Heck, his smile smoked her insides, leaving her breathless with anticipation. "I...I...thought..." She swallowed hard and tried again. "I thought this was just a kiss."

"No point tiptoeing around the truth. I want to fuck you."

"But...but..." Words failed her.

His grin widened. "I thought you wanted plain speaking."

"I have no idea what I want," she finally said, and it was nothing less than the truth. The two men had her confused and befuddled.

"We'll go with instinct." Charlie swooped, not giving her a chance to argue.

Oh hell. No point lying to herself. She wanted this—whatever *this* turned out to be.

He kissed differently than Gavin, cajoling instead of demanding. Their lips slid together with warmth and sultry promise, and every one of her objections whimpered and died. His fingers branded her flesh while he held her in place to wreak havoc on her emotions. The taste of him, along with his scent and confident manner, drove her crazy. He nibbled her top lip and soothed it with his tongue before pulling back to study her expression.

"Kissing you makes me happy."

Leticia tilted her head to stare at him. "As much as kissing Gavin?"

"This isn't a competition," Charlie said, laughter crinkling the corners of his eyes. "I like kissing both of you. Why don't you take off your T-shirt so I can see you properly?"

"Good change of subject." A spike of fear hit her and she chewed on her bottom lip, indecision whispering about rash decisions. This wasn't right, so why did she want to obey?

"I try."

Leticia stalled, wanting to follow his directions yet hesitant because she hadn't been with anyone else for ages. "Gavin likes you. I've never seen him look at anyone like he looks at you. No way can I come between mates. I won't."

"Gavin likes you as well. He's your mate."

"No, he's not." A harsh note entered her voice. "He's your mate. You shouldn't be here with me, and you should be jealous of the fact he kissed me."

"Are you jealous of Gavin being with me?" Charlie countered.

She wanted to lie. "Yes," she blurted the truth. Her teeth clacked together before she said anything else incriminating.

"I've seen the way Gavin looks at you. At first envy hit me, then I took a good look at you and understood." He tugged at the hem and pulled the T-shirt over her head. Leticia didn't think about protesting. Not once, even though he'd see her ugly scar. The cotton inched upward, baring her stomach, the lower curves of her breasts and finally taut nipples, one reddened by the plucking of his fingers.

Charlie stopped, the T-shirt bunched around her neck. "Beautiful."

She tensed, knowing he'd seen the scar. Puckered and still red despite the time since it had happened. Part of her waited for questions. They didn't come.

"Exquisite."

A sigh eased out. It was a long time since anyone had called her beautiful. She'd lost a lot of weight, although her breasts were still plump. Nerves jumped inside and the urge to babble struck. "I'm too skinny. You shouldn't do this." *Way to tell him, Leticia. Weak.*

"Don't. Just let me go a bit further. I'll stop as soon as you tell me."

127

Huh, the man had bricks in his head if he thought she wanted to stop. She was nervous—yes—not stupid. Leticia held her tongue, watching him with nerves scampering like frisky kittens as he studied her. He cupped one breast, stroking, his hand tan compared to her pale skin. She hadn't spent any time basking in the sun after running in feline form, and her normal tan had faded. Biting her lip, she fought the self-conscious thoughts and the urge to say how terrible she looked, how ugly her appearance.

Her flesh filled his hand, and she quivered at the exquisite sensation of his callused fingers dragging across the curve of her breast. The friction of his fingers stopped short of her nipple and drove away some of her reservations. It felt *so* good. Exquisite. She caught her breath, silently urging him to pinch and pluck again, to give her the bite of pain that would make her come alive.

He lowered his head and breathed a stream of warm air across the taut peaks until her blood flowed hotly through her veins. A moan escaped, the sound holding every ounce of emotion pummeling her inside. His touch. Gavin's touch. Between the two of them, they'd dragged her from the gloomy fog she'd inhabited this week. Shocked her out would describe the change better.

She loved them for it, would remember with gratitude when she was too sick to leave her bed.

"You still with me?"

He'd noticed she'd drifted. Damn. The last thing she wanted was to discourage him.

"Don't stop." Her hasty words drew a laugh from him and it lit up his entire face. Not handsome—no Gavin was much prettier. Charlie's profile struck her as strong and rigid, his jaw suggesting a determined streak some might call stubborn. When he smiled, his pale eyes glittered and a hint of a dimple flickered to the right of his mouth. Mesmerized, she reached up and traced the tiny dent with her fingertips.

"Don't stop?"

"No. Kiss me." She grasped his shoulders and puckered up, hungry for another illicit kiss.

"My pleasure."

Instead of tasting her mouth, he took her nipple between his lips, sucking hard at first until messages of lust pumped straight to her pussy. She jumped at the faint sting of teeth, the lick of his tongue and heard the suction. Moisture gathered between her thighs and she stirred restlessly, needing, wanting him to move faster, give her more.

"Charlie."

He lifted his head, glancing at her before turning his attention back to a glistening nipple. "Pretty."

Their gazes connected and a frisson of pleasure streaked straight to her lower belly. Just with a look. Wow! As if he could read her thoughts, he smiled and licked the underside of one breast. He skimmed his hands across her rib cage and tiny tingles skittered in the wake of the contact. Her eyes widened when his hand drifted lower still, the ridges on his fingers causing a hitch in her breathing. He flashed her another grin. "You can touch me back. I like my lovers to participate."

"What are you trying to say? Are you complaining about my technique?" Horror stripped away the feel-good mood. Her ex used to put her down. She had done nothing right and that included bedroom activities. Like fucking a dummy—her ex's words—which, according to him, was why he'd strayed. "We shouldn't be doing this anyway. It's not right."

"Steady. I didn't mean to insult you. All I meant was that I'd love you to touch me. I *crave* your touch, and I wouldn't be doing this if Gavin didn't agree. He does."

"But how do you know? It's cheating on your mate."

"There's a bond between the three of us. It's there. You know it too. You can try to lie to yourself but it's there inside you. Touch me. Go on, Leticia. You know you want to."

It was true. Everything he said.

Leticia sighed, losing a fighting battle. She needed his touch, and it was clear from his expression and words he knew it.

"How do you like to be touched?" It was like being a virgin again, uncomfortable and out of her depth. Tension filled her, desire seeping away, replaced with an acute case of anxiety. What if she did something wrong?

"Touch me however you want." Charlie rolled off her and into the middle of the large mattress. "I'm yours."

All hers. Her gaze stroked his body from feet to face. Her tongue moistened her lips and a trembling hand reached out, coming to rest on his chest. His skin was warm, the reassuring thud of his heart soothing her fears. Taste. She needed to explore him with her mouth, to learn if he'd enjoy her touch. She tried not to think of the alternative. No, she refused to spoil this moment...

Leticia fingered one nipple, jerking back in surprise when he shuddered. Wide-eyed she stared at him. Damn, he'd scared her. For a moment she'd thought he'd harangue for hurting him or handling him like a novice.

"I'm putty in your hands, babe. Touch me however you want. It's all good."

Was her fear that obvious? Did he think she needed encouragement? Well, he'd be right. Touching him terrified and elated her at the same time. So much at risk, so many images to store in her mind to make her last days memorable. Happy.

Damn, she didn't want to die.

She swallowed and knew she needed to focus because Charlie seemed to read her easily. The last thing she wanted was to fall apart in front of him.

"As long as all of you isn't putty." When she realized what she'd said, she clapped her hand over her mouth in consternation. She flicked a quick glance the length of his body, her eyes coming to rest on his erection.

"No putty there," he whispered, laughter shimmering in his eyes. "Shift closer. I can't wait for you to touch me again."

Leticia licked the tip of finger and drew it across the engorged tip of his shaft. His cock jerked at her touch, his loud intake of breath bringing a delighted smile. Yes. She could do this. No pretense here, he really wanted her touch. Her hand curled around his shaft, and she forced aside her lingering reservations about right and wrong. Warm. Hot even, and smooth. His hips jerked when she tightened her grip, a hiss of pleasure escaping him. She eyed him with uncertainty.

"Yeah, do that again. More. Please, Leticia."

Leticia went with gut instinct, exploring his cock and testicles. The stroke of her finger across the head brought a shudder from him. The pump of her hand made him groan. She scraped her fingernails across his balls, back and forth in what she hoped was a stimulating manner. At least she'd stopped trembling inside, worried about doing the wrong thing, about the enormity of touching someone else's mate. The thing was, it didn't seem so wrong. Touching Charlie seemed so right...

Her hands glided along his length, the swollen head of his cock taking on a liquid sheen as pre-cum beaded at the slit. Charlie's eyes glittered when she checked his reaction, and she realized he'd scrutinized her, taking in her every reaction. It made her want to pace like a caged lion in an exhibit. Why did he have to watch her like that? Too personal. Way too personal.

"Carry on," he encouraged. "Anything you'd like."

She licked her lips. "I want to use my mouth."

"Babe, I can't think of anything I'd like better."

Charlie had to steel himself to hold still. It was obvious someone had hurt her, leaving her hesitant. The ragged scar that snaked across her shoulder looked recent. The look on her face told him not to ask questions. Not yet. Hopefully, he and Gavin could fix her wariness and show her how special she was to them.

Two mates. Hell, he couldn't believe the way the three of them locked together puzzle-perfect.

Meanwhile, she stared at his cock as if it might bite her. Charlie smothered a laugh. Oh yeah, he'd love to bite her, except according to Gavin that was how she'd caught FIV. The last thing he wanted to do was bring back bad memories, not when pleasure lay so close.

To his disappointment, she released his cock and touched a tentative finger to his inner thigh. Damn. Even that turned him on, his cock bucking at her touch. She used her fingernails and made small circles, moving closer and closer to taut balls. Her finger glided across them, rolling and tracing the delicate skin between. No one had ever taken this much care with him. With Gavin, their lovemaking had been quick. Hot and hard. Pleasurable, yes, but this was different again. Despite his rising desire, Charlie let her explore. For the moment...

She licked her lips again, giving away her nervousness, and after each time she touched him in a different manner, she checked his reaction. Charlie decided to start talking, to tell her what her touch did to him. Not something he would've done in the past, but there was a connection between them—he sensed it—and it burned as strongly as his tie to Gavin. Damn, he wished Gavin were here to help. The last thing he wanted was to frighten her, so he talked, hoping to soothe her fears.

"When you touch me like that I think about pushing my dick into your wet pussy."

Leticia gasped, her hands jerking off his body. In consternation, she stared at him. "But I'm sick. Look at me."

"I have looked. You're gorgeous—a bit skinny, but Gavin and I will make sure you eat more and put on weight. I bet you're very curvy at a healthy weight."

"Pleasantly rounded." And the way she said it wasn't complimentary. Another piece of the puzzle fell into place. Charlie stored it away for a moment when he could talk to Gavin in privacy.

"My favorite kind," he said, and he ran his fingers down her biceps. She shivered, losing her pinched expression when he touched her. He liked that his touch did that to her and decided a talking and touch combo would work even better. He cupped a breast, brushing the underside, loving the way she quivered at the scant touch. "I can't wait. I'll flick my tongue across your swollen clit until it vibrates and you clench around my fingers."

"You talk a good game, mister." Her fingers curled around his dick again, the exquisite friction making him impatient.

"You're good at that," Charlie said, willing himself to relax. "You gonna let me have a turn? I thought I could wait. Not possible. I need you now."

He didn't give her a chance to answer. Charlie moved swiftly, smirking at the tiny squeak she emitted when he flipped her

134

onto her back. Seconds later, he was between her legs, lifting her to his mouth. His tongue lashed the length of her slit. He hummed, loving the spicy flavor of her. "You're wet. You want me."

"I—we—shouldn't be doing this." It was a weak protest.

"Why not?"

"Because I'm sick. I'm—" She broke off, her mouth firming.

"Gavin said it's nothing I can catch. We have condoms, so unless you want to stop right now or you're not well, then I'm continuing." Charlie finished his sentence with a delicate lick over her clit. The bundle of nerves jumped beneath the pressure of his tongue. His finger slipped in and out of her with hot, easy glides. He hooked his fingers, searching for the special spot that would give her even more pleasure. "How does that feel?"

"G-Good."

"You don't sound certain."

"I'm scared."

His heart clenched at the vulnerability in her voice. "Why? I won't hurt you. Gavin and I both want you very much." One look at the longing on Gavin's face when he left the room had made this decision easy. He'd do anything for the man, not that making love to Leticia was a hardship. It was something he wanted, and the need was as driving as it had been the first time with Gavin.

A flush flooded her cheeks, and she refused to look at him. "I know, but it's not easy. Flashbacks."

"I can't be doing this right then." Charlie stroked her inner walls with his finger, loving the flushed dewiness of her skin. With gentle suction, he used his mouth to push her higher, wanting to give her new memories to flash back to in moments of stress. She writhed beneath him, responding beautifully to his touch, her hips canting upward as she silently begged him to push her into climax.

"Ooh," she whispered, paying attention again.

"Describe the sensations to me."

Leticia huffed out a breath. "Do you always talk so much?"

Charlie couldn't help his snort. Talk? Him? Oh yeah, he was Mr. Sensitive and sought after by all the girls. *Not*. "Tell me." He put demand in his voice, slashing the words through the air like a whip.

"I'm wet." The words came out grudgingly, South Africa heavy in her abrupt reply. She still had misgivings.

Charlie disregarded her trepidation and continued yammering. "Yeah. That's good. Tell me more."

He could listen to that sexy accent for days. His groin throbbed. He ignored it to concentrate on Leticia. He licked across her clit again before backing up and lapping her scalding honey from every crease, every fold of her pussy lips.

When she didn't utter another word, he smiled against her heated flesh. Withdrawing his finger very slowly, he whispered to her about what he intended to do next. "First, I'm going to find a condom." After a last languorous lick and a quick thrust of his tongue into her entrance, he pulled away. Luckily he knew where Gavin kept his stash of condoms and lube. Charlie retrieved a condom from the bedside drawer and ripped it open.

Leticia flinched at the crackle of the foil.

"Do you want me to stop?"

"No." He had to lean toward her to catch her whisper.

"Last chance to say no." He rolled the condom onto his dick, gritting his teeth at the surge of pleasure. It wouldn't take much before he exploded. Somehow, he had to hold back, had to keep control until he took care of Leticia and gave her pleasure. This was not the time to fuck up. Once they knew each other better it wouldn't matter, but when she still wore her scars, he needed to work without haste. At least she'd lost the pinched expression and, apart from her slenderness, she seemed healthy today. The rest had done her good. He bent to suck on a nipple.

"*Charlie*." Her hands clutched at his shoulders.

"I'm trying to go slow." Nothing less than the truth.

"Take me." Her eyes closed, and her lips screwed up as if she expected pain.

"Do I need to find a flogger? Gavin said he has toys somewhere."

"Huh?"

"You look as if you're expecting pain." He moved over her, settling between her parted legs, and kissed her. Slow sips of her lips, giving her the sense he wasn't in a hurry, even though urgency rode him, his balls drawing painfully tight. The silky skin of her cheek met his bristly chin. Leticia didn't seem to mind, her harsh breathing sounding like purrs. Her nails dug into his shoulder, clutching him close and encouraging him. He nuzzled her neck and took a bite at the juncture of her neck and shoulder. A loud groan escaped and her fingernails dug in cruelly.

"Charlie, now. Please. Now!"

A slight readjustment of his body and his cock lined up perfectly. He pushed just the head of his cock inside the scalding heat of her pussy and stopped, wanting to hear the hungry noises from deep in her throat again. The graze of his teeth at her shoulder brought forth the same sexy noise. Her hips jerked, impaling herself a little more.

"Don't tease. Please don't tease. I need you to fill me."

Damn, he wanted that too. With a deep breath, he pushed deeper, the snug fit making him grit his teeth. "Your flesh is parting for me. Feels amazing." He kept up the pressure, thrusting deep into her pussy until her warm flesh cradled him. Balls-deep, he enjoyed the fiery heat clutching at his cock. He nuzzled her neck, taking tiny bites until he reached the marking spot. He scraped his teeth a little harder, remembering when Gavin had bitten him—the pain mixed with indescribable pleasure.

When Leticia shuddered, he lifted his head. "Does that hurt?"

"No. It's good. Too good. I forgot what it could be like. The sheer pleasure of intimacy and physical closeness." Leticia bit her lip, shooting him an uncertain glance, as if she'd said more than she intended. "Sorry. No, it doesn't hurt. I-I like it a lot."

Charlie grunted and moved. He plunged his fingers into her hair and pressed his forehead against hers. They stared at each other, the slow, rocking pace of invasion and retreat sending sensual flames licking from his balls. Every sensation—he wanted to draw them out to give as much pleasure as he received. Each spear of his cock into her dew-slicked flesh tugged at his heart. Hard to believe he could have such heart-pounding sex with two people in such a short amount of time. Hell, it would be so hot with the three of them together. He grabbed the taut globes of her ass, lifting her so his strokes went deeper. Leticia whimpered, and he realized he'd increased the pace, starting to pound into her. The bolts of pleasure increased, a fine sheen of sweat coating his body.

She seemed so fragile, yet the flush of arousal filled her face and crept down her neck to her beautiful breasts. Lifting up, she strained to meet his thrusts, the wet sounds of fucking filling the air. "Am I hurting you?"

"Nooo," she wailed. "Make me come. Please. Please. *Pleeease*."

"That I can do." Sparks of desire ignited almost continually and his balls drew up tight, the pressure to come nipping at his willpower. He removed his hands from beneath her butt and smiled at her. "Touch your breasts. Show me how you'd like me to touch you."

"That won't make me come," she muttered with a dark glare.

"If you show me what you like, I'll return the favor later on. Hell, I'm secure. You can even critique my performance."

139

Pleasure surged through him when she laughed. It made him realize she didn't laugh much.

"Deal." With an expression of concentration, she cupped her breast and squeezed a nipple between finger and thumb, rolling it. As he watched, the color changed from pink to dark red. She groaned, arching upward and grinding her clit against him in a needy move.

His breath went shallow and in a silence thick with sensual tension, he withdrew until only the head of his cock rested in her before surging back inside with a seamless stroke. The heat. Damn. It was alluring. It was amazing. Addictive. He reached between them, rolling his finger across her swollen clit, keeping to the same rhythm she used when fingering her nipple. She gasped. Sighed. Charlie paused, intrigued by the emotions playing across her face before continuing to drive them both to climax. His strokes became shorter, more erratic while his finger massaged her slippery clit, giving her enough for pleasure without pushing her over the edge.

"How much more can you take?" Slow. He needed to go slower. Far too good to rush. He reduced the speed of his strokes, drawing a sob of protest from Leticia.

"Please. It's been so long. I need this."

His finger strummed across her again. Each leisurely stroke into her wet heat contradicted the pounding need, the bubble of desire in his balls, almost ready to erupt. She was right. No more. Not right now. He stopped trying to prolong their lovemaking, using a firm stroke on her clit and increasing the speed again, driving into her with hard digs. Her sheath flexed, gripping him sweetly. Another touch of her clit and she cried out. A final strum sent her over the edge. She shattered, her cry of pleasure almost a scream. Her flesh rippled around his cock, his rapid strokes and the relaxation of his resolve to hold back did the rest. He pounded into her, semen rushed up his cock and exploded from him while her pussy milked him of every drop.

"Damn. Leticia." He wanted to say a lot more, except that was all he could get out. Hopefully she'd put it down to a male thing and basic communication. He liked to praise his partners, tell them how sexy they were and how beautiful they looked with the flush of arousal shining on their skin. This time he had nothing. Instead, he grasped her tight, only moving when her insistent shoving at his shoulders told him his weight was a problem. Charlie rolled until she lay on top of him.

"Thank you," she said in a solemn voice.

"Are you being polite?"

"No. That was good. I didn't think I'd ever have sex again."

"Why not? You're beautiful. Sexy. Any male would be lucky to have you in their bed." The thought of another man with his hands on Leticia brought a frown.

"I have FIV. Gavin must have told you I'm dying."

Shock whopped him in the chest. "He said nothing about dying." He'd said she was worse...

"It's true. I have all the symptoms. None of the shifter males looks at me, apart from Gavin. I've lost weight, sleep little—"

"Don't say that. You're beautiful."

"I'm going bald!" she blurted.

It was as if someone had wrenched his heart and squeezed it in a cruel grip. For fleeting seconds he didn't know what to say, how to make it better. Tears sparkled in her eyes, and as he watched one ran free, tracking down her cheek.

"Babe." He rubbed away the tear with his thumb. Then he held her and let her cry. He murmured soft words of nonsense and ran his hand up and down her tense back until she relaxed and the hoarse sound of her sobs didn't fill the room.

About five minutes later he realized she'd fallen asleep. She didn't even wake when he released her and gently rolled her into the middle of the bed. He removed the condom, covered her and left the room, closing the door after him. Although he'd intended to shower here, he didn't want to wake her and decided to let her sleep. Charlie grabbed his bag and after writing a note telling her to join him at the café later if she wanted, he left the house to have a shower at his own place. Running away perhaps, but he needed time.

When he parked outside the police station ready to start work, turmoil still churned inside. In one magical week he'd found two people to love. Logic told him it was impossible, although that didn't stop his heart from lurching at the thought of holding and touching either Gavin or Leticia. Kissing them. His fingers prodded the mark at his neck, desire sizzling painfully through him. He'd found his future. An exciting time, yet how could he celebrate when one of them was going to die?

Chapter 7

Jealousy

G avin left the foal in safe hands, quietly confident about its chances of survival since they'd managed to get it to drink. He glanced at his watch and knew he didn't have time to go home, yet he turned his vehicle in that direction anyway. Charlie's car wasn't there when he arrived at his house so he went to the police station, deciding it would be best to talk to him before he saw Leticia.

"Charlie, are you busy?"

"Good morning, Gavin," Laura said, a brow rising to remind him of his manners.

"Laura. Hi. I need to speak with Charlie. It's important." His gaze darted to Charlie, trying to communicate his urgency.

Inquisitiveness blazed in Laura. Gavin could tell she wanted to ask questions. She opened her mouth but Charlie stood. "I'm going to the café. Can I bring you back a coffee?"

Laura nodded. "Sure. I'll take my usual."

"Right." He stood and rounded his desk, brushing a casual kiss on Gavin's lips. "I left my wallet at your place. Do you have money?"

Some of the tension trickled out of Gavin. He caught the startled expression on Laura's face, followed by her grin. "Yeah, I have money. Is Leticia okay?"

"I left her sleeping."

Aware of Laura's wagging ears, Gavin asked no more questions. They'd already given her enough private information, and he could see she was dying to voice her curiosity. "Good. I don't have long. I'm meant to be over at the Jensens' farm to look at one of their cows."

Charlie stalked over to the door and opened it for him before turning back to Laura. "Won't be long."

"I wasn't sure if you wanted to let people know about us," Gavin murmured.

"I refuse to hide our relationship. We're mates." Charlie shot him a quick glance before starting down the steps. "Sorry to hurry you, but I don't have long either."

Even more of the tension left Gavin's shoulders, and he jogged to catch up with Charlie. There was something else they needed to discuss. Gavin knew it, except he hesitated. He could smell Leticia on Charlie, and it pushed at his feline. But what else could he expect since he'd left them in bed together?

"Leticia cried herself to sleep."

"What happened?" Despite his worry, a hint of jealousy tugged at him. He'd wanted Leticia for so long. He knew none of this was Charlie's fault but it didn't stop his regret or envy.

"We made love." Charlie stopped walking, his expression one of caution. "Is that a problem?"

Jealousy swelled into a gnawing ache in his gut. "Don't mind me." Gavin strode away from Charlie, attempting to get his riotous emotions under control. Leticia—damn, this wasn't bloody fair. Finding a mate should be a time of celebration. Instead, envy festered in him at the thought of Charlie and Leticia together.

"Dammit, Gavin. Don't do this. You left us alone. You must have known what would happen." Charlie grabbed his shoulder and dragged him to a halt.

"What about me?"

"What about you? You're my mate. You're Leticia's mate. We both need you. Get a grip and help her. She thinks she's dying, Gavin."

Gavin swallowed, the truth hitting him with blinding force. It was possible she would die, and the thought of it killed him, worse than the resentment eating him. "I won't lie to you. It's not looking good for her. And it's true I'm having a problem handling my feelings about you being with Leticia. If it weren't for the virus, we'd be together."

Charlie's mouth firmed, his eyes flashed as he shoved open the door to the café. The doorbell tinkled when they entered. Emily appeared from out the back. "Hi, Emily. I'll take my usual and a takeaway coffee for Laura."

Fuck, that hadn't come out too well. "I'll take an orange juice," Gavin said. "Grab a seat and I'll pay." He tugged his wallet out of his rear jeans pocket and handed over a twenty-dollar note, joining Charlie in the far corner. "Sorry. I shouldn't have said that. I...sorry, okay?" To his relief, Charlie gave a curt jerk of his head in acknowledgement. Gavin's breath eased out as he surveyed the inhabitants of the café.

A harried mother sat at one table, drinking a coffee while keeping an eye on her two toddlers. Two elders occupied another table, both members of the council who governed the felines in the area. A chessboard sat between them. Gavin gave them a respectful nod before turning his attention to Charlie again.

"How was it when you were with Leticia?" Gavin had to force the words out, mostly because he didn't like to think of Leticia with another male. He held his breath, waiting for the answer even though he didn't want to know. His hands fisted on his lap and he consciously relaxed them.

"It was as if we belonged, the same as me and you." Charlie forced a smile at Emily when she delivered their drinks and waited until she left before speaking again. "I wanted to bite her shoulder. I don't understand because I'm not feline."

Gavin sighed. "I'm not sure I understand either." The doorbell tinkled, and he cast a disinterested glance at the new arrival—until he saw her. "It's Leticia."

"I left a note for her," Charlie said. "I figured she'd do better with normal things."

"Good thinking." He cast a quick professional eye over her. She looked brighter than the previous day, a delicate flush in her cheeks instead of the paleness. Too thin though. "Hi, sweetheart. How are you today?" He stood and pulled out a chair for her.

Leticia sat, her gaze flickering over to Charlie. The color in her face intensified. "Still a bit tired. I think I could sleep for a week."

Charlie took her hand. "So you sleep. No problem."

"Leticia, what do you think about Charlie?"

Her mouth dropped open. "That's personal," she snapped, tossing her head. Her brown eyes flashed, shooting golden lights at him.

"Tell me."

"I...I think he's my mate, except that's not possible. Right?" Confusion clouded her eyes when she looked to him for answers. "Because you and I..."

Gavin let out a slow breath because it was the same with him—they were both mates. It was what he'd told Saul and Lucas. "I've never heard of a three-way mating before."

"And now you have," Charlie said. "Get over it and deal. We're together—all three of us." He rose abruptly. "Gotta go. I'll see you both tonight at your place." He paused to scowl at both of them. "We're sleeping together. Get plenty of sleep this afternoon, babe. You're gonna need it." He took two steps

147

before stopping. Turning, he returned and brushed a kiss over Leticia's lips. He squeezed Gavin's shoulder before kissing him too. "See you later."

They both stared after him while he collected a takeaway coffee from Emily and strode out the door.

"He's serious?" Leticia asked.

"Oh yeah." Gavin stroked the back of her hand, light of mind after Charlie's blunt speaking. "Sounds as if we have quite the night in store for us."

"Are you sure Leticia is well enough to do this?" Charlie grabbed two beers and a juice from the fridge.

Leticia planted her hands on her hips. Her glare held a glint of frustration. "Hello. I'm right here. I have FIV. I'm not deaf." She watched the two men communicate without words, a flutter of nervousness trembling through her.

What if she lost control and used her teeth? She couldn't bear it if she spread the disease to Gavin.

"Maybe this isn't a good idea. I might hurt you." After accepting the juice she'd asked for, she sank onto a chair at the small kitchen table. Already she could imagine the reaction if she passed along the infection—the mass hysteria and panic amongst the feline residents of Middlemarch. They'd run her out of town. A shudder worked through her body and her hand trembled so bad she set her juice onto the table. "This is a bad idea."

"I want this," Gavin said, crossing to her side. He pulled out the chair next to her and sat down, taking one of her hands between his. Warmth filled his green eyes, and she struggled to remain calm, not to pull away from his touch. She swallowed in an effort to hide her nerves. Gavin had filled her dreams for months, yet she'd told herself to keep away. She'd managed well too—until this week.

"You didn't hurt me. What we did together was amazing." Charlie took possession of the chair on the other side of her. He scooted close so his thigh touched hers.

Warmth crept down her leg and she swallowed again, not sure whether to move or not.

"Besides," Charlie said. "I have a plan to keep your mouth very busy while Gavin fucks you."

Leticia flinched, his candid speaking bringing conflicted feelings. "I...um..."

"Everything we do tonight and in the future will be consensual," Gavin stated. "If you don't want this, Charlie and I will retire to our own room. But you will stay here with us so I can monitor you professionally."

The silence seemed to throb. Leticia didn't know what to do, what to say. The hairs at the back of her neck and on her arms and legs lifted, and she knew if she were in feline form, she'd appear larger due to her discomfort. A ragged sigh whispered past her lips. Despite the temptation...no, she couldn't do this.

She had to do the right thing. "I don't want this."

Gavin's hand tightened on hers. "Define *this*."

"Sex. I don't want sex." She refused to look at either of them, her chest tight with both fear and acute disappointment. Never let anyone say she hadn't done the right thing.

"You had sex with Charlie."

"I know, and I'm sorry. I shouldn't have." Damn, why was she such a bitch?

Charlie's intense gaze scanned her before his shoulders lifted in a faint shrug. "It's all right, Leticia. We won't force you to sleep with us. I'll start cooking dinner."

"Fine." Gavin released her hand, the loss of contact like a rejection. "Charlie's right. Neither of us is interested in forced sex. While Charlie's starting dinner I'll get you set up in the spare room."

"Okay. Thanks," Leticia said. At least they weren't making a big deal out of her refusal.

"I thought Leticia would say yes." Gavin sprawled out on the bed, naked and watching his mate's every move.

"She's scared. We need to give her time." Charlie unbuttoned his uniform shirt and tossed it aside. Making short work of the rest of his clothes, he strode to the bed and dropped down beside Gavin. "Forget about Leticia. Kiss me. I need attention."

A snort escaped and he rolled toward Charlie to find him grinning. His mate understood and wanted to distract him.

Gavin read it on his face. His gaze dropped to the small bruise near his mark. He hadn't left the bruise on Charlie. *Leticia*. Damn, he had to get a grip on his jealousy.

"Any particular place you'd like me to kiss you?"

Charlie smirked. "I could draw you a diagram. Let me grab the can of whipped cream out of the fridge."

Gavin grabbed his forearm before he could roll away. "Don't need a map. I'm skilled with anatomy. It's my specialty." Leaning over, he brushed a light kiss to Charlie's lips. When Charlie took the initiative, deepening the kiss, Gavin groaned. Instant heat reverberated between them. The lazy stroke of Charlie's tongue against his sent pleasure surging. He let his weight settle on his lover, trapping their cocks between their bodies.

When he lifted his head, Charlie grinned at him. "Damn, I think you're right. Anatomy is one of your best subjects."

"You ain't seen nothing yet."

"Show me," Charlie whispered, spreading his thighs and relaxing beneath him. The trust on his face humbled Gavin and made him happier.

"You bet." Gavin pressed another soft kiss on Charlie's mouth while his hand smoothed across the raised marking site. He kept the kiss easy with gentle suction of his mouth while his hands skimmed with purpose and skill, driving the pleasure between them. He rocked his hips, grinding his cock against Charlie's belly. With each pump of his hips, he pushed up the tension between them until Charlie moaned without reservation, bucking against him to get the pressure he needed on his cock.

Gavin strummed his fingers across the mating mark and watched Charlie's face lost in pleasure. His dick wept freely against Gavin's stomach, yet still Gavin took his time. His lips lingered against Charlie's throat, the rasp of five o'clock shadow bringing a shudder of desire.

"Soon I'll get the lube and stretch you ready for my cock. I'll fill you, slide deep and make you hot for me." Gavin's mouth sought the mark, rasping his tongue back and forth.

Charlie gasped, angling his head to give Gavin better access. "How hot?"

"So hot you'll whimper with it."

"Don't do whimpering." A choked, breathless sound squeezed past his lips when Gavin used his teeth on the mark. "Shit. Yeah. Okay."

Gavin grinned, his heart lightening. "That's what I thought."

"If I'm going down whimpering," Charlie said, "then I'm taking you with me."

"Yeah?"

"Yeah." Charlie rocked against him, hissing when their cocks rubbed together, the friction incredible.

Gavin couldn't prevent his moan of pleasure. This—being with Charlie—he could get used to big time. He dipped his head and kissed his lover, accepting the eager pressure of Charlie's lips, the open giving in return. Charlie needed him, and he needed Charlie.

The creak of the bedroom door lifted his head. Gavin turned his head, growled at the interruption.

"I couldn't sleep." Leticia stood in the doorway, her tawny blonde hair hanging around her shoulders. Her oversized T-shirt hung in loose folds around her slender body. "I—" She broke off, a delicate flush flooding her cheeks. "Sorry. I'll go."

"Don't go, babe."

Gavin hid his amusement. Charlie looked distinctly predatory and damned if it didn't turn him on. His hips shifted, and he ground his dick against Charlie.

"Wouldn't you like to watch?" Charlie purred.

Hell, the man even sounded like a feline now.

Charlie didn't wait for Leticia to reply. "Come closer. You'll get a better view."

Leticia hesitated, and after sending a warning glance at Charlie, Gavin climbed off his mate and went to her.

"Come on. You can sleep in here. There's room for three."

"But...but I shouldn't be here." Deeper color suffused her face when Gavin caught her ogling his erection.

"Of course you should." Gavin suppressed a satisfied smile, clasped her hand and led her to the bed. He hoped like hell that they didn't scare her off again.

"Come on, babe," Charlie said. "I need a hug."

She slipped into his arms, and Gavin let his breath ease out with relief. He returned and reached for the bedside lamp, flipping the switch and plunging the room into darkness.

Gavin slid across the mattress until his body lay flush with Leticia. She clung to Charlie, although this time jealousy didn't stir. He smoothed aside her long hair and nuzzled her neck. Before he could think, his tongue flicked out to lick. Her spicy flavor filled his mouth. Temptation rocked him and he gave in, pressing a kiss against a throbbing pulse point. For an instant, she froze before the tension seeped away and she relaxed, giving him free rein without objection.

"Gavin. Charlie," she whispered.

"Now we have you right where we want you, babe."

Gavin chuckled at Charlie's lascivious tone. "We certainly do. The question is what are we going to do to you first?" A quick glance at Charlie and they decided. Just like that, without a word spoken.

With his right hand, Gavin stroked the smooth skin of her throat before grasping her left shoulder and exerting enough force to make her lie on her back. She blinked once, long lashes falling to screen her eyes. Nerves. He'd seen them before her lashes hid her thoughts from view. Understandable. The faint tremor in his hands spoke of his own anxiety. He could scarcely believe this was happening—the two people he cared for most were in his house, his bed.

"What are you going to do?" The bleed-through of uneasiness was evident in her voice, the throaty drawl uncertain.

Gavin opened his mouth to speak, except nothing came out apart from a croak. A searching look from Charlie transformed into understanding. The reality of being with both his mates

154

had thrown him into a place he'd never imagined and now worry and satisfaction combined inside to bring distinct apprehension.

Charlie answered her question for him. "We're gonna love you, babe. Give you pleasure and receive it in return. We're gonna make you see how it could be with the three of us together in one tight unit. Can you deal with that?"

"I...I'm frightened," she said in a rush of words.

"Gavin is terrified too," Charlie said, taking him by surprise even though every word was truthful. "Just as well you both have me here to act as an anchor."

The moment Charlie spoke, Gavin understood the accuracy of his statement. An anchor. One human and two felines. Charlie was the cement to make them strong if only he and Leticia were brave enough to take this step.

"This will be good," Charlie said with quiet confidence. His certainty eased some of Gavin's nerves, and Gavin noticed Leticia relaxed a fraction too. Charlie trailed his fingers over Leticia's shoulder, sending an encouraging wink in his direction. Taking a deep breath, Gavin mirrored Charlie's actions. He traced Leticia's collarbone and shoulder, savoring the gift of being able to touch. A purr of contentment erupted from him, rivaled only by Leticia's soft sighs as she succumbed to their touches. Every tight muscle unclenched and she seemed to melt into the mattress.

"Let's take off your sleepshirt before you get too comfortable." Charlie helped her to a sitting position and lifted her to whisk the oversized T-shirt over her head before she had time to blink. Dressed in only brief white cotton panties, she relaxed into the mattress again. It was the first time for ages Gavin had allowed himself to look at her as an attractive and sexy female instead of his patient. His cock lifted in reaction and unbidden his hand reached for one breast.

He must have made a sound because Charlie leaned over and placed an unhurried kiss on his lips, soothing and gentling him. For a second their mouths clung and a groan escaped. His groan. Damn, this man made him forget everything. When Charlie drew back, he smiled and turned his attention to Leticia.

"Would you...ah, like me to go?" she asked.

Gavin had never heard her sound so diffident, and her uncertainty shored his own flagging confidence. "No. Didn't you listen? We both want you here with us."

With a conspiratorial smile at Gavin, Charlie dipped his head and kissed the curve of one breast. Good idea. He couldn't wait to touch her more intimately and let the passion build. Gavin bent and copied Charlie, mirroring his actions. His mouth settled on the plump curve of a breast. Damn. Emotion rushed through him, tightening his throat and stinging his eyes. He'd never thought this would ever happen, and he wondered if he'd wake up and find the entire situation nothing but a fabrication made up by his desperate mind.

"Take her nipple into your mouth, Gavin," Charlie ordered.

Gavin stared at his mate, their gazes connecting and holding. He couldn't believe this man wanted him, wanted Leticia as badly as he did. Yeah, dream territory.

"Go on," Charlie said. "You know you want to. Touch her how you've always dreamed. Do it. Now."

A harsh breath whistled through his lips. How he'd dreamed... A quick look at Leticia showed her tension. Their thoughts ran in parallel. Hell, Lucas would kill him if something happened to Leticia because of him, and nothing Saul did would save him from Lucas's wrath.

Shoving aside his unease, he cupped her jaw with his hand and kissed her. His tongue slipped into her warm mouth. Heaven—more, better than he'd dreamed. He savored the soothing touch of Charlie's hand at his shoulder as he deepened the kiss, excitement soaring through him. His heart thumped in erratic stutters while the rest of his body reacted in a purely masculine manner.

Sexual. He snorted, knowing he wouldn't last long. Touching and kissing Leticia wound him tighter than a feline teenager about to experience a first shift. When he lifted his head, Charlie squeezed his shoulder again.

"You could follow my order now," he said. "Get with the program and suck her nipple."

Gavin's brows rose. "Or what?"

Charlie snorted. "Probably a punishment of some sort in there, except I don't have the energy to think of it right now. Let's just say if you don't follow my orders—and make no mistake I am in charge here—there will be consequences in the future."

"What about me?" Leticia asked.

"Consequences for you too, princess. Obey and there won't be any trouble."

"I guess we'd better do as he says," Gavin said, a spurt of happiness taking him by surprise. Charlie—the catalyst for change. Dang, he was glad he'd found the human. Still smiling, he leaned over Leticia and teased a little first, taking tiny bites out of the creamy flesh of one breast. Her soft sigh of pleasure filled him with satisfaction, made him want more.

"Gavin." The warning in Charlie's voice jolted him, an electrical charge rushing through his body to settle in his shaft. Grinning against Leticia's breast, he finally obeyed. His mouth opened and closed around one pouting nipple. He laved it with his tongue, heard Leticia's throaty groan, felt it vibrate through him.

Charlie moved and settled at Leticia's other breast. When Gavin lifted his head a fraction, their eyes met. Charlie's cheeks hollowed as he sucked, and Gavin followed suit. The heat in Charlie's eyes intensified, and Gavin could read his mate's thoughts. He loved the soft cries coming from Leticia. He liked being with both of them, and Charlie loved being in charge. It was giving him a real buzz. Hell, Gavin was finding it strangely liberating giving up control for a change and following orders instead of being the one issuing them. He hadn't realized how much the stress in his job ate at him. Giving over control might benefit him. Something to ponder later once he was alone.

Charlie lifted his head. "You stay up here for the moment. Kiss her mouth, her breasts and make her desperate to take us."

"Don't I get a say in this?" Leticia's eyes glowed in the same manner his did when his feline came to the surface. An answering surge came from his feline, as if he recognized a mate.

"Not today," he whispered against her lips. "Charlie's in charge tonight." He cradled her head and kissed her again, savoring the slow dance of tongues and lips. Damn, he'd missed out on so much time. The back of his eyes stung as he glided his fingers over her thin blonde hair beneath his fingers. It brought home what they faced with the progress of the disease.

His lips slid across her firm jaw and he forced thoughts of disease and death away. He was bloody lucky to have this time with Leticia. If it weren't for Charlie, he didn't think he'd have progressed this far with her. His lips nibbled at her neck, moving downward toward her chest. He savored her tentative fingers running through his hair, and as her confidence built, the firm press on his shoulders, the teasing swish across the marking site.

He swallowed, the sizzle of pleasure brutal. Intense. Gasping hoarsely, he struggled against the need to tease, to bite in return. A low groan slipped free when she repeated the move, using her teeth. "Damn, Leticia. Don't tease me. I can't...I'm not sure if I can keep control if you do that."

"Leticia. No teasing. Close your eyes and concentrate on what we're doing to you. I want you to let the pleasure build. Part your legs for me, babe."

Gavin started, having forgotten about Charlie for a second, although he was glad of the reminder, the buffer between steering a straight line and jumping straight into stupidity. Leticia's fears of spreading the disease to him weren't groundless. Blood contact would do it easily enough.

Sensations flooded Leticia, running so close together and with such power if felt as if she were in a vast undertow. Two men paying attention to her, telling her to close her eyes and suffer through it. Heck, she was suffering all right. A pair of lips brushed over hers, a barely there touch. Gavin's musky scent with the underlying sandalwood and citrus flooded every panting breath.

"Lift your hips for me, Leticia."

Like a mindless robot, she followed the husky instruction, pushing up with her legs. Charlie whisked off her panties, leaving her as naked as the two men. She swallowed, suffering a moment's hesitation. Two men at once. It wasn't right. She shouldn't...

A kiss at her breast broke into her tortured thoughts. Gavin. He drew her nipple into the warmth of his mouth and sucked hard. A ribbon of sensation twirled through her body, heading straight to her pussy. A slow-trailing finger moved the length of her slit, and like an echo, the magical sensation zapping straight back to her breast. She gasped, her body straining, alternatively arching upward into mouth and finger, wanting more touches, more pleasure. *Just more*. A moan sounded, and it took a while to realize the sound came from her.

"Spread your legs a little farther for me, babe." Charlie's husky voice ratcheted up the pleasure and sense of acute anticipation. She followed the order without hesitation.

"Damn, you are perfect, Leticia." Gavin punctuated the words with a kiss that stole her breath. At the same time, there was a swish of a tongue that ran the length of her slit. Oh hell. A garbled protest rushed off her tongue, but Gavin's mouth trapped it. He stroked and kissed her, soothing her initial panic until she relaxed again.

"Good girl," Charlie murmured before he resumed his assault on her flesh. The stroke of a finger, the probe of his tongue. The sensations layered one on top of another until she panted. Pleasure rose, swirling through her in waves. Charlie increased the friction and her hips strained upward, wanting more of his teasing touch. Every nerve seemed to light, glowing inside her.

"I need you inside me."

"I'm conducting the party here," Charlie murmured seconds before he swirled his tongue around her clit and back down to delve in her folds. Leticia groaned and both she and Gavin stared at Charlie. He lifted his head and grinned at them, his lips shiny with her honey. "That's so good. Gavin, is it safe for you to taste too?"

161

"I...it should be." Gavin cleared his throat and refused to look at her. "The virus is spread by biting, although prolonged exposure can hold a risk of infection."

"Kissing?" Charlie asked in a harsh voice.

"It should be okay."

Charlie reached over to switch on the bedside lamp and glared at Gavin. "But you're not sure."

Leticia wrenched from Gavin's touch, staring at him in horror. "How can you bear to touch me, knowing I could give this disease to you?" Horror swept through her, driving away every bit of banked passion. It was like a balloon bursting, all the euphoria exploding out with one pinprick.

"Contact with blood through biting—" Gavin broke off when he noticed their expressions.

"You're not sure. That's not good enough. Leticia and I don't want to lose you, not now that we've found you. Gavin, we both need you."

"I can't...can't..." Leticia shuddered, fear and loathing filling her mind. This disease—it had wrecked her life, changed her brother's life irrevocably. There was no way she could subject Gavin to the disease. Nothing had changed. Nothing. "I can't do this."

"Don't leave. Please." Gavin cast a beseeching glance at her, and she swallowed before looking away.

"I can't. It's bad enough now, knowing about the disease inside me. I couldn't live with myself if I knew I'd given you a life sentence." She sniffed, trying valiantly to stem the rising tears. "I don't want you to die too."

"Aw, damn," Gavin muttered.

Leticia sat up and hid her face against her raised knees. Deep down she'd known it was a bad idea to come into Gavin's room. A bad, bad idea, but the loneliness had become too much. She could hear Gavin and Charlie, the murmurs, the creak of the bed.

The mattress depressed beside her and Charlie's arms wrapped around her shoulders. "Gavin knows what he's doing."

"He doesn't," she sobbed. "He's lonesome, like me, and that's making him take chances."

"That's not true," Gavin said. "I have a mate."

Oh yeah. That was right. Gavin had Charlie. The tears that had slowed, picked up pace again. For the first time she understood what if meant to be alone in a room with other people.

"Stop thinking so hard, Leticia. Both Gavin and I want you here with us. We can work around your FIV."

Gavin smoothed his hand over her shoulder. How she knew it was him rather than Charlie she didn't know. She sensed it. Damn, she was such a fool, making one mistake after another. Why had she succumbed to her impulse to come into the bedroom? She snorted—a derisive sound aimed at herself. Heck, simple answer to that one. Loneliness. She was so tired of her solitary state.

"Lie down, babe. You need rest."

"No," she said.

Gavin pulled away so she could see his face. Oh boy. His doctor face. "Yeah, you should sleep, Leticia." The words confirmed it. "You need all the rest you can get to regain your strength."

She wanted to say she had plenty of time to rest when she was dead. She didn't, guessing the shocked response she'd receive. People were uncomfortable with death. Hell, she was uncomfortable with it, but she was also a realist.

"I'm not tired." The yawn that opened her mouth an instant later made both men laugh. "Fine," she snapped. "I'm a little tired."

Charlie chuckled. "Lie down then. Sleep." Gentle hands forced her down toward the mattress, and sighing, she gave up the fight. At least she'd had sex this morning with Charlie. Her lady parts hadn't dried up or atrophied from lack of use. Things weren't all bad.

With a sigh of defeat, Leticia followed instructions and the two men settled, one on either side of her. Gavin leaned over, flipped the switch on the bedside lamp and plunged the room into darkness. They both cuddled into her, cocooning her in warmth. Her eyes closed, and she sighed again, their presence filling the solitary spots inside.

Charlie watched Leticia drift into sleep. Poor thing. It couldn't be easy going through what she was, through no fault of her own. He thought about her, he thought about Gavin. He thought about the three of them together. Finally, he moved away from Leticia, and after he'd checked he hadn't woken her, he climbed from bed and left the room. His mind was way too busy to attempt sleep. Perhaps television would settle him.

Down in the lounge, Charlie shut the door and grabbed the remote. The blare of music had him scrambling to find the volume button. With the sound problem sorted, he sank onto one of the leather chairs, staring at the screen while his mind chewed over what had just happened with Leticia. Gavin... He shook his head, his gut churning with fear, with anger.

"Charlie? Are you okay?" Gavin stood in the doorway, naked.

"Fuck, yes, there's something wrong." Charlie vaulted to his feet, letting his fear spill out in fury. "You would risk your life to be with Leticia? Don't you care about me at all?" He winced when he heard his words, his anger.

"I...fuck! Okay, what I did was stupid. I admit it. Are you satisfied?"

"But you still did it. You still kissed Leticia, and if she had said nothing, you would have gone down on her, knowing there was a risk you could catch FIV."

"A tiny chance."

Charlie took one look at Gavin's face and swore. "You'd do it again." He dragged a hand through his hair and turned away, fists clenched at his sides. Long strides took him across the room until he ran out of space. He turned and crossed the room again, dodging both a faded brown leather chair and Gavin. Difficult to believe he'd mated with a man who had suicidal tendencies. Shit!

"Understand what it's been like for me. The proximity to Leticia with both of us naked…"

Charlie stalked another circuit of the room before coming to an abrupt halt to glare at Gavin. "Do you have a death wish? What happens if you die, if you both die? Have you thought of that?"

Shock bleached Gavin's face white. "I'm sorry. I didn't think."

A derisive snort escaped Charlie. "That's a piss-poor excuse."

"I know. I know. It's all I have."

Another speedy circuit of pacing did nothing to settle his anger. It made him realize how much he'd come to care for Gavin in a short time.

Gavin leaned against the wall, watching him. With another curse, Charlie spun away, finding a measure of control in the physical movement. He sensed Gavin scrutinizing him, and despite his irritation, arousal crept through him, filling his cock.

"You realize it's difficult for a guy to pace naked," Gavin said.

"Yeah, well. You don't look so dignified propping up the wall in your naked state either."

"I'm sorry, okay? It was stupid. I was stupid, although I'd like to point out the chances of passing the virus via a kiss or sexual fluids is small. Leticia could even have kids and the chances are something like ninety-eight percent that the child would be healthy. The only way she could pass the virus on to me or another feline would be for her to bite and draw blood."

Charlie raked a hand through his hair. "Damn, I hate this."

"And you think I don't? Jesus, Charlie. She's my mate. She's your mate too, and she's dying. What the hell are we going to do?"

Chapter 8

We're Gonna Lose Her

Charlie sensed Gavin's anguish. The same pain that filled him, clutching his heart. It made him think of his mortality. "Are you sure there's no cure?"

"I've researched until my eyes hurt. So far there's no known cure, not once the disease is passed by a bite."

"We're gonna lose her," Charlie said.

"Yeah. I think so. I...despite my training I'm so bloody helpless."

"Fuck." Charlie swallowed, the onset of tears close when he seldom cried. He went to Gavin then, crossing the room in two long strides and hauling him into his arms. Raw and primitive grief threatened to overwhelm him. Wetness dampened his chest from Gavin's weeping and tears leaked from his eyes too.

They clung for a long time, needing the comfort and each other's touch to counteract the despair.

Gavin lifted his head, his dark lashes spiky with moisture. "We should try to sleep."

"Yeah." Charlie didn't move though, his mind on something else. Probably best to spit it out and go from there. "Would you consider fucking me?"

"Now?"

"Yeah. I need to feel alive. Is that wrong?" Honesty as far as it went. A sliver of jealousy had crept into his thoughts. While he physically craved Gavin, his mate wanted Leticia as well as him. Granted, he enjoyed Leticia's company, and the lovemaking had been hot between them. His connection with her was like a piece of a jigsaw slotting into place, but Gavin filled his mind now. He wanted—no needed—to stake his claim.

Damn, he was figuratively pissing to mark territory. A bark of laughter rang through his head. Too bad the knowledge didn't knock sense into him. He still wanted to make love with Gavin. Tonight. Now.

"No, it's not wrong. You want to go to the spare room?"

Charlie nodded. "Sure." Because Leticia was in Gavin's—their room. He narrowed his eyes on Gavin. "You're not trying to keep this a secret from Leticia?"

The swift expression of shock answered his question. "Hell no. You're my marked mate. I will not hide you or pretend anything but the truth when it comes to us."

169

Gavin's words went a long way toward settling the unease gripping his chest. The band of tension released, and he could breathe again. He nodded, thoughts whirring through his head. They didn't know each other well, yet given time, he was sure they could work out any difficulty facing them. Yeah, time would fix everything, apart from Leticia.

Without another word, they both padded from the room, Charlie pausing to switch off the television and the light. When they reached the bedroom, Gavin closed the door behind them and turned to him.

"We'll talk more tomorrow."

"Okay." Charlie knew it wouldn't be easy. Their relationship had become important to him though, and he'd do everything he could to work things out between them. "Kiss me."

"Yes." Gavin prowled across the floor, almost tackling him. They fell to the bed in a tangle of limbs, lips melded together, while they fought for control to see who came out on top.

Charlie laughed as they wrestled. With a grunt, Gavin rolled him and he found himself staring up into his mate's green eyes. A distinct twinkle glinted in them. Charlie tried to throw Gavin off and failed. "Now you have me," he said. "Exactly what do you intend to do with me?"

"I'm going to love you." Gavin's mouth came down on his again, a gentle kiss that ignited into passion. Charlie's arms wrapped around Gavin's shoulders while they communicated with actions rather than words. The slide of lips. The flicker of a tongue. The brush of cocks and the rasp of stubble. Gavin's mouth was hot and wet, the lazy stroke of his tongue arousing. His lips parted from Charlie's to drift across his jaw, then down his neck. Charlie knew where Gavin's attention headed, and a hungry groan escaped as a moist breath caressed his face. His shaft bucked, urgency and desire coalescing into a tight sensation in his groin.

"Damn. Gavin." He spread his thighs, hips canting upward in silent entreaty.

"Patience." His lips settled over Charlie's mark and he sucked.

A blast of fiery heat engulfed Charlie. His cock jerked, and he slipped his hand down between their bodies to soothe the ache. "I will come if you keep that up." His hand curled around his dick. The crown was damp with pre-cum, allowing an easy pump of his hand. Intense pleasure sizzled through him, the musky scent of Gavin filling his every breath. The suction of Gavin's mouth and the massaging grip of his fist had him shuddering, gasping. "You're making me crazy."

"That's the object," Gavin said, lifting his mouth. He rubbed his thumb over the raised scar and moved down the bed. Seconds later his lips wrapped around Charlie's cock. The wet heat sent pressure rampaging the length of his body, made him gasp and want to plead.

Damn, making love pre Gavin hadn't packed the same punch, it hadn't made him whole as it did now. Another gasp squeezed out. His hips jerked upward, rocking his cock deeper. Gavin's tongue swirled over the head, teased the sensitive underside and sucked until the sparks of heat frayed every bit of control. The pressure of Gavin's fingers massaging his mark pushed him even higher. With a convulsive heave of muscles, he shot his seed into Gavin's mouth, the swallowing action lengthening the pleasure.

His cock softened, and with a final swipe of his tongue, Gavin released him. He picked up the bottle of lube he'd grabbed from their room before they left Leticia to sleep and squeezed some onto his hand. Charlie watched his lover's face, anticipation making his cock fill again. It was true. He'd never experienced this before, needed his lover quite as much. The intensity of the hunger, the urgency was almost scary. Almost. Not enough to make him stop though. Every time he saw his lover, he wanted to touch.

"I want you," Gavin said.

"I'm all yours. Take me." Nothing less than the truth.

Gavin took him at his word, but instead of stretching him, he explored with his mouth, teasing his balls and licking down toward his puckered hole. Charlie groaned, the intense pleasure growing into hunger. The moist sensation of a tongue, teasing across his entrance shot his arousal to pre-orgasm heights.

"Damn. Gavin."

Gavin lifted his head and grinned up at him. "You don't have much of a vocab."

"We'll see how much conversation you have when I'm tonguing you."

Gavin laughed and went back to his teasing. After a final lick, he used his fingers, the lube now warmed from his body

172

heat. A second finger soon joined his first. Charlie squirmed, shuddering when Gavin pegged his gland. This time the tempo wasn't as urgent. "How are those fingers? Can you take another?"

"Yeah, give me more." The burn of pain melded with the explosive sensations to produce a rock-hard erection. He shuddered, his eyes closed to concentrate on Gavin's every touch.

"You're singeing my fingers. Tight. I can't wait to get my cock into you."

Charlie snorted and opened his eyes to study his lover. "So what's stopping you? I don't need more stretching. You're just teasing me now."

Gavin removed his fingers, grabbed more lube and rubbed it on his cock. Charlie caught his breath, anticipation soaring when Gavin guided his cock to his entrance. "I want to watch your face this time."

"Yes." Charlie caught Gavin's gaze and held it, a rocket of heat, pleasure and the sense of belonging filling him.

Gavin watched Charlie the entire time. The desire in his eyes went a long way to erasing the envy Charlie harbored toward Leticia. A purr sounded, and Gavin laughed. "Sometimes you're more feline than me." His laughter turned predatory and hunger vibrated between them as Gavin pushed, going slowly, forcing his way past the ring of muscle. Charlie sighed, relaxing into the pleasure-pain of the initial intrusion. Gavin pulled back a fraction before gliding back inside, moving deeper each time until his balls slapped against Charlie. Fully seated, he paused, breathing hard.

"You're so fuckin' tight. Hot. Good." Gavin retreated and slid back inside with a sigh of enjoyment. "Really good."

"I'm not fragile. Take me hard."

"If you have trouble sitting tomorrow, remember this was your idea."

Charlie snorted a laugh of amusement that ended on groan when Gavin took him at his word and slammed home. "Sitting. Yeah. And I say payback is a bitch."

Gavin withdrew, then thrust home, increasing the pace of his strokes. They both groaned, a fine sheen of sweat coating both their bodies. Charlie's cock brushed against his stomach, trapped between them.

"I'm gonna come," Gavin said, his voice harsh while they strained together. He grasped Charlie's cock and pumped it.

Charlie kissed Gavin's shoulder, letting his teeth graze the marking site.

"Damn. Do that again," Gavin ordered.

"You've healed. No one would know I've bitten you."

"Which means you should bite me again. I like you marking my body."

Charlie licked Gavin's shoulder again, and this time let his teeth sink in a little deeper. Gavin let out a low groan and sought the mark on Charlie's shoulder. He sucked deep.

Charlie's heart pounded, a choked, breathless sound escaping him. He gritted his teeth, wanting the enjoyment to last, to balance on the cusp of climax instead of toppling over straightaway. Didn't happen. Gavin pumped his cock again and Charlie's seed shot from him, blasting against his stomach. His rectum flexed and clasped Gavin's cock. He felt the surge of wetness inside and heard his lover's gasps of enjoyment as he came. Gradually their breathing returned to normal, and after a final rasp of his tongue over Charlie's mark, Gavin pulled free. He attempted to rise and dropped back against Charlie's chest, clasping him around the shoulders.

"I'm not sure I can walk," Gavin muttered, kissing him lightly.

"Good to know I can wear you out."

"Yeah." Gavin tried again, and this time rolled off the bed. When Charlie attempted to follow, he stayed him with a lifted hand. "Nah, stay there. I'll bring a cloth so you can clean up."

Charlie relaxed, watching Gavin's arse as he walked from the bedroom. Not long after he heard the faint sound of running water. His eyes closed and his thoughts wandered. There had to be some way of moving forward—the three of them—because he thought he'd lose it if something happened to Gavin. He couldn't lose Gavin, and Gavin needed Leticia with him. They had to work it out.

"Are you going to sleep?"

"Nah, restin' my eyes."

The mattress moved and a warm cloth drifted across his chest and stomach, wiping away the drying semen. Gavin cleaned his cock and tossed the cloth aside.

175

"Move over."

"There's no room to move over," Charlie countered. "Single bed, remember."

Gavin grunted and shoved at his shoulder, leaping onto the space he'd made. He wrapped Charlie in his arms and said, "We should talk now. We need to present a united front for Leticia."

A flash of anger hit Charlie, rushing through him like a vehicle without brakes. His gaze speared to Gavin, and this time he refused to let the emotion and hunger in his lover's sexy green eyes sway him. "You should have fuckin' told me about Leticia. I would have understood if you'd explained everything."

"Yeah, I know. I haven't handled this well."

"The way I see it, there's only one thing to do. I will share you with Leticia." Charlie tried to keep the caustic note from his voice and failed. The more he thought about it, the harder the jealousy bug bit. *Second choice*. The thought reverberated like a bell inside his head. He didn't bloody want second choice. "That's if you want me."

Gavin erupted into movement, spinning and rolling Charlie onto his back. Breathing hard, he gripped his biceps, holding Charlie in place. "This is the last time I'm gonna say this," he said in a hard voice. "I want you. Here with me. You are my mate."

"But—"

A harsh growl vibrated in Gavin's throat, his top lip curling up in a snarl of displeasure. "Don't piss me off. If I didn't want you, I wouldn't have marked you. We belong together."

"What about Leticia?"

"Have I mentioned you fucking her? Knowing what you had done together...do you think it wasn't like a kick in the gut, smelling her on you? Hell!" His eyes closed, his face twisted up in anguish. "I hate this."

Shame spread in Charlie. Gavin was right. This wasn't easy for any of them. He imagined Leticia suffered jealousy too. "I don't want anything to happen to you, Gavin. We can both be with Leticia, but you can't take risks. The community counts on you. I want you, so you have to keep control over your feline."

Gavin released Charlie's arms, relaxing into his embrace. "I'll try. It's difficult having Leticia in the same house."

"Maybe she could go back to the farm or, if the drive back and forth between Alexandra and Middlemarch is too much for her, she could stay with one of the Mitchells so you can still keep a close eye on her."

"No! I—oh hell." Gavin rubbed a hand over a whiskery chin, a harsh sigh filling the silence between them. "The disease is progressing so fast I need to see her each day. You've seen how exhausted she gets. The travel will be too much for her."

"So she stays and you keep your hands off."

"I don't think I can do that either," Gavin confessed, his tone rueful. "Not now that we've progressed as far as we have already."

"So the rules are easy. No biting. No intimate contact with your mouth, not if you're not sure of the consequences."

"Yeah. Okay. I'll try."

Charlie cursed. "No trying involved, Gavin. Either you follow the rules or you stay the hell away from Leticia. I'll tell Lucas if I have to. I'm sure he'd like to know we're both fucking his sister."

"Brave words. Lucas would thump both of us. You wouldn't escape the battle unscathed. Besides, I haven't fucked her."

"Yet." Humor filled Charlie then, and he said, "If you value my hide intact, you'd better play by the rules. This single bed sucks. Should we go back and sleep with Leticia?"

"Yeah." Gavin slid off the bed and hauled Charlie to his feet. Together they returned to Leticia and slid into the bed, one on each side of her.

Charlie pulled the covers up and closed his eyes, attempting to sleep. Despite Gavin's promise to do things safely, worry gnawed at his gut. The connection between them seemed to grow with each passing day. In the past, the future hadn't worried him. Things changed. He'd changed because now, he sure as hell harbored a shit load of apprehension.

Leticia woke slowly, once again toasty warm and happier than she'd felt for ages. Cautiously she sniffed, recognizing both Charlie and Gavin were in the bed with her. They'd left her alone for a while last night, leaving once they'd thought she slept. When she inhaled again, she caught the faint muskiness of sex and resentment sliced through her.

"I know you're awake, babe."

Leticia's eyes flew open to see Charlie's grin. Her heart knocked against her ribs when she recalled the previous morning and the way Charlie had loved her. She wanted that again. Every morning, until she was too sick to keep up with him.

"Morning, Leticia." She turned her head to see Gavin's intense gaze. His eyes glowed and a twist of arousal shot to her lower belly.

"Hi." The breathless quality to her voice gave away her longing.

A hand crept over her breast, toyed with her nipple, her arousal swift and instantaneous. When Gavin touched her other breast, mirroring Charlie's actions, a groan escaped.

"What are you doing?" she asked, breathing evenly in an attempt to control her pulse rate.

Gavin's eyes twinkled in a mischievous manner. "If you don't know, we're not doing a very good job."

They were doing a perfect job, and they both knew it. Every touch sent her soaring, made her want more. Arousal raced through her body, the intensity of it no longer taking her by surprise. Yesterday with Charlie hadn't been enough. She wanted Charlie again. She wanted Gavin. "I...I want both of you. That can't be normal."

Gavin shrugged, the shift of his shoulder bringing him closer to her. "It doesn't matter what anyone thinks, except the three of us." His mouth replaced his hand on her breast, the deep suction sending her from zero to go in seconds flat.

On her other side, Charlie moved down the bed, parting her legs. His warm breath moved across her folds, fingers and mouth slowly moving over her flesh. The twin suctions hurtled her into passion. Her body moistened, the liquid arousal as Charlie pushed a finger into her bringing a wash of color to her cheeks. A tremor raced through her. Gavin saw and chuckled. He rolled away from her and grabbed a condom, handing it to Charlie.

"No," Charlie said. "You use it."

"Would you like me to fuck you, Leticia?" Gavin's intense green eyes seared straight into her. She'd always thought he was sexy, but this was more intense. Her heart beat a rapid tattoo against her ribs. The sane part of her wanted to tell him to leave because the connection between them scared her and she feared it would only become worse. She'd become dependent. Bad enough now that she had to seek medical help all the time. What would it be like when she could no longer care for herself? She took a deep breath, ready to tell him no, that one of them had to act sensibly.

"Yes," she whispered.

His lips peeled back in a feral grin, his eyes stark and glittering with raw, male desire. Her body hummed, even though she knew this was a bad idea. Charlie smoothed his hand over her hip, the faint drag of his callused fingers eliciting a shudder, an explosion of hunger. The heat in her face told her she must appear flushed. A slow lap along her slit, down and back up to circle her clit. She twisted against Charlie's body, decadent warmth flooding her, driving away the lingering chill. Erotic promise filled the air, and selfishly she wanted to roll in it, play and linger. Snatch up memories while she still could.

"How are we going to do this?" Gavin asked Charlie.

Her lips tightened a fraction, annoyance dispersing some of the anticipation. *This.* "I'm not an object that needs special handling."

Pain flashed over Gavin's face. *Bitch.* She didn't need to act so catty. She'd drive both of them away if she weren't careful.

"Gavin wants to keep us all safe," Charlie said, the soothing of his hand stroking her flesh in direct contrast to the chiding note of his voice.

Damn, she was a bitch. Lucas had warned her that her snippy attitude would drive away men. "Sorry."

"Don't apologize. We know you're apprehensive. Gavin and I are too." He brushed a kiss over her inner thigh and moved away. "We'll do it this way. On your back Gavin."

Leticia caught her bottom lip between her teeth and bit down, trapping her protest inside. Was it too much to want spontaneous and spur-of-the-moment? All this planning and careful discussion took away the gloss and pleasure. Yesterday with Charlie... She cast him a longing glance before turning back to Gavin. Her chest expanded with a deep breath and she acknowledged the primitive hunger pulsing inside. Although she'd enjoyed things with Charlie, she needed Gavin.

"Give me the condom," Charlie said.

"I thought I—"

A smirk crossed Charlie's face, taking him from serious to mischievous. "It's an excuse to touch you. Leticia and I will put the condom on for you. Come on. Lie on your back and get ready for some fun." He winked at her, and Leticia's ruffled thoughts settled.

With a wry look at both of them, Gavin followed instructions and settled in the middle of the bed.

"Get him nice and hard," Charlie said. "Hands only this time. Don't make him come."

A quick glance at Gavin confirmed he wouldn't need much in the way of stimulation. His cock jolted while she studied it. "What are you gonna do?" Leticia asked, not taking her gaze off the long, hard length.

"I'm going to tease him a little. A few kisses."

"Bring it on," Gavin said, although Leticia noticed he seemed a trifle worried.

Moving closer, she grasped his cock, taking comfort from his gasp. She wasn't the only worried occupant in the room. Hard and hot to the touch. Smooth. Leticia ran her hands up and down his shaft, enjoying the velvety sensation and the underlying strength, the way he pulsed beneath her ministrations. A single fingertip traced across the broad head and dipped to brush the sensitive underside and the prominent vein.

"You won't hurt me," Gavin said. His trepidation had faded, replaced by frank interest. "Go on. I dare you."

"Good one, Gavin," Charlie said, chuckling. "She'll tease you unmercifully now. We're gonna gang up on you. I bet we can make you suffer." His glance at her held a clear challenge, and she returned his grin. "Roll the condom on him and after that, use your mouth, if that's what you'd like."

Leticia understood and approved. No intimate contact via mouth for her and Gavin. Unable to resist teasing Gavin, she stroked his cock again, massaging the bulbous head, the curved glans until a drop of liquid appeared at his slit. She dipped her head, moving closer, wanting to taste before she realized it would be too intimate. Damn. Almost angrily, she ripped open the foil packet and rolled it on, fumbling a little with the unfamiliar task. It had been a while.

"Good girl," Charlie said.

When she looked up, she realized both men watched her. "What? Have I done something wrong?"

Charlie shook his head. "Nothing we do together is wrong."

"Agreed," Gavin said. "Do you think we could move this along? Please?"

"I don't think we've teased you enough." Leticia smirked at them both and lowered her head again. The condom tasted artificial but the heat of Gavin's cock pierced the thin latex. If she ignored the rubbery flavor and used her tongue, she could almost imagine it was his bare flesh.

Gavin bit back a groan when Leticia rolled the condom on

his dick. His eyes fluttered closed, and he concentrated on the sensations, greedy to experience everything he could with her before...before he had to go to work, he thought hastily.

"Like that, Gavin?" Charlie's whispered words were close to his ear.

Leticia swiped her tongue across the head of his cock.

"Yeah." His strangled reply didn't cover the heaven he'd dropped into, the searing heat and magic. Even though the rubber came between them, it still felt bloody good.

"I thought you'd like it." Charlie nibbled on the column of his neck, his fingers rubbing over the marking site. Gavin bit back a groan of pure pleasure. The attentions of two lovers at once was indescribable.

"Kiss me," Gavin said.

Charlie's mouth settled on his, and Leticia explored a little more. Soft hands fondled his balls while her mouth sucked, tightening and loosening around the head of his cock. Charlie's tongue pushed into his mouth and sensation twisted through him. The more they pushed him, the more the hunger grew. He hadn't realized what he'd been missing until now. Muscles rippled and flexed as he shifted position on the bed, fighting the pleasure. Charlie lifted his head to smile down at him. Gavin's nostrils flared, dragging in the musky scent of Charlie and the sweet overtones of Leticia. His feline pushed, the pinprick at his fingertips telling him how close he was to shifting. Panicked, he struggled for control, panting with effort.

"That's enough for now, Leticia," Charlie said.

A protesting sound escaped Gavin when she lifted her head, because despite the weak control he had on his feline, he wanted more.

"Easy," Charlie whispered next to his head. "Leticia, straddle Gavin's legs and take him inside you."

Hell. A shudder of anticipation swept him. Longing. Excitement. It all combined into a pulsing hunger that threatened to undo him.

"Concentrate on me, Gavin," Charlie murmured in a stern voice.

Surprise sent his gaze straight to his mate. "Can you feel...?"

"I can sense your unease, your excitement. Breathe deep. Focus on me." Charlie kissed him, achingly slow. Passion swirled through Gavin, and every breath he took seemed filled with Charlie's scent. So familiar. Arousing. Their lips tangled in an unhurried manner, and for a few seconds he could ignore Leticia and her fumbling moves at the lower end of his body.

"Concentrate on me," Charlie said, his tone insistent. "Otherwise you'll hurt my feelings."

Gavin blinked, startled by Charlie's disclosure. "I'm sorry. I..." Belatedly he noticed the gleam of mischief in his lover. "Bastard," he said, although it lacked heat.

Grinning, Charlie kissed him again, an easy slide of lips and a hint of tongue. Seductive this time, designed to draw his attention. Hold it. And it did until Leticia took him inside her body. His breath hissed out of him like a balloon pricked with a pin. His heart jumped and dang near bust out of his chest.

"Easy." Charlie soothed him with kisses. Soft murmurs. He pressed his fingers over the marking site, using purrs of encouragement.

Oh God. It was too much. Way more than he'd ever imagined. The heat claimed him as she impaled herself on his cock. A deep shudder racked his body, and for an instant he thought he'd come prematurely. A sharp pinch at his nipple snatched back his control and a second pinch gave him a measure of restraint.

"Feel good?" Charlie's warm breath drew his attention. He gripped Gavin's hand in silent understanding.

"Yeah."

"How you doing, Leticia?"

"He's big." She panted, and when Gavin looked past Charlie, he caught his breath at the delicate flush on her cheeks. She wanted this as desperately as he did. The knowledge steadied him, made him realize Leticia fought demons too. Her demons trumped his, so he had no right to self-pity. Charlie was right. Together they were stronger. They could do this, make it work and support each other.

She pushed down the last bit and Gavin decided he'd reached heaven early. The tight clasp of her pussy made him sigh his enjoyment.

"I like it," she added.

"Am I allowed to offer an opinion?" Gavin asked.

"Go for it," Charlie said.

Gavin could hear the lightness lurking in his words.

Leticia rose and pushed down again on his cock. Her blonde hair moved in loose waves with each sway of her body. Her brown eyes glowed, golden glints more distinctive than normal, and her beautiful breasts beckoned.

"Lean down so I can suck on your breasts," he said.

"Good idea," Charlie said.

Leticia slumped toward him and his mouth settled over one nipple. Charlie grasped her other breast and took her nipple into his mouth. Gavin sucked and, judging by the movement of Charlie's mouth, his lover did the same thing. Leticia moaned, the husky sound filling the bedroom. Her sheath clenched his cock, hugging his shaft and testing his willpower.

Damn, he loved this woman, had for a long time. He'd fought it. Having her now... Fuck, he didn't want to lose her. His heart cried out, and he closed his eyes to hide his roiling emotions. Panic gripped his mind. Every avenue, he'd followed and nothing made the slightest difference.

"More. I need more," Leticia pleaded. "I need to move, for you to fill me, fuck me. Please."

Both he and Charlie released her breasts. She straightened, rose until he could see his length, shining with her honey. Slowly, she impaled herself again. It was the sexiest thing he'd ever seen. Sharp canines pushed through his gums, his feline stirring again, snarling in the confines of his mind.

Panic—fear, it nipped him, fueling every insecurity. "What if I lose control and bite?"

The stricken expression on Leticia's face made him want to eat his words. Idiot. She thought he meant the disease.

"I don't mean I'm frightened of the disease. I mean I don't want to hurt anyone." The last thing he wanted was to hurt either Charlie or Leticia. They meant everything to him.

"You will not lose control," Charlie said. "And the only one you will bite is me. It's hot. I like it," Charlie whispered, brushing his lips over Gavin's neck and mouth. "I have something for you. No biting until later though." He moved closer and pressed his cock to Gavin's mouth. "Open wide."

"No biting, huh?"

"That's right." Charlie leaned closer to Leticia and Gavin watched them kiss. It was a thorough kiss yet unhurried. Hot. A jolt of sensation struck his groin and settled in his balls. He sensed it then—the connection between the three of them. It throbbed through his body, through the air. He traced his tongue over the crown of Charlie's cock, sucked lightly, savored the hint of pre-cum.

Tension built in him with each unhurried move by Leticia. Hands touched and teased. Charlie caressed both of them, and he returned the favor, stroking everywhere he could while continuing to suck on Charlie. Like a rogue wave, the pressure built inside him, inside the bedroom. Soft moans and sighs of pleasure fueled the magic, each sensation layering on top of another until all he could do was float in satisfaction. Gavin held on for as long as he could, but without warning, the tension became too much. He exploded, spurts of semen blasting from his cock. A groan roared up his throat, vibrating around Charlie's cock. At least he had the presence of mind not to bite. He felt the tight, rhythmic clasp of Leticia's pussy and relief sizzled through him. He hadn't stuffed things up.

"Come on, Gavin," Charlie murmured. "My turn."

He applied himself, wanting to please his mate, sucking and licking until Charlie's guttural groans filled the room. When he glanced up, he noticed Leticia was kissing Charlie, and this time instead of jealousy, relief spread through him. Charlie rocked, pushing his cock deeper into his mouth. His dick seemed to lengthen even more, then he pulsed, climaxing. Semen shot down Gavin's throat and he swallowed, drawing back once Charlie softened in his mouth.

Leticia lifted off him and he rolled off the bed, removing the spent condom. Tossing it into a trash bin, he turned back to the couple sprawled on the bed.

"Thanks, Charlie."

Charlie nodded and Gavin rejoined them, his throat tight with emotion. Thanks to Charlie, they'd worked out things—the three of them. Charlie was the glue that would hold them together.

Chapter 9

Two Weeks Later

"How's Leticia?" Laura asked.

"About the same. Not getting better or worse." A pang of anxiety darted to Charlie's heart, the ever-present worry gripping him, stirring his fears. He knew Gavin had tried everything and hated his lack of progress. It ate at him. Although they maintained a cheerful, positive attitude around Leticia, they both worried about her. The knowledge she could die and they'd lose her hovered in the background like a resident ghost.

Their lovemaking had taken on a sense of urgency. None of them had spoken of it, but stress rode them all. He'd moved in with Gavin and Leticia, bringing most of his clothes and personal gear, and they tried to work it so one of them was with her most of the time.

The phone went and Charlie picked it up, pleased for an interruption to halt his thoughts of Leticia. "Middlemarch police." He listened before saying, "I'll be right there."

"Problem?"

"Yeah, Mrs. Barry crashed her car through the camping ground fence. She says a sheep ran in front of her car. The camping ground manager says she's been drinking."

"Do you need me?"

"Nah, I can cope," Charlie said.

"Why don't you head home once you're done with Mrs. Barry?" Laura asked. "I'm on call tonight."

"Yeah. I think I might. It's been a long day."

A real long day, he thought two hours later as he opened the door and toed off his black boots. To top that off, Mrs. Barry had been drinking—any idiot could identify the fumes—and when he mentioned it, she'd lost her temper and decked him. The woman threw a mean right hook. His jaw still ached.

"Anyone home?" he called. His shoulders slumped when no one replied. Damn, if ever he needed a hug and a kiss, it was now. Charlie trudged into the kitchen and opened Gavin's fridge to grab a beer. With a sigh, he pulled back the tab and took a sip, enjoying the crisp rush of hops running over his taste buds.

With calving and lambing season underway, Charlie presumed Gavin was out on a call. Sometimes Leticia went with him.

Charlie headed down the hall to the bedroom, intending to change out of his uniform and do laundry. Unfortunately, his clothes didn't wash themselves, and although Leticia sometimes did the chore, he didn't like to impose when she wasn't well and tired so easily. She still slept a lot.

Before he reached the bedroom, a soft sound told him he wasn't alone. Pausing, he cocked his head to listen. Leticia. Damn, she was crying. He hesitated, took a deep breath and pushed the bedroom door open to slip inside. The bedroom was dark, the blinds drawn to keep out the approaching night. Charlie stumbled his way to the bed and flicked on the bedside lamp. On seeing Leticia, curled into a light ball with only her head visible, he sucked in a harsh breath. A huge knot formed to block his throat, and he gulped, schooling his face to impassive.

"Sweetheart, what's wrong?" He set his can of beer on the bedside table and slid onto the bed, wrapping his arm around her waist.

"Go away."

"You can't make me," he said, keeping his tone light. "Where's Gavin?"

"He had a call-out. He didn't know how long he'd be." Leticia sniffed and turned to face him. Her eyes were red and her face tear-stained. The pillow looked damp, which showed she'd been crying for a while.

"Are you gonna tell me what's wrong?" Charlie grimaced inside. After a quick glance, he was certain he had a good idea of the problem. His stomach clenched while he fought to maintain a cheerful exterior. "Did Gavin do something?"

"We made love. Gavin and I."

Charlie sucked in a hasty breath. Maybe he was wrong. "Did he hurt you? Did either of you bite?"

"No, it was fine. Perfect. I don't want to die, Charlie." The tears trickled down her cheeks, and he tugged her against his chest, comforting in the only way he could. He held her, smoothing his hands down her slender back. When he touched her hair, a long lock came free. Bloody hell. Horrified, he swept it aside. No wonder she'd been upset.

"You're not gonna die, babe."

"I'm not getting any better. I have to sleep all the time, and now my hair is falling out in hunks." A sob broke free. "I'm going bald."

"Babe, you're gonna be okay. Gavin and I are here for you. We both love you."

"For how long? I'm getting weaker. I used to think I'd find a mate and have offspring, that I'd live a happy life. You'll never believe this, but I used to pity Lucas. I knew he was gay, and I thought I was so much better. Talk about a fool. I concentrated on my career when I should have grasped all the other opportunities that came my way." She looked him straight in the eye then. "At least you and Gavin will have each other once I'm gone."

What the hell could he say to that?

He'd tried to offer hope—both he and Gavin had tried to make the best of a bad situation. Hoped for the best. The only thing he could do was continue. He pressed her against his chest and held her while she cried again. Gradually she relaxed, no longer holding her body so tense. Her sobs faded, her breathing became more even.

Charlie stayed where he was for another half-hour. When he heard the faint rumble of a car, Charlie slid from her grasp and stood. After switching off the bedside lamp, he paused, but her breathing remained steady. Good. She needed her sleep.

Gavin looked tired when he entered the kitchen.

"Tough day?"

"Yeah. I had two ewes with trouble lambing and some idiot hit one of Jacob Foley's stud rams."

"Near the campground?"

"Yeah, how did you know?" Gavin grabbed a beer and handed one to him.

Charlie accepted the beer. "That idiot would be Mrs. Barry. Drunk in charge. She took out a fence at the camping ground with her car and belted me in the jaw when I asked if she'd been drinking. You made love with Leticia."

Gavin pulled out a chair and sat at the table. "Yeah, I did. Where is she?"

"In the bedroom. She's asleep."

"She okay?" Gavin picked up on the undercurrents. "Did I hurt her or something?"

"She was crying. Her hair has started to drop out in big handfuls."

"Shit. I'll go to her."

Charlie stayed him with a raised hand. "Nah, let her sleep. Besides, it looks like you need to chill. We can watch television and afterward you can shave my head for me."

"What?" Gavin's gaze snapped away from his beer to Charlie's face. "What the hell do you want me to do that for? I like your hair."

"I figured if Leticia was losing her hair, I'd lose mine."

Gavin buried his face in his hands before glancing up at Charlie. "Damn, I knew there was a reason I hooked up with you. I think I need a haircut too."

"My sexy bod?" Happiness swelled inside Charlie and a goofy grin formed.

"You have a good heart. I can't imagine being without you. It's bad enough—"

"Don't say it. I feel the same way."

"Did she say anything else? Anything about us making love?"

"Other than it was good—no. Did you want to bite her?"

Gavin snorted. "Oh yeah. I made a hole in the pillowcase. It was good between us, although not as good as it is with the three of us together. Are you okay with us doing that?"

"Of course I am. Come here." Charlie stood and hauled Gavin to his feet when he dawdled. He pulled his mate close and hugged him.

"I'm so glad you're here with me, Charlie. I don't think I could get through this if it weren't for you."

Their lips slid together. The need for comfort and reassurance filled Charlie, and judging by the desperate grip Gavin had on his shoulders, he figured the same feelings coursed through his mate. Their mouths met with clear desperation, an erotic assault on the senses. When they parted, they were both breathing hard.

Gavin's eyes glittered. He pressed his forehead to Charlie's. "Thanks, I needed that."

Charlie cupped his jaw, his fingers rasping across the stubble covering Gavin's jaw. "We're in this together, man. I care for Leticia too."

Gavin swallowed audibly. "I don't know what else to do. I've tried everything I know, everything I've read. She's still losing weight."

"I know you've done your best. You've done everything possible." He rubbed his thumb over Gavin's bottom lip and stepped away. "Stop beating yourself up about it. I don't want to lose you too. Have you eaten?"

"I wasn't hungry."

"I'll cook something."

They prepared a meal together, cooking extra for Leticia in case she woke. Once the dinner was ready, Gavin went to see if she was awake, returning a few minutes later.

"Her hair. Hell, she has huge bald spots. This afternoon it was fine."

Charlie squeezed his shoulder, not attempting to speak because he knew his voice would break.

"I should ring Lucas and Saul. Let them know things aren't too good."

"Do you want me to do it?" Charlie asked.

"Nah, I'll talk to them. It's my job."

But this was more than a job for both of them. Leticia was their mate. "How long…" Charlie trailed off, unable to say the words. It was hard enough thinking them. Stating them made the situation seem all too real.

Gavin cleared his throat. "I don't know." The shiny glint in his eyes hinted how close he was to losing control.

"Eat first. We'll ring Lucas after we've eaten." Charlie served the steak, potatoes and salad, forcing himself to eat. Everything lacked flavor, reminded him of cardboard, but he kept eating. He noticed Gavin was playing with his food and coughed, a significant jerk of his head indicating he should eat. Gavin finally ate, although with little enthusiasm. Charlie set his knife and fork down and pushed his plate away. "You finished?"

"Yeah. Sorry. I guess I'd better ring Lucas." Gavin disappeared into his surgery.

Part of Charlie wanted to offer support, to hold his lover while he passed on the bad news. Instead, he cleaned the kitchen and went to the bathroom to get his hair trimmer, shaving cream and a handful of razors.

Back in the kitchen, he fidgeted while he waited for Gavin to return, arranging and rearranging the items he'd retrieved from the bathroom. He sank onto a chair only to spring to his feet again when he heard footsteps coming from the surgery.

"Gavin?"

SHELLEY MUNRO

"Yeah." Gavin walked straight into his arms, his eyes damp with unshed tears. Burying his face against Charlie's shoulder, he shuddered. "That was the hardest thing I've ever done."

"You okay?"

"Not really. Damn, I feel so bloody helpless."

"Are Lucas and Saul coming?"

"Yeah. They're driving to Middlemarch tomorrow. They will stay with Saber and Emily for the night so they don't have to worry about driving back to Alexandra late."

"Help me with my hair," Charlie said.

"You sure you trust me?" Gavin held up his hands to demonstrate the faint tremor.

Charlie winked, wanting to lighten the heavy atmosphere, even though he couldn't erase the problem. "Don't worry. If you cut me, I know the local doctor. We can call him to fix me up."

A snort erupted from Gavin. "You've been warned." He gestured at a chair. "Take a seat. The barber shop is open for business." When Charlie sat, Gavin ran his fingers through the blond locks. They'd grown since Charlie first arrived, and Gavin liked the longer length. "Are you sure you want to do this?"

"It's only hair. It will grow back. Besides, I figure Leticia could do with the show of support. This loss of hair upset her. I don't care if my head has weird bumps or my ears stick out. I'm doing it for Leticia. She needs us in her corner right now."

The heavy weight of emotion clawed at Gavin's chest. Damn, he loved his mate. He hadn't told him yet because everything was happening so fast between them. With Leticia. He swallowed and switched on the clippers. "Don't make a sudden move."

"I know I'm safe with you."

"Jeez, don't ramp the pressure up too much. I might not handle it."

Charlie smirked and some of the burden on Gavin's shoulders lifted. Thank God for Charlie. He didn't think he'd have made it this far if it weren't for his mate. He ran the clippers over Charlie's head and the short blond locks fell to the floor.

"I was glad to come home today. Apart from dealing with Mrs. Barry, I had a call-out to investigate missing apples."

Gavin picked up the can of shaving cream and squirted some on his hand, smoothing it over the short stubble on Charlie's head. He picked up one of the disposable razors and shaved off the last of his mate's hair. Five minutes later, he patted away the remnants of the shaving cream with a towel.

Charlie's blue eyes twinkled up at him. "So how do I look?"

"You look sexy."

He batted his lashes. "Yeah, but do you want to jump me?"

"Anytime." Gavin fought a smile. "My turn. Is your hand steady or do I need to call the local doctor?"

Charlie stood, brushed a quick kiss over Gavin's lips and nudged him toward the chair. "You'll have to wait and find out."

Fifteen minutes later, Gavin handed a broom to Charlie. He swept up the hair while Gavin checked on Leticia.

"Is that you, Gavin?" Leticia's voice was thick with sleep.

"Yeah. You want something to eat?"

"I'm not hungry."

Gavin frowned, concern prodding him into doctor mode. "You need to eat."

"I've been eating. I had sandwiches after you left for work." She leaned over to switch on the bedside lamp. "What the fuck have you done with your hair?"

Charlie came up behind him, slinging an arm around his shoulders. "We decided on a change. I think we look sexy."

"You look...pale. Shiny." Her mouth clamped shut as if she thought she'd said too much.

"I like it." Charlie winked at him. "Gavin looks so damn sexy I made him shave my head too."

Not true. A glance at Leticia told him she didn't look so sure. While Gavin struggled for something to say, Charlie squeezed his shoulders. He kissed him, and as usual, Gavin's feline stirred, a purr rumbling through his head when their lips caressed and tongues tangled. The agitation in his mind faded a fraction, his arms tightened around his lover. When they pulled apart, they were both breathing hard. Charlie leaned in, pressing his forehead against his. His mate's musky scent wound through his senses, his presence calming and centering him.

"Hey, what about me?" Leticia asked. "I could do with a few kisses and cuddles."

"Are you up to taking on both of us, babe?"

Gavin turned to study Leticia, taking in the pale cheeks and sparse hair. An invisible fist clenched around his heart, the beat stalling before kicking into a rapid thump again. She shouldn't exert herself, but he didn't tell her that, not if it was what she wanted. He wasn't about to issue orders and restrictions. Leticia had enough to deal with now.

"Please. I want you both inside me. I'm not tired since I've slept for the last few hours."

Gavin hesitated until Charlie nudged him, his head dipping in a slight nod. *It's what she wants.* The words echoed through his head as if Charlie had uttered them aloud. Forcing a smile, one Gavin hoped passed muster, he stepped toward the bed with Charlie at his side.

"Do you want to undress us or should we strip for you?"

Leticia sat and plumped the pillows, propping them up against the headboard. "Strip." A glint of feminine interest filled her eyes, melting away the last of Gavin's reservations. Charlie was right. If she wanted sex, then that was what she'd get. He was up for the job. A glance at Charlie's groin told him his mate was in the same condition. This was about Leticia and her needs.

"Take off your shirt," Charlie ordered.

Gavin grinned and unfastened his shirt one button at a time. Both Leticia and Charlie stared at his bared chest. With the final button undone, his shirt slipped to the carpet with a soft thud.

"Don't stop there," Charlie said. "We're enjoying the view. Right, Leticia?"

"Oh yeah," she said, smiling with clear expectation. "Although I'm sure it will only improve."

Charlie scanned Gavin's chest, the sensation like a physical touch. His cock pressed against his fly with distinct interest. A few months ago he couldn't have imagined being with two mates about to make love.

"Off with your trousers," Charlie's insistent voice dared him, and Gavin wasn't about to back away from a challenge. He promptly unfastened his trousers, dragging off his boxer briefs and his socks at the same time. Naked, he posed to let their gazes rove his body. Unbidden his hand dropped to his cock, and he squeezed, stroking and teasing until goose bumps pebbled his skin.

"That is so hot," Charlie whispered, stepping closer to kiss his neck. He nibbled the marking site and Gavin groaned, raw and guttural. Needy.

"Come over here," Leticia suggested, and Gavin shook himself from the sensual spell he'd fallen into the minute Charlie touched him. She whipped the T-shirt she wore over her head, a sunny smile lighting up her pale face. When she saw she had their attention, she tossed aside the covers and parted her legs, flashing her pussy at them. With a glint of mischief lighting her eyes, she licked her forefinger and slipped it between her legs. A stroke of her finger later, she sighed.

"Let us see," Charlie said.

Delicate color rose in her cheeks and she lifted her finger. It shone in the light of the lamp. Desire rose in Gavin and he took half a step toward the bed before Charlie stopped him.

"Grab a condom and the lube."

Gavin wanted to argue. He wanted to shove Charlie aside and lick her juices from her finger before slipping his cock into her pussy and sliding home. He wanted it so bad he shook with it.

"Gavin?"

One glance at Charlie told him his mate knew exactly where his thoughts lay and sympathized. The swelling ball of jealousy in his mind imploded with a sense of shame. It wasn't right to want more, not when he had more than he'd ever expected. "Yeah. Okay." He circled the bed and opened a drawer, pulling out several condoms and a bottle of lube. By the time he turned, Charlie was naked and on the bed with Leticia. He was kissing her, and this time Gavin kept his envy at bay, merely hastened his steps so he could join them.

"Condom?" he asked Charlie.

"Sure. You want to put it on for me?"

Gavin's nostrils flared, the clawing tension inside finding an outlet in his hardening cock. He placed the condoms and lube on the bedside table, retaining one. He ripped the foil packet open and kneeled beside Leticia, taking in the smooth skin and vulnerable curve of her spine. Her pink tongue lashed one of Charlie's nipples, rasping over the nub until it hardened. He gripped Charlie's shaft and unable to resist, dipped his head. With his tongue, he lapped across the crown. Charlie's ragged breath brought a rush of satisfaction. Wanting to tease, he sucked hard enough to spike sensation, to bring a rush of pleasure. With a final swipe of his tongue, he pulled back and rolled on the condom.

"Come here, Leticia," Charlie said.

Excitement and anticipation flashed through Gavin. He watched Leticia clamber over Charlie and Charlie guide his cock into her pussy. Slowly, she sank down, and Gavin held his breath, watching the careful impalement. It was the sexiest thing.

"Okay, babe. Come here. Kiss me while Gavin suits up and stretches you a little."

"You have done this before?" Gavin asked her.

"Yeah, not recently, but I have had anal sex before."

He smoothed his hand over her shoulder, unable to resist touching her. His heart twisted when he noticed a shiny bald spot. Damn he hated this.

"I can't wait to fuck you," he whispered.

"It's gonna be epic," Charlie promised. "Both of you at the same time."

Leticia exhaled noisily, indicating her impatience. "Enough talking. I'm ready. I want both of you inside me. Now."

"Don't you want warm lube?" Gavin teased, removing the lid and squeezing gel into his palm.

"I can handle the chill. I'll heat up soon enough. Besides, if you don't hurry, I'm going to move without you," Leticia warned.

Gavin laughed, enjoying the glimpse of the old Leticia with her fire and determination. "Coming right up, Ms. Bossy." He smoothed a slippery finger over her puckered entrance, determined to take things slow even though she vibrated with impatience.

"Kiss me, babe," Charlie said, winking at Gavin. "Concentrate on me for the moment."

Gavin took his time, taking pleasure in exploring Leticia's body. With his excellent hearing, he picked up her soft sighs into Charlie's mouth. They grew louder when he slipped a finger into her. Her sexy little wriggle, designed to drive his finger deeper drew a laugh from him, a chuckle from Charlie.

"Our little puss is impatient," Charlie murmured.

"I'm impatient," Gavin said. "But this is so much fun. She's so responsive."

"I know. Every time you stroke her, she clenches around my cock."

"Yeah. She's clenching around my finger." Gavin added more lube and another finger. The heat seared him, and he couldn't wait to bathe his cock in the same fiery pleasure. "How are you doing?"

"Impatient," Leticia said. "Still impatient."

Gavin winked at Charlie, relaxed and at ease. When his fingers slipped inside her easily, he removed them and rolled on a condom. Arousal curled through him and his hand trembled when he guided his dick to her puckered entrance. Taking a deep breath, he pushed the head of his cock inside, closing his eyes to savor the moment and hold it close.

Leticia winced and he stopped. "You okay?"

"It's been a while. Just give me a moment."

Gavin pressed a trail of kisses to her shoulder, keeping well away from temptation. He met Charlie's gaze for an instant, the flash of understanding and silent encouragement bringing an unmanly sting to his eyes. Charlie kissed Leticia and Gavin watched the slide of lips, the flicker of pink tongue, the entire intimate exchange. While they kissed, Gavin pushed deeper, past the ring of muscle, taking his time until he bathed in her heat. Gavin met Charlie's gaze again and nodded. They moved in rhythm, one withdrawing while the other surged inside. The friction, the warmth, the intensity. Gavin thrust automatically while his mind and body collected the sensations and enjoyed each erotic caress, hoarding it for him to think about later.

The brush of Charlie's hand against his mark pushed him higher, harder, each breath coming with a harsh gasp. Leticia shuddered, her cry one of animal pleasure. His feline rose to the surface, glorying in the sharing.

"We're gonna have to do this again," Charlie said.

"Good, huh?" Gavin asked.

"Oh yeah." Leticia gasped, a soft cry breaking free. "I can't wait much longer."

"Thank God for that," Charlie muttered.

Gavin laughed, surprising himself. Despite the intensity, this was fun. Charlie made everything enjoyable and new. He withdrew and pushed back inside Leticia, his cock brushing against Charlie's through the thin membrane separating them. Gavin kissed Leticia's shoulder and a harsh breath hissed from her.

"Oh. Oh," she whispered, and seconds later, she bit down on Charlie's shoulder. Charlie bucked, his cock jerking against Gavin's. Climax rushed through Gavin, so good it was almost painful. Leticia's entire body jerked, her hot passage clamping down on his cock. He was vaguely aware of Charlie crying out and felt the slight pulse before he pulled free. On shaky legs, he made his way to the bathroom to discard the condom and clean up. A sense of satisfaction, even contentment filled him as he dampened a cloth with warm water, squeezed it out and walked back into the bedroom.

"I marked him," Leticia said in a flat voice as she registered Gavin's presence. "I didn't mean to do it. I lost control. It was so good, so normal being claimed by both of you and I wanted to be part of it."

"Shush, it's all right." Charlie stroked her arm. "You didn't hurt me. There's no harm done right, Gavin?"

Gavin hesitated, picking up on Leticia's unease, yet he dithered about saying anything. "Turn over, Leticia, and let me take a look at Charlie's shoulder."

The mark appeared red. Angry. Charlie winced when Gavin touched it. Gavin jerked his hand away.

"Damn, do that again," Charlie said. "Please."

A slow grin spread across Gavin's mouth. He brushed a single finger over the raised red mark and bent to kiss Charlie, capturing his groan with his mouth. His body arched, and he groaned, a splash of semen hitting Charlie's hip.

Lifting his head, Gavin grinned. "I guess you're okay."

"Men," Leticia muttered. "Yeah, it's all fun and orgasms now, but what the hell are you going to do if Charlie gets sick from my bite? I don't want him to die like me."

"Don't panic, babe," Charlie said. "You will not die, and I can't catch anything from you. Remember, Gavin told us that. As long as you don't bite him then we're sweet."

She scowled. "But what if—"

Gavin was going to speak but Charlie cut in first. "You won't, but if you're worried we'll get you a mouth guard. That should do the trick."

Chapter 10

Matching Hairstyles

"What the fuck have you done with your hair?"

"Good morning to you too," Charlie said, standing aside to let Lucas and Saul enter. He cast a quick glance down the passage before saying in an undertone, "Leticia's hair is falling out in clumps. Gavin and I decided we'd shave ours off in solidarity."

The *oomph* went out of Lucas. He slumped against Saul, took a deep breath. "Thank you for all you're doing for Leticia. I don't know how to thank you."

"No thanks necessary," Charlie said. "We love her." Nothing less than the truth. He loved both his mates, thought about them regularly when he wasn't with them. His stomach clenched as he recalled Leticia's words from the previous night.

She was going to die.

A quick glance at Gavin had confirmed the truth of Leticia's words. Gavin had done everything, tried every method at his disposal and didn't think she'd beat the disease.

"Gavin and Leticia are in the kitchen eating breakfast. I'll see you later tonight. I've gotta go to work."

Lucas moved off, leaving him alone with Saul.

"You love her," Saul said.

"Yeah." His hand rubbed across his twin mark. Even with his uniform shirt over the top, a spike of pleasure, of awareness shot through him. "They're my mates. I love them both." But he hadn't told either of them. Tonight. He'd tell them tonight. "Catch ya later." And with a wave, he left.

"Hey, Lucas. Saul." Leticia forced a smile and stood, shoulders back and head high, despite the knowledge her physical appearance would shock them.

"Hey, sweetheart." Lucas didn't hide his shock. She caught a flash of emotion before he yanked her into his arms, almost crushing her in his embrace.

"Can't breathe," she gasped, struggling weakly.

"Hell. Sorry." Lucas stepped back.

"You have a cute scalp," Saul said, entering the kitchen behind Lucas. He hugged her and ran his hand over her shaven head.

"Charlie did it for me this morning." She flashed a grin at Gavin. "I was the odd man out because I had the most hair." Leticia paused, took a quick summation of their expressions and ruffled up like a bristling tomcat. "What? Ah, heck! Don't look at me like that. I know I'm dying. It doesn't take a genius to know I'm growing weaker by the day. There's no point skirting around the problem."

"Coffee?" Gavin asked.

"You can't pretend there's nothing wrong with me," Leticia snapped.

Gavin rose, his chair scooting back. "We don't want our noses rubbed in it either." He dragged a hand over his head, surprise flashing before he remembered he no longer had hair.

Leticia knew the feeling well. The lack of hair on her own head kept surprising her too.

"Hell." Gavin scowled at her. "Once you're done here come into the surgery and I'll do more tests."

"Enough already." Leticia's shoulders rose and fell again in an irritable shrug. "I'm tired of being poked and pried at like a specimen in a jar. All the tests in the world won't make me better." Her bottom jaw stuck out in a pugnacious manner, daring them to argue. "I'm not having any more tests."

"Don't you think you should listen to Gavin?" Lucas asked in a mild tone. "He's the expert."

Fury swirled through her gut, compressing until it exploded into a fireball of caustic words. "All the expertise in the world hasn't saved me. I just want to be left alone."

"Fine. If that's the way you want it." Without another word, Gavin stomped from the room, the sharp intake of breath and the firm pad of his feet as he retreated spelling out his displeasure. At the end of the passage, a door clicked shut.

Finality. It sizzled in the air.

Saul clapped his hands slowly. "Way to go, Leticia. Piss off the one man who has gone out of his way to help you."

"What the fuck do you know? You're not sick. You're not dying. Try stepping into my shoes and see how you like it. I can bite you any time and give you a taste of hell." Her chest rose and fell, anger whipping through her and finding an outlet in clamped fists. She took half a step toward Saul before Lucas let out a low growl. It made the tiny hairs at the back of her neck prickle, and the blaze of fury in his golden eyes when he stepped between her and his mate brought a wave of shame.

Without taking her gaze off her brother, she backed away to slump into a chair. Tears stung her eyes, and she blinked to ward them off. This wasn't right. Intellectually she knew her behavior was wrong, but she couldn't seem to help it.

Two mates. She had so much to lose, and it hurt like hell. It was the first thought that popped into her head in the morning and the last waking one before she dropped off to a fitful sleep.

Death.

Knowing it was happening, seeing her energy decreasing each day brought fear, and now that she'd spent time with both Gavin and Charlie, made love with them, it seemed far worse.

"I'm sorry." She couldn't look at either Saul or Lucas, frightened of the pity she'd see on their faces.

"It's all right," Saul said, joining her at the table.

"No it's fuckin' not," Lucas snapped. "Never threaten my mate like that again. It kills me you have FIV. Don't you think I'd change things if I could? Trying to push us away isn't smart, and especially Gavin and Charlie."

"I didn't think you approved," Leticia snapped.

"That was before I saw how much they care for you," Lucas snarled, not backing down. "You're the one who will suffer if you push us all away."

Damn. Did he think she didn't know that? No matter what she did, she lost. She'd figured that if everyone hated her, it wouldn't be so dreadful once she died. Twisted logic, yeah. Tough shit. She felt guilty enough as it was for marking Charlie. A quick glance at Lucas confirmed he'd sensed her inner turmoil and picked up on some of her fear and confusion. Sometimes the mental connection between her and her brother freaked her. She wished she could control it but mental anguish made a great conductor. Might as well admit the truth to both of them.

"I marked Charlie. I didn't mean to."

"And the guilt is getting at you," Saul said.

"No. Perhaps," she amended, checking Lucas's reaction again. His raised brows told her he knew. "Yeah. Okay. Yeah, it is. I shouldn't have done it to Charlie. It was a spur-of-the-moment thing. My thoughts went AWOL."

Lucas scowled and dragged out a chair, straddling it while he concentrated on raiding her frenzied thoughts. "What did Gavin say? And Charlie?"

"What could they say? It was too late. I'd already done it and couldn't take it back." She shrugged again, pretending unconcern when inside the guilt ate her. Charlie would suffer when she died, more than he needed to, and that was what she hated most of all.

"Do you want to come home with us?" Saul asked.

"Yeah." She didn't even need to think about her reply.

"Dammit, Leticia. That's running away," Lucas barked. "You're staying put with your mates. I'm not coming between the three of you because you're running scared. I love you but you're not coming home to Alexandra with us."

Leticia opened her mouth to snarl back at her brother when Gavin spoke from the doorway. "I'm glad Lucas sees things clearly. You belong here and we're not letting you hide."

"And yet you're all sidestepping the death issue," she retorted. "What's fair about that? It's concealment in a different form."

Gavin closed the distance between them, cupped her cheek and stared into her eyes. "Nothing. You're right. We'll try to do better, but you can't leave. We'd both miss you if you left us now. We're a team, Leticia. Charlie and I need you." He swallowed, and she noticed the circles of tiredness beneath his eyes. He'd lost weight. An ache sprang to life near her heart and the fight oozed out of her limbs. She didn't want to leave. Not really. She wanted to live, to celebrate life and love with her two men, and that was the problem.

"I'm sorry. I'll stay," she said. "But I'm done with tests. No more. The results say I'm sick. We know that already."

Gavin glanced at Lucas and Saul before he turned his attention back to her. "Deal. No more tests. What would you like to do today?"

"I might go to see Emily at the café. Have a cup of coffee and one of her chocolate brownies. She and Saber are heading off on their holiday tomorrow. I'd like to say goodbye and wish them a happy holiday."

"In that case, I'm buying," Saul said. "I have a yearning for some of Emily's chocolate brownies myself."

The day passed quickly enough, yet surrounded by people she'd never seemed so alone. They ended up having dinner with the Mitchells and around nine she drooped, so tired she could scarcely stay upright in her chair.

"I think that's our cue to leave," Charlie said. "Leticia needs to sleep."

"She can sleep here," Emily said.

Beside her, Gavin stirred, placing his hand on her shoulder. "No, we'd prefer to sleep in our own bed. Besides, you're off early tomorrow. You don't need us underfoot."

The warmth from his touch seeped into her body and glowed in her face, although his words might have had something to do with her high color.

"I prefer sleeping in my own bed." Emily's lips twitched a fraction, belying her somber expression.

"That's because you share it with me. I'm sure Leticia finds her bed very comfortable." Saber didn't even attempt to hide his amusement, bringing another rush of heat to Leticia's face. The teasing brought normality, and she loved them for it.

"Thanks for dinner, Emily," Charlie said.

Leticia yawned, wavering on her feet when she stood. Damn, she shouldn't feel this exhausted, not after the three-hour nap she'd had during the afternoon. Gavin slipped his arm around her waist and her breath eased out. Part of her wanted to unleash her tongue and tell him she could walk on her own. These men coddled her, sometimes too much, even though they meant to help. The sad truth was she didn't think she could make it on her own tonight. She'd done nothing except sit and sleep, which shouldn't leave her with achy limbs and a heavy weight pressing on her entire body.

"We'll drop by in the morning." Lucas stood to brush a kiss on her temple. "Stay strong," he murmured, and Leticia knew he'd somehow picked up on her thoughts again.

The drive home to Gavin's house passed in a blur. Charlie carried her into the bedroom. He dropped her onto the bed and stepped back to switch on the bedside lamp.

"I don't need any help to undress." Leticia pushed upright and kicked off her shoes. Gavin entered the bedroom and came to a halt right by Charlie. They both watched her, two silent men with baldheads and intent eyes. "Are you coming to bed now?"

The two men stared at each other and she could see their silent communication. They wanted sex. It was as clear to her as it was to them.

"Nah, we might watch some television first," Gavin said.

Leticia's temper flashed. "If you're going to make love, why don't you just tell me?" She yanked off her blouse and unfastened her bra, tossing them aside. Her jeans and panties landed on the pile and breathing hard, frustration burrowing through the pit of her stomach, she ripped back the covers and naked, slid between the sheets. "Please, don't exclude me. Make love here where I can see. I'm too tired to participate but let me watch you. You've made me love you both." Her voice caught, and she had to push out the words. "Don't close me out now."

"You got it, babe," Charlie said, bending over to brush a kiss over her temple. She wanted to turn her head and sink into his kiss. Her body wouldn't obey the command, so she lay there with her eyes closed, panting to breathe past the series of aches that clutched her body like a lover.

Gavin sat on the bed beside her. "Are you okay?"

"Tired," she lied. No way did she want to tell Gavin of this new development—the extreme physical and mental tiredness and the aching in her joints. "You guys didn't let me sleep much the night before."

"That's true," Charlie agreed. "You go to sleep now. We'll both be back soon. We won't leave you alone."

Leticia heard their footsteps when the two retreated. She didn't stir, kept her breathing easy when she wanted to weep at the surge of pain. The aches intensified, pulsing in irregular waves. A groan squeezed past her clenched lips. For an instant she considered calling Gavin but didn't. She'd meant what she said earlier about rejecting more tests. She curled her knees up to her chest, and that eased the pain. Damn, she was so tired, so exhausted.

Soft voices woke her, and it took a while for her brain to kick into gear. Her eyelids fluttered, her eyes adjusting to the dark room. Gavin and Charlie had come to bed while she slept. They lay on their sides, facing each other. Charlie's hand stroked down Gavin's back, dislodging the sheet screening him from her sight. They kissed and her breath caught. She heard their soft laughter and wished she could see their faces. As if they read her mind, Charlie rolled, pushing Gavin onto his back.

The smile curving Gavin's lips made her heart beat faster. Sexiness blazed from them like an attitude, the pair gorgeous together. Charlie kissed Gavin again, the suction of lips loud and playful. She caught a flash of tongue and a tinge of arousal swept to the pit of her stomach.

"You look good together," she murmured.

"You're awake," Charlie said. "Do you want to join us?"

"Not this time." She didn't think she could move if she tried. After flexing her biceps, she realized the pain had faded to a manageable level. Good. She didn't want to worry either of them. Preferable to remember them like this—full of laughter and sexy teasing. Love.

Gavin grinned at her, a wide, honest reaction that reached all the way to his eyes and made the corners crinkle. Laugh wrinkles suited a man, made him attractive and magnetic. "Guess we'd better give you something to watch then."

"I'll probably fall asleep." A pity she wouldn't be around long enough to get wrinkly. The idea sounded more attractive now that she'd run out of time.

Charlie snorted. "Did you just insult us? I think we should be offended, but I'm too mellow to argue the point."

"I need more practice if you're not sure." She spoiled the comeback with a jaw-cracking yawn.

"You're exhausted." Gavin frowned and pulled out his professional doctor mantle while he scrutinized her.

"So I'll sleep," she said. "Don't worry. I'm a big girl. I can tell you if I hurt or ask for help if I need it." How she maintained her glare, she wasn't sure, but to her relief, Gavin backed down. He reached out to stroke a finger across her cheek. His touch slipped over her skin, soft as a feather yet packing a powerful punch of emotions. *Regrets*. She had a few, wasting so much time. "Don't let me stop you. Really, I'm happy to watch. Please."

Charlie peeled back the coverings on their side of the bed so she could see their naked bodies without difficulty while making sure she'd remain warm. Another small courtesy. The two men spoiled her, making her feel like a storybook princess, wanted and loved. Special. Charlie kissed her lips, a gentle kiss that devoured and made promises. When he pulled back, her heart raced.

"I see the attraction in watching," Gavin said in a husky voice. "I want what she had."

"My pleasure." Charlie turned back to Gavin, a blaze of love and pure joy sparkling in his eyes. He looked at her in the same way so Leticia knew what the smoldering gaze did. She heard Gavin's sharp exhalation, saw the flush of desire high on his cheekbones before Charlie's back blocked her view. Then Charlie rolled on top of Gavin, pressing him into the mattress, and she could see again. When their lips touched, her breath hitched, pressure building low between her legs. Charlie cupped Gavin's jaw, the slide of palm over cheekbone and lower face creating a whispery rasp.

Leticia swallowed, shifted her legs and had to bite her bottom lip to halt the groan of pain. She froze, held her breath, waiting for the sharp muscle-stabbing needles to cease.

Damn, what was wrong with her? A cautious breath later the pain receded, leaving her body coated with perspiration. Okay. So maybe she wouldn't move again until necessary.

A low masculine moan snared her attention, and she held on to the noise, focusing on Charlie and Gavin, every sound, every move they made while they loved each other. The stroke of a hand over a biceps. The grunt of pleasure when Charlie grazed the cords of Gavin's neck with his teeth. The scent of their bodies as they heated into arousal. It was a ballet, excitement running like music through her head while the two men touched, the pace surging then slowing. Her body hummed, nipples pulling taut and brushing the cotton sheet with each inhalation. And when Charlie kissed Gavin's nipples, biting and scraping his teeth over them, sucking them, it was almost as if he did it to her.

A jolt of pleasure shot to her core and moisture coated her folds, yet when she tried to move, warning twinges zapped up and down her spine. *Okay*. Best she keep still. Frustration bled through, her nails digging into her palms.

Concentrate on Charlie and Gavin.

Breathe. Focus.

She watched Charlie move down Gavin's body, kissing, nibbling, licking the residual sting away to leave his mark. They whispered to each other, loving words that should've isolated her. But somehow watching brought her closer and made her just a little envious. This was better than sleeping in a separate bedroom. There was plenty of time for that later.

"Enough with the teasing. Suck my cock," Gavin ordered.

Charlie's chuckle filled the air. "But I'm having too much fun." He punctuated his words with another kiss, sucking on Gavin's hip until the blood rushed to the surface. When he pulled back, Leticia saw his grin of satisfaction and echoed it.

"Sucking my cock will be fun. I promise," Gavin purred.

Charlie moved closer to Gavin's cock, brushing his cheek against Gavin's shaft. "Fun for you."

"Then fuck me already." His words were a plea. Leticia saw a tremble work through him, the way his hips thrust upward in silent appeal. She held her breath, intent on watching them both. How long would Charlie draw out the pleasure? How far would he push Gavin?

"Soon," Charlie promised. "Very soon." His tongue glided across one taut ball before he opened his mouth, taking it inside.

Gavin reached for his cock, getting in one sly stroke before Charlie knocked his hand away. He lifted his head to smirk. "Do you want me to handcuff you? Then you'd really know sensual torture."

Leticia thought about restraints, being at the total mercy of her lovers. It would've been nice. Well, maybe nice wasn't quite the right word.

"You'd do it, wouldn't you?"

"Yep," Charlie said. "I have a set of handcuffs in the other room. Another day."

"And I could torture you, see how you like it."

"Not a problem. I know I'd enjoy anything you dish out to me." Charlie spoke between licks, and Leticia sensed the warm mist of air over her folds. She gasped, a quick intake of air that drew the men's scents deep into her lungs. Heat emanated from their bodies, warming her, dragging her into the building passion.

She watched Charlie stroke his tongue from the base to the tip of his cock, lapping at the crown before enclosing him in the heat of his mouth. His lips slid down the shaft, taking more of Gavin's cock, and it was the hottest thing she'd ever seen. She couldn't take her eyes off the moistened flesh vanishing into Charlie's mouth. Gavin started to shake, and she understood why. She'd experienced Charlie's talent. Hot and wet. The tension inside crackled as she imagined his stabbing tongue, the scrape of his beard on her inner thighs.

"Fuck, Charlie. I'm gonna come if you keep that up. There's lube over there."

Charlie lifted his head, humor digging into his lean cheeks. "Still trying to order me around."

Leticia swallowed. "I think you should get the lube for Gavin."

"Ah, so she didn't fall asleep," Charlie teased, turning his head to grin at her.

"And she agrees with me." Gavin arched upward, grinding his cock against Charlie's hip. He groaned, his dark lashes lush semi-circles beneath his eyes. Primitive hunger strained on his face as he writhed against his lover.

"Damn, that is so hot." Charlie reached for the lube. With fumbling fingers, he popped the lid and squeezed the liquid into the palm of his hand. Seconds later, he circled Gavin's rosette and pushed a finger inside. Leticia's face flushed at the raw, male desire on Gavin's face, the concentration on Charlie's.

"No more, Charlie. I don't need slow. Please fuck me now."

The two men exchanged a glance so hot Leticia quivered with the firestorm in the air.

Charlie palmed his own cock, using the last of the lube and pushed inside Gavin. His muscles rippled as he thrust, working into Gavin, invading him. The expression on Gavin's face riveted her attention—the passion, the love. His stark male lips were firm, a hint of color shading his cheekbones.

"Charlie," Gavin whispered, watching his lover with a blaze of passion in his expression. "Bite me, Charlie."

The marking site on her shoulder tingled the second Gavin made the soft demand. Charlie leaned over Gavin, clasping him and obscuring her view. The sounds of their loving kept her connected. She'd never considered watching others having sex as something enjoyable. She knew better now. It was...consuming and exhilarating.

Charlie increased the pace of his strokes, the slap of flesh loud, almost brutal. Charlie wasn't as careful as he was with her. A guttural moan drew her attention back to the action. Sweat coated Charlie's shoulders, his buttocks flexing with each frantic stroke. He nuzzled Gavin's jaw, peppering it with kisses, gradually working down to the marking spot. Gavin arched beneath him, bucking and moaning again.

Leticia bit back the whimper building in her throat, her torso hot and shivery. Who knew she'd be such a voyeur?

The two men writhed together. Kissed. Gavin shouted, his entire body stiffening beneath Charlie.

"Damn, that is so hot. I love you, Gavin," Charlie said, and he bit down on the marking site, his big body convulsing as he climaxed. The pair stilled, clutching each other tight and murmuring lovers' words.

When Charlie lifted his head, she caught the gleam of his teeth in the faint light and smelled the coppery scent of blood. A soft cry broke from her, attracting their attention.

"I thought you were asleep, babe," Charlie said.

"No." Her heart pounded so hard, her chest burned with the frenzy of motion. She couldn't tear her gaze from his lips.

"Gavin, you okay?" Charlie pulled free of his lover and strummed a finger over the mark. "Damn, it's bleeding."

"Clean it up for me in a sec," Gavin said.

"I can do it now." Charlie bent to lap his tongue over the bite mark. Gavin groaned, clutching Charlie's shoulders. "It's stopped bleeding. It must be handy healing so fast."

"Feline genes have their uses," Gavin said.

"One day soon you and Leticia have to show me your cat forms. Isn't there somewhere private we can go where you can shift?"

"We can run on the Mitchells' land. Saul and Lucas might like to run with us. How does that sound, Leticia?"

"It sounds great," she said, although her agreement held no conviction. A shift hurt at the best of times, the reforming of bones and muscles not a pleasant sensation. The way she hurt now, she didn't want to attempt one, even though a shift to feline had helped her health in the past. When the time came, she'd make an excuse to set their minds at ease.

"Good. It's a date." Gavin climbed off the bed and padded to the bathroom.

"I was gonna grab something to clean up with," Charlie said.

"Stay there," Gavin said, a light coming on in the passage. Seconds later Leticia heard water running.

"Do I get a goodnight kiss?" she asked.

"Anytime, babe." Charlie leaned over and she caught the scent of Gavin's blood on his breath. Normally that would have repulsed her, but right now, the coppery aroma pushed at her feline. Her canines pushed through her gums along with a groan. Charlie's lips settled over hers, their breaths mingling. The kiss went straight to hot and heavy, their tongues exploring and twining together.

She wound her hands around his neck, ignoring the twinges of shooting pain darting in a crazy pinball motion to her fingers. Instead, she focused on his mouth, his hands, the building passion and the taste of both Charlie and Gavin. When they came up for air, both were breathing hard. Leticia's gaze dropped to Charlie's mark. She leaned over and sank her teeth into his shoulder without a second thought, ignoring his jolt of surprise. Then he held her close, pressing her head to his shoulder. The heavy weight of his hand on her back brought her back to reality. She rasped her tongue over the mark and cleaned away the blood.

"Sorry. I don't know why I did that. Are you okay?"

"I'm fine, babe. I love you too. I'm glad you're with us both."

"Hey, what's this? The minute my back is turned you two are at it," Gavin teased.

Charlie pulled away and stood. He accepted the cloth from Gavin and cleaned himself. He grinned at them both. "I'm irresistible. What can I say? Some of us have it and some of us don't."

"You bit him?" Gavin asked, eyes narrowing.

"He said I didn't hurt him. I didn't mean to do it. I guess watching you both turned me on more than I realized."

226

"He's bleeding. You can't keep biting him, Leticia. Charlie doesn't heal as speedily as we do."

"It's no big deal. Leticia didn't hurt me. Come back to bed." Charlie brushed the blood away with the back of his hand, leered and gripped his cock. "We can play some more."

Gavin frowned but returned to the bed. "Leticia? What about you?"

She let her breath ease out, trying to fight a flinch of pain. "No, I really do intend to sleep." If she was lucky she'd make it through the rest of the night before she gave in to the building pain and had to confess to Gavin.

Chapter 11

Pained Awakening

Leticia woke slowly, aware immediately that something was wrong. Every muscle telegraphed pain, nerves singing like an ill-played violin. A hoarse groan emerged, and she dragged in a cautious breath. Even that sent fiery slivers of agony to pepper her limbs and torso. Her face contorted, and she gritted her teeth while tears tracked down her cheeks. With a groan, she curled in a fetal position.

"Leticia? Leticia, what is it?" Charlie peered at her through the gloom. He placed his hand on her shoulder and she let out a strangled cry of pure anguish. With a curse, he removed his hand, turning to Gavin who lay on his other side. "Gavin, wake up."

"Waz up?" Gavin muttered.

Leticia groaned as Charlie turned back to her and knocked her shoulder by mistake.

"Damn, sorry, babe," Charlie spoke over his shoulder. "Something's wrong with Leticia. Switch on the lamp by your side."

With her eyes clamped shut, the pain swamped her, bombarded her. A drummer pounded in her head, an accompaniment to the demon violinist.

"Leticia, tell me where it hurts." Gavin crouched beside her, his face a blur. She couldn't focus. A knot blocked her throat. She coughed, and even that hurt. Sweat slicked her torso and limbs. A pained moan escaped, then a whimper at the reverberation.

"Hurts," she croaked.

"I know, sweetheart. Let me pull back the covers so I can take a look at you."

"It's an excuse to perv," Charlie muttered.

She tried to laugh, but it emerged as a distressed cry. "Hurts."

"Tell me where it hurts," Gavin repeated, tugging at the sheet and duvet she'd burrowed into during the night.

"Every...where." She shivered, the pressure on her ribs with each labored breath excruciating. When Gavin tugged on the bed coverings, jolting her, fiery cramps attacked her arms and legs. She screamed, the end of the shriek exiting as a full lion's roar.

"Hell." Gavin fired orders at Charlie. Charlie ran from the bedroom, the thud of his feet firing daggers into her brain. "I know it hurts, sweetheart, but I need to check your stats. Charlie will be back in a sec."

"Hurts." She panted, trying to breathe past the knives stabbing her entire body. More tears tracked down her cheeks. Without warning, she convulsed, her body arcing upward in a tight bow. She screamed, the agony the worst thing she'd ever experienced. Another seizure racked her body and her world faded to black.

"What the hell are you doing to her?" Charlie thrust Gavin's bag of medical instruments at him, breathing hard, his features stark with fear. Gavin set the bag aside.

"I have done nothing," Gavin snapped, pressing his finger to her neck to check for a pulse. "She started convulsing and blacked out. You'd better ring Lucas and Saul."

"Fuck," Charlie said, pressing close to Gavin. "Are we going to lose her?"

Charlie's telltale tremor communicated his fear, and it enveloped Gavin, chasing every bit of medical knowledge from his mind. He froze for an instant, then Charlie stepped back, bursting through his uncharacteristic indecision. "I don't know. It doesn't look good."

"Right. I'll ring Lucas now. Is she unconscious?"

"Yeah, but I won't know more until I do tests."

Gavin heard Charlie leave the room. He muttered a soft prayer under his breath and checked Leticia. She was breathing but seemed unresponsive to every test he administered.

Charlie appeared at his side, stark anguish in his face. "Lucas and Saul are on their way. They'll be here any minute. Lucky they hadn't left for the farm yet."

Gavin set aside the pin he'd used to prick Leticia's big toe, closed his eyes and swallowed. He turned to Charlie, stepping into his arms to seek comfort. Charlie's arms wrapped around him in a tight embrace. For tense seconds they held each other, united in their pain.

Finally, Gavin pushed away. "We'd better get dressed before Lucas and Saul arrive."

"Yeah." Charlie grabbed a pair of jeans and stepped into them. A car pulled up outside. "I'll let them in."

Gavin pulled on sweatpants and dressed before covering Leticia to keep her warm. No time to fall apart right now. No time. He had to hold it together, at least while Lucas and Saul were here.

The low murmur of masculine voices sounded, moved closer. Lucas prowled into the bedroom, his face pale and terrified. "Leticia?"

"She's in a coma, Lucas," Gavin said.

Charlie stopped beside him and squeezed his hand in silent reassurance.

"What happened?" Lucas stroked his fingers over Leticia's pale cheek. She didn't react to his touch. Saul stood by Lucas and gripped his shoulder.

Gavin stepped forward to stand beside them. "I don't know. She seemed okay last night, tired but that's all. This morning she woke in extreme pain. She lost consciousness soon afterward."

"Will she wake up?" Saul asked.

Tension throbbed and swelled in the bedroom while Gavin considered his answer. Grief clutched his heart while they stared at him in silent hope. Searing pain carved his gut, agonizing as if the blade of a sharp knife sliced into him. He'd failed, and their silence struck like blows of accusation. Well, they could get in line. He blamed himself most of all. He'd missed something, some snippet on the net or in medical books that might have helped Leticia beat the bloody disease. Ready for anger and a possible attack, he scanned their faces and told the truth.

"I don't know. Leticia isn't behaving like the other cases I've read."

"But it doesn't look good?" Saul asked.

"No. I'm sorry. I should have—"

"Fuck!" Lucas's eyes glowed an eerie gold and his hair bristled, making him appear bigger, more formidable.

Gavin took half a step back, stumbling when he knocked into Charlie. Charlie steadied him, offering silent reassurance. When he took a deep breath, Charlie's scent filled his lungs, calming his angst.

"I hate this," Lucas snarled. "I'd like to rip the cowardly bastard who did this to her to shreds and stomp on his bloody corpse."

"So why didn't you?" Charlie snapped.

The sharp anger in his mate's voice made Gavin realize he wasn't the only one suffering. Charlie and Leticia were marked mates. It would be harder for him, and selfishly he hadn't even considered this. Turning, he wrapped Charlie in his arms.

"I battered his face," Lucas said in a frustrated growl. "Leticia wouldn't let me do any more because the feline authorities where we lived would've ordered me killed, but he doesn't look so handsome now, not after I finished with him."

"She loved him," Gavin said.

"She may have loved him, but she loves us now." Charlie pulled away from Gavin and strode to the bed. He stared down at her with an anguish that tore at Gavin's heart. "We're her mates. We make her happy."

"You do," Saul said. "Lucas and I wouldn't have left her here with you if we didn't think you cared for her. We all love her. She's an amazing woman. What..." His voice broke. "What are you going to do now?"

Gavin stared at Leticia's pale face. "All I can do now is monitor her, hook her up to an IV and see what happens. She's breathing on her own, which is encouraging. Unusual actually, but then I've never seen a feline go into a coma before. When we die it's normally quick."

"Quick how?" Charlie asked, a sliver of fear and unease swirling across his features.

"Most felines die of a heart attack. We live long lives, longer than a human and get a flu-like illness, which seems to bring on a heart attack. Once a feline goes down with that flu they never recover. I assumed it would be like that for Leticia. The other FIV sufferers died like that. I thought Leticia would go the same way."

Lucas jerked his gaze from his sister, turning to stare at him. "So she might regain consciousness? I mean she's holding her human form."

"I don't know. I don't think so," Gavin said. "If she doesn't wake, it will be hard to pump enough nourishment into her. You've seen how much weight she's lost." His chest ached so much he had to stop speaking. He fumbled in his pocket for a hanky, couldn't find one and swiped the back of his hand over his nose. "The longer she remains unconscious..." He trailed off, unable to grasp his professional mantle when Leticia meant so much to him.

The truth as he saw it. She was pretty much dead now. They'd lost her.

Chapter 12

The Aftermath

Three Weeks Later

"Damn it, Charlie. Eat. You can't carry on like this. I can't...can't lose you too." Gavin thumped a plate of food in front of his mate. He grabbed another plate full of food and sat opposite Charlie. "Eat."

"I didn't think this would be so hard. Until Leticia...I didn't realize what the bond between mates meant and how adrift I'd feel. Sometimes when I'm sitting with Leticia I want to crawl into bed with her, go to sleep and never wake again."

Gavin fumbled the knife he was holding, the stainless steel implement hitting the edge of his plate and thumping to the tabletop, taking gravy and mashed potato with it. He dropped his fork and glared at Charlie. "Don't even bloody think it. How the hell do you expect me to get through this without you around? I love you, dammit. You're my mate. I need you."

"You keep pushing me away."

He thought... Pushing him away. Gavin closed his eyes, enjoying the solid weight of his heartbeat, smelling the bloody scent of rare beef. He opened his eyes again, seeking Charlie's gaze. "It's the guilt," he said, his voice hoarse with emotion. "Logically I know I did everything I could, but the thoughts hover. I keep thinking I should've done more, done things differently."

"What? What more could you have done?" Charlie glared, his expression mean and highlighted by the light blond stubble shading his head. Gavin almost smiled. He looked like a tough biker with his scowl and the hard glint in his pale blue eyes.

Gavin shoved his plate away, the beef tasting on par with a spoonful of sand. "You're right."

"We can't keep on like this, pushing each other away. Leticia wouldn't have wanted us to do that. It would have pissed her off."

Gavin snorted. "True."

"I don't want food. I need you." Charlie's taut voice told of his inner pain, his hurt, and Gavin acknowledged again that in his suffering he'd pushed Charlie away. They were marked mates, and he'd ignored Charlie, buckling under stress and remorse.

"All right." Gavin stood and held out his hand. "Let's go."

Charlie blinked. "Go where?"

"To our bedroom, after I do a last check on Leticia."

Charlie nodded and stood. After placing their discarded meals in the fridge, they walked down the passage to the spare bedroom. Gavin had to steel himself to enter, as he did every day. It was Leticia, but not the woman he knew.

"If you ignore the medical equipment and the disinfectant and spicy scent, it's almost as if she's sleeping."

Gavin wrapped his arm around Charlie's waist and squeezed. She had the appearance of a sleeping princess, albeit on the skinny side. "She looks as if she might wake at any moment. So beautiful."

"She'd look better if she wasn't so skinny and you didn't have her on that oxygen machine." Charlie spoke bluntly. "But her hair's growing back."

A frown curved Gavin's mouth. "Yeah, it is. It's weird the way her hair is growing so even. I would have expected it to drop out again. Her blood work is the same."

"Is the virus mutating somehow?"

Gavin issued a frustrated sigh. "I don't know. I know nothing." He snorted. "Yeah, what sort of doctor does that make me?"

"Man, let it go. You're a great doctor and everyone around here counts on you. You saved Laura's life."

"It's the ones I don't save that haunt me."

"You've done your best, running every test you can. We all see the way she's deteriorating. Lucas doesn't blame you."

True, but it didn't lighten the burden of guilt. He'd keep trying to bring Leticia back. She wasn't dead. Not yet.

One glance at Gavin told Charlie his mate was stressing again, blaming himself for failing to cure Leticia. With her weight-loss, she couldn't last much longer. It hurt, knowing she was dying. He'd give his left nut to bring her back. *Wasn't gonna happen.* Not in this lifetime. He'd never witness Leticia and Gavin playing in their feline forms or try to run with them. Just him and Gavin now. His breath caught, the swell of pain like a bleeding wound. They couldn't continue like this, existing instead of living.

"I'll be in the bedroom." His voice emerged stiff and abrupt. "I won't be long."

In the bedroom, Charlie stripped and slid between the sheets. His muscles throbbed with fatigue, so bloody tired. Along with insomnia, he'd had late-night call-outs for emergencies. When he closed his eyes, all he could see was Leticia. In his mind's eye, he saw her as he'd first seen her wearing a hat and a miniskirt, all smiles and attitude. The same night he'd hooked up with Gavin.

The pad of footsteps and the rustle of clothing had him opening his eyes, and he smiled faintly. His eyes drifted over Gavin's naked chest, the flexing muscles and wide shoulders. "Hey."

Gavin's answering grin lifted some of the tiredness and stress from his features. The shadows under his green eyes remained. "Hey."

He slipped into the bed and into Charlie's arms. Charlie pressed close, enjoying the steady beat of Gavin's heart and his soapy scent from the shower before dinner. Their groins brushed and a shot of desire flared to life. He wriggled again and took heart from Gavin's sharp inhalation and the burgeoning erection pressing against his belly. Their mouths met and they kissed. Excitement and pleasure battled inside, along with relief. He needed the intimacy to affirm their love, to tamp down the loneliness. He used the tip of his tongue to outline Gavin's lips, nibbled at them, and then licked the sting away. Hunger rippled inside, his body humming to life. Muscles rippled as they rocked against each other in lazy thrusts.

"Damn, that is good. I've missed this so much, but it doesn't seem right with Leticia…"

"Yeah. Me too." Charlie writhed against Gavin again and sucked on the marking site, pulling the blood to the surface. He reached between them to grasp their cocks. Gavin moaned when Charlie pumped them and sought his mouth, kissing him again. So good. He'd missed the physical connection. "Leticia wouldn't want us to turn from each other."

"I'm close already," Gavin muttered, ignoring the comment.

Charlie decided to leave it. He'd make sure they didn't become distant again. They needed to make love. The last three weeks had been weird and although they'd hugged and kissed, they hadn't made love. That drought couldn't repeat. He wouldn't let it.

"Just let go." A shiver rocked through Charlie, pleasure building in his balls. Drops of pre-cum eased the rub of his fist over their cocks. Their cheeks rasped together then Gavin spread a trail of kisses down his neck. He worked his teeth back and forth over the mark on Charlie's shoulder, a shudder arcing to his cock. His heart lurched and an intense burst of heat exploded from him, semen washing across his hands as he came. Charlie released his own cock to concentrate on Gavin. He gripped his lover's shaft, coaxing a response from him, pushing him harder until Gavin climaxed with a hoarse groan.

"I love you, Charlie. Love you so much."

Charlie hugged him close. "Love you, Gavin. I need you. Don't leave me alone. Leticia—I need you, man."

"I'm sorry." Gavin pulled away to cup his cheek, frowned at Charlie's unshed tears. "I never meant to alienate you. You've given me so much. Because of you, we had a few weeks with Leticia, and that's longer than I predicted. I know I've concentrated on Leticia recently, but never forget you're my mate and I love you."

"What are we going to do?" The tight sensation in his chest came back with vengeance, reminding Charlie of the huge gap in their lives without Leticia. She'd slotted in so well, knitting the three of them into a close relationship, making them into a team.

"Take one day at a time." Gavin sighed, a gust of warm breath against his neck. "That's all we can do." He reached over to switch off the light and curled back into Charlie, despite the stickiness. Charlie didn't argue, content in his mate's embrace. Yeah, one day at a time might get them through this nightmare.

Gavin woke from a deep sleep, the best he'd had for weeks. Darkness shrouded the room, the steady rhythm of Charlie's breathing reassuring and bringing a measure of comfort he hadn't experienced in weeks. He relaxed into his mate's body, savoring the closeness. His belly rumbled with hunger. He didn't move a muscle, preferring to stay with his mate. He could eat in the morning. Thank God Charlie had pushed him. They'd needed the closeness again. They'd needed each other in the way of feline mates. It brought home to him his responsibilities as a mate. Leticia was lost to both of them now. The reality was, she couldn't lose more weight and live. As a feline, she needed more nourishment than they could pump into her. Nothing to do but wait. At least they had each other. For a while he'd forgotten that. He wouldn't forget again.

A thud at the far end of the house slid through his mind, piercing his comfortable doze. He lifted his head, waking Charlie with the abrupt motion.

"What's up?"

"Me, if you don't stop that sexy wriggle," Gavin answered.

"I'll wriggle if I want to." Charlie sounded more alert, interested in pursuing the matter.

A repeat of the noise attracted Charlie's attention. "There's someone in the house," he muttered, his voice hard. Tense. Cop-like.

Despite the tension, or perhaps because of it, a streak of lust slammed Gavin's body. He groaned, the tension going straight to his cock.

"Hold that thought," Charlie said, sliding from the bed. A wave of sex and male musk filled the air.

"Dammit, you're not going without me."

"Stay. It's my job."

"This is personal. You're not working now."

"Lucas and Saul would have told us if they intended to visit."

Gavin gripped Charlie's forearm, jerking him to a halt. "Yeah, they would've told us. Besides, they're coming tomorrow morning."

"It could be someone after drugs. Stay behind me," Charlie ordered. "I don't want to lose you too."

Gavin rolled his eyes. As a shifter, he had a better chance of survival during a run-in with a thief. He'd protect his mate with everything he had. No way would he lose Charlie, not now when he needed him for survival.

Charlie paused outside the internal entrance to the surgery.

"They're in the kitchen," Gavin said, pinpointing their location after hearing another thump.

"What the fuck are they doing there? There's nothing to steal."

They prowled the remaining length of the passage, a stream of light spilling through the open doorway to pierce the darkness. They glanced at each other. What kind of thief turned on lights and didn't worry about discovery? Gavin read Charlie's intent with ease and nodded. Together, they burst through the doorway, coming to an abrupt halt.

A feminine screech filled the air and an almost full bottle of milk hit the floor with a liquid splat.

"Fuck." Gavin gaped, taking in the empty plates and remnants of food on the table. His heart dive-bombed against his chest in staccato attacks.

"What?" Leticia arched her brows, her posture defensive. "I was hungry."

"Leticia?" Charlie croaked.

Gavin pulled out a chair and shoved his mate into it. His own legs trembled so bad, he sank onto a chair next to Charlie. They shared a glance before turning to stare at Leticia in consternation.

She'd been close to death. So weak, he'd had to put her on an oxygen machine so she continued to breathe. Unresponsive to every test he'd given her, he'd intended to discuss pulling the plug when Lucas and Saul visited in the morning.

How was this possible?

He rubbed his eyes. When he focused again, she remained in front of him, sawing on a piece of roast beef with her knife. As he watched, she thrust it into her mouth and chewed.

"Why are you staring at me as if I have two heads?" Leticia waved a fork in the air, her chin lifting in pure arrogance. "At least I'm dressed." She gestured at her cotton nightgown.

"Uh, maybe I'll make coffee," Charlie said.

Gavin scowled at Leticia, his heart racing so fast he could scarcely hear himself think. "Make mine a whiskey." *How was*

243

this possible? The thought ran through his head like a video on a continual loop.

"Whiskey is a good idea."

Gavin noticed Charlie staggered as he made his way to the alcohol cupboard. He understood Charlie's reaction. With a gulp, he turned his attention back to Leticia, he tried to study her with the eye of a medic. He failed. Instead, he scrutinized her as a man. A lover. Her breasts rose and fell beneath the white cotton. Healthy color filled her cheeks while she forked cold green beans into her mouth. The bloom of pink that hadn't been present the last time he'd checked on her.

"What? Why are you staring at me?"

"Are you going to eat all that?" he asked, referring to one of the meals he and Charlie hadn't eaten the previous night. An empty plate attested that she'd already eaten one meal.

"Yeah. I'm starving."

"How do you feel?"

"I already said I was hungry." Her brow wrinkled when she caught Charlie's perturbed stare. She turned back to glower at him. Gavin had never realized how much her glare turned him on. Pure lust sizzled in him and he had to grip the edge of the table to halt the urge to grab her.

"Why are you staring at me? Jeesh, I sound like a stuck record. I'd stop asking the same questions if you gave me answers."

"Never mind that," Charlie said, fumbling two glasses. He set them on the table and sloshed a generous measure of whiskey into both. The base of the whiskey bottle struck the table with a dull thud. With a trembling hand, he shunted one at Gavin and picked up the other. He drained it in one go, reaching for the bottle to pour more.

Oh yeah. Gavin experienced the same mental confusion. He picked up the glass of whiskey Charlie had poured for him and drank it in one long swallow. Charlie refilled his glass without hesitation.

"Before we answer your questions, apart from hunger, how are you?"

"What is up with you two?" She spoke around a mouthful of mashed potato and gravy.

Despite his earlier hunger, the rich, meaty gravy scent turned his stomach. The slug of whiskey hadn't helped. "Answer the question," he barked, losing patience. He didn't believe this. *Did not believe it.*

"I'm fine—a bit weak when I stand up but better now that I've eaten." Her eyes narrowed as if she'd remembered something. "I was on a machine." She gestured at a bloody spot on her left hand. "You attached me to a drip."

"They were there for a reason," Charlie snapped. "Didn't you think to call out?"

"But I was hungry." Leticia shrugged. "That's all I could think about."

"You've been in a coma for over three weeks. You needed the oxygen machine to keep breathing."

"Three weeks? I don't remember—no, that's not true. I remember unbearable pain and...and that's all." Her knife and fork dropped onto her plate with a crisp clunk. "I've been out of it for three weeks?"

"The machine was keeping you alive."

"I was dead?" Her eyes rounded and when she realized her right hand trembled, she slipped it out of sight below the table.

"I need to run tests." Gavin sent her a challenging glance. She opened her mouth and shut it again, apparently rethinking her intention to complain.

"I'm glad you didn't protest," Charlie stated. "Because I will sit on you, if necessary, for Gavin to do his tests. You won't enjoy that. No, stay there. Don't move."

Leticia ignored his order. "I wanted to check the fridge for more food."

Gavin left them to their bickering and hurried to find the things he needed to check Leticia's current state of health. A blood test first. *Bloody fucking amazing*. That was what this was—a miracle. He burst into the kitchen, half convinced he'd find her slumped in Charlie's arms. Dead. Or he'd discover he'd been dreaming.

Very much alive, she'd found more food and concentrated on demolishing the contents of her plate. Charlie scrutinized her, taking an occasional sip from his glass of whiskey. If anything, Charlie seemed more in need of his medical services than Leticia did.

"Do you have to take more blood?"

Charlie placed his glass on the table. "I meant what I said about sitting on you, if that's what it takes for Gavin to do the tests. Don't make me prove it."

"You're bullies."

"You haven't had to live through the last three weeks. You owe us," Charlie said in a grim tone. He reached for the whiskey bottle again, cursing when the contents didn't cover the bottom of his glass.

"This won't take long," Gavin promised. "I'll do bloods, and we can do the rest tomorrow."

Charlie drank the last of the whiskey and reached for the phone. "While you do that I'll ring Lucas. I don't think they'll mind an early morning call."

"Do you have to call them right now? Two males hovering over me is more than enough."

"You haven't been around recently," Charlie snapped. "I'm ringing them."

After a huff to show her displeasure, Leticia pulled out her chair and relaxed her left arm, extending it for Gavin. The procedure didn't take long. Gavin took the sample to his surgery and started work in the small lab, equipped by months of fundraising by the local felines. He went through the process, concentrating on each step.

This wasn't possible. In his medical opinion only the machine had kept her alive, yet right now she seemed fine. He stared at the slide containing the blood sample, blinked and squeezed his eyes shut before he looked again. *Well hell.* The virus was still

SHELLEY MUNRO

present but not in the same numbers. How? For months, the virus had multiplied, becoming dominant over her antibodies.

Somehow, her body was fighting the virus. He'd done a blood test two weeks ago and things had appeared the same. Another study of the slide showed a foreign component. A gasp escaped, whistling past tight lips. He stood and returned to the kitchen.

"Charlie, I need to do a blood test on you."

"Why?"

"Don't be such a baby," Leticia said with a sly smirk at Gavin. "I'll sit on you if you refuse."

"You and whose army," Charlie scoffed. "I presume you have a good reason," he said extending his arm.

"Do you realize that neither of you is wearing clothes? My brother and Saul are on their way here right now."

"I don't think they'll mind," Charlie said. "Besides, they're coming from the farm. It will take them a while."

Gavin took a blood sample and strode back to the surgery. Charlie followed him, leaving Leticia alone in the kitchen.

"Leticia is right about the clothes. I'll bring you a pair of jeans." Charlie paused. "Is there a problem?"

Gavin snorted. "I know nothing. I'll know more after I take a look at your blood."

A sliver of fear hit Charlie's face. "Do I have FIV?"

"No, but there's something odd going on with Leticia's blood. A mutation. I'll know more once I can compare your blood. I'll test mine too."

Charlie sat in silence while he prepared a slide. "Is that it?"

248

"Yeah."

Charlie stood and disappeared down the passage while Gavin continued his tests. Half an hour later he'd formed a hypothesis. He had no idea if his theory was right, but it was his only one. When he entered the kitchen, Charlie cupped a mug of coffee while Leticia ate a pile of toast slathered with jam.

"So what's the verdict, Doctor?" Leticia asked. "Will I live?"

"Frankly I'm not sure what's going on with you. My best guess is that when you mated with Charlie he gave you some of the antibodies I'd passed on to him. Something about the combinations seems to have killed off some of the FIV virus."

Charlie stood and pushed Gavin into a chair, pouring him a mug of coffee and pulling out another chair. "Is it a permanent change?"

"You mean I'm getting better?"

Gavin hated to wipe the excited expectancy off her face, yet he couldn't leave her with a false sense of security either. "It looks that way, although I'm not a hundred percent sure. You still have FIV but it seems mild compared to what it was before."

"I'm not going to die?" Leticia's smile lit up the kitchen.

"Not today at any rate," Gavin said. "I'll need to do more tests but I think the disease is in remission." A broad grin tipped up the corners of his mouth. Charlie grabbed Leticia and danced around the kitchen. With an exuberant laugh, Gavin stood and joined in the dance, wrapping his arms around his lovers. They had a second chance and maybe a future. He had two mates. He had love. Acceptance. He kissed both Charlie and Leticia on the lips then exhaled with a long sigh of contentment, basking in the glow of love.

Chapter 13

Epilogue

A gentle breeze blew over the hill. Leticia walked between Charlie and Gavin, crossing the tussock grasses to reach a private spot not visible from the road. Despite the onset of autumn, the warm and sunny stretch of weather provided the perfect day for a run. The distinct scent of mud, dried salt and plants filled every breath. Heat shimmered through the air, the sky a brilliant blue without a single cloud. It was a great day to be alive.

"Here looks good." Gavin stopped and dropped the blanket he'd carried from the SUV.

Leticia yanked her T-shirt over her head and bent to remove her boots. A grin surfaced when the two men fired clothes left and right, trying to beat her to strip. Although she still carried the FIV virus, it continued to lessen, and they were hopeful she'd make a full recovery. Life was good. "I'm ready to shift!"

"Wait," Charlie said. "I want to watch." He spread out the blanket and sprawled on it, wearing nothing but a grin.

Both she and Gavin moved back, glanced at each other. Gavin winked and together they let the change take them. Fur sprouted, bones lengthened, reshaped. The usual sensation of displacement, laced with pain, zipped through Leticia while she shifted to lion. With a gasp, she fell to all fours, the sparkle of magic filling the air. Suddenly every sense worked at top speed, sensations pouring through her—the dried grasses, the tang of salt, the sharp note of cow manure and the lemon of the soap they'd used in the shower this morning.

A soft growl claimed her attention and a black leopard nudged her on the shoulder before smooching. He purred, a sound of contentment. Pleasure.

"Wow, that looked amazing." Charlie stood, his expression a trifle uncertain and one of awe. He took half a step before, both in accord, they jumped him, playfully knocking him to the ground.

"Ow," he muttered, rubbing his butt. "I will make you both lick my bruises tonight."

Sounded like a plan to her. Gavin liked the idea because he purred and rubbed his head against their mate's chest. Charlie grinned and reached out, stroking them both at the same time. Damn, his caress seduced her, the rough scratch of fingers bringing a rumble of contentment. Judging by Gavin's continual purring, he enjoyed Charlie's touch as much as she.

"Are you going to run or stay here and annoy me?" Charlie's soft laughter told her he loved their attention and reveled in seeing them this way. He truly loved them, just as they loved him in return. Happiness spread through her at the acknowledgment.

Luck, love and laughter. Family. She had all of that now, along with hope for the future. That was the most precious thing of all.

Gavin licked Charlie with his rough tongue and jumped away when his mate tried to retaliate. She dived after him, playing a rough game of chase. They snarled and mock-growled at each other with Charlie clapping and cheering.

After half an hour, she submitted to Gavin, sides panting with tiredness while she quivered beneath him. He let out a questioning growl and released her, letting out a bark. A second abrupt bark communicated his desire for her to shift back to human. Sounded good to her. She visualized her human form in her mind and seconds later, she walked over to join Charlie where he sprawled on the blanket, enjoying both the sun and the view.

"You okay?" Concern tinged his voice.

"Puffed. I haven't exercised much recently."

"And it doesn't help that I pushed you too hard," Gavin said, dropping to the ground beside them. "Any pain?"

"Don't treat me like an invalid." Leticia sniffed to make sure they understood her irritation. Their twin grins didn't bode well. They knew all right and were unapologetic about their concern.

"Don't be angry with us," Charlie said, tugging on a short lock of her hair. "You scared us half to death when you went into that coma. We need time to adjust. That's why Lucas and Saul ring every day and visit as often as they can. Why London fusses at you to eat and Tomasine asks you to share her lunch. It's why Ramsay asks for help with his exercises and Emily and Saber call every few days to check on you. We're clingy and we're not apologizing."

Gavin's grin widened as he nodded. "What Charlie said. Now are you okay?"

Leticia heaved out a put-upon sigh, but it was for form. Inside she celebrated the love and caring she'd found with Charlie and Gavin, with her friends. She leaned over and kissed Charlie, a slow mating of mouths that she gradually took deeper. Her heartbeat raced when she slipped her tongue past Charlie's lips, teased and tasted until they each pulled away, both of them breathing harder.

"I'd like to kiss you, Gavin. A proper lover's kiss. Do you think it's safe?"

"Yeah, I do. We'll still need to use condoms during sex but I think kissing is safe. No biting though."

"Kisses are good." Leticia grabbed his head and held him while she slid her lips over his, not that he put up much of a fight. His lips were firm yet soft, his scent familiar. They took their time, tasting and teasing each other until Charlie complained.

"Hey, I'm a bit left out here."

Without haste, they parted and jumped Charlie, pinning him to the ground and kissing his face and chest, gradually working down his sun-warmed body. Leticia licked his pectoral muscle with raspy licks, taking pleasure in his contented sigh, the way his eyes closed, his lashes a dark fan on his upper cheeks.

"Don't bite there," he gasped.

Leticia lifted her head. "I'm not doing anything."

"I am." Gavin's tone was smug. "But you're right. We don't want to finish this before we've started."

Leticia closed her left eye in a wink. "True. We should make this last."

"You don't need to stop altogether," Charlie protested.

Leticia went back to kissing, working down his body. Occasionally, she paused to kiss Gavin, pleasure springing to life inside her. The stroke of Charlie's hand in her short hair added another point of connection. Desire flared to life, shimmering inside, warming her. Gavin caught the tip of her breast between his lips and sucked until the pull echoed between her legs. The rough and sensual play of his teeth brought a surge of liquid arousal, and when she stirred, the way Gavin stilled told her he scented her readiness. A low moan rumbled at the back of her throat.

"Are you ready for us, babe?"

More than they'd ever know. Every time they made love—the three of them—it was as if she affirmed life over again. She treasured each precious moment. Her hand reached for Charlie's throbbing hardness and with an instinctive rhythm, she pushed at his control.

With a bark of laughter, Gavin joined in the teasing, concentrating on both of them. A touch of her shoulder. A kiss on her belly. A finger lightly circling Charlie's nipple. The rasp of his tongue along Charlie's cock. Soft sighs of pleasure filled the air. Low moans of desire. Like a slow dance, they cemented their love until they shivered and needed more from their erotic duel.

"Condoms. Lube. Where did we put them?" Charlie demanded in a hoarse voice.

"My jeans," Gavin said.

Charlie searched through the scattered clothing, muttering under his breath until he triumphantly produced a handful of foil packets and lube. He kept one for himself and chucked the rest to Gavin. After ripping it, he rolled it on and lay back on the blanket.

"I'm all yours, babe."

"Good to hear," Leticia said, bending over to stroke his powerful chest. She straddled him and guided his cock into her before impaling herself.

"Damn, that is hot," Gavin said. "I love watching the two of you together."

"Well, we like it better when you join in," Charlie said. "Hurry and stop prolonging our agony."

"Since when is pleasure considered agony?"

"There's a thin layer between pleasure and pain. You know that," Leticia chided. "Besides it's easy for you to say that right now. Payback is a bitch, and there are two of us to gang up on you."

Eyes crinkling at the corners, Gavin ripped open a condom and rolled it onto his erection. Seconds later, he squeezed lube into the palm of his hand and slathered it the length of his shaft.

Leticia shivered, looking forward to the pleasure-pain of his possession, the closeness that came from being with both of them, the sense of flying. Freedom.

Slippery fingers stretched her, and it wasn't long before he pushed inside her body. Charlie kissed her, a light and tormenting touch of lips. The caress of lips along her spine brought new sensations then her lovers surrounded her, filled her. They rocked together, sliding in and out until she shuddered, helpless with the pleasure. Her heart thundered as her two men increased the power of their thrusts.

"Each time we do this I can't believe it can get better," Charlie muttered.

"It does," Leticia said.

"Oh yeah." Gavin withdrew and pushed inside her again. "That's because we're mates."

Leticia groaned at the sense of fullness. *Amazing*. Perspiration covered her body, and Gavin's heartbeat pulsed against her back, Charlie's at her chest. Pleasure bloomed, Charlie's next stroke brushing her swollen clit. Molten fire exploded through her, squeezing her lovers' cocks with each silken clasp.

At her back, Gavin grunted, stroked once and climaxed while Charlie licked across her marking site, the rasp of his jaw sending another pulse of pleasure zapping through her. He groaned, shuddered and let go while she luxuriated in the aftershocks.

Gavin pulled out and rolled over to discard the condom. She clambered off Charlie, and Gavin tugged her against his chest. Charlie squeezed closer, and they held each other. Sandwiched between the two, she relaxed, her eyes closed, security and confidence about the future filling her. Only one thing could make it better.

"I want to have a baby," she murmured.

Both men tensed, and if she'd opened her eyes, she'd have bet she'd catch them exchanging silent messages.

"Who would be the father?" Charlie asked.

"Both of you, silly. We're a team."

Gavin released her and moved away. "I don't think it's a good idea."

She missed his warmth and opened her eyes to protest. "Yes, it's too soon. I still want a baby. I never thought I'd have the opportunity."

"I'm in favor of the idea. Gavin's the doctor, though, and he's right. I'd like more time with just the three of us. You're not fully fit again yet."

Leticia speared Gavin with a hard stare. "So you're not saying no? Are you worried about the baby getting the FIV virus?"

"The chances of passing the virus on to a baby are medically low, the same as it is with a female human with her baby. Once you're fit you and Charlie can make a baby."

"No," she said. "It will be our baby. Test tube if that's the way we have to do it. Our baby," she repeated. "The three of us."

"That's a great idea," Charlie said. "Mix our sperm together and wait to see what happens."

"I love you both," Gavin said, his voice husky with sudden emotion.

"We know," Charlie said, leaning back and using his clasped hands as a pillow. "You tell us every day."

Leticia smiled so wide her mouth hurt. Charlie did the same thing—told them he loved them. She kind of liked it and decided in that moment, she'd follow suit, staring now. "I love you both. You make me feel special."

"That's because you are extraordinary," Charlie said, and Gavin nodded.

"It's the three of us together that makes us a tight unit," she said, something she truly believed. A feline girl didn't get much luckier than this.

Oh yeah. Her lovers were very special.

Chapter 14

Bonus Chapter

Storm in a Teacup café, Middlemarch, New Zealand

Feline Shapeshifter Council Meeting.

Present: Sid Blackburn, Agnes Paisley, Valerie McClintock, Benjamin Urquart

Apologies: Saber Mitchell

Sid Blackburn sat at a table for six and nursed a flat white while he waited for his fellow council members to arrive for their meeting.

Valerie and Agnes arrived first, and after a brief stop at the counter to order coffee, they hustled over to join him.

Ben entered the café next and headed straight for Sid. He pulled out an empty chair, his usual happy expression absent and his brow creased in worry lines. "Kenneth will be late for the meeting. He asked me to give his apologies and told me he'd be here as soon as he can."

"Something wrong?" Valerie asked.

"He hasn't been well for the last week," Ben said. "His daughter persuaded him to make an appointment with Gavin."

Agnes's eyebrows rose. "Kenneth couldn't work the appointment around our meeting?"

"Gavin is working reduced clinic hours at present while Leticia is recovering. I heard he's busy with vet work for the local farmers and is only taking emergencies outside the clinic hours. He needs an assistant," Sid said. Something they needed to consider for the future. They didn't want the lad to burn out from stress.

"Well, in that case," Agnes said, wrinkling her nose. "It's strange without Saber here."

"Lad deserves his holiday." Ben waved at a new arrival. "What's on the agenda today? The Sevens Rugby tournament?"

Sid pulled a notebook from his shirt pocket and opened it. He peered at his writing as it wriggled about the page in big blurs. His darling mate was always telling him to use his glasses, but they got in the way, so he conveniently forgot them. Unfortunately, he'd truly forgotten them today when he could have used the aid.

"*Psst*," Valerie hissed. "Where are your reading glasses? Here let me read your notes. What are they about? Our plan of attack?"

Sid handed over his notebook to Valerie. She pushed her glasses up her nose and started reading. "Teams invited."

"Done." Sid leaned back in his chair. "Saber and I contacted the local clubs plus those in Dunedin, Queenstown and as far south as Invercargill. We've had an excellent response."

Valerie consulted the notebook. "Referees?"

"We have a team of six organized plus two reserves. We've also arranged ball boys from the school. No shortage of volunteers," Sid added as he scanned the busy café. Emily Mitchell worked hard, and it showed with the continual stream of customers. London Allbright was doing the baking while Emily and Saber were away, and if he wasn't mistaken, she'd just taken a batch of cheese scones from the oven. Delectable scent, and one of his favorites to have with a cup of strong tea.

"Refreshments?" Valerie glanced up and scowled. "Sid, are you paying attention?"

"Multi-tasking," he said and aimed for the serene smiled that always ruffled his mate.

"I can answer that one," Ben said, before Valerie went all schoolmistress on them. "I've organized two barbecues to cook sausages for a sausage sizzle. The scouts are running those. The Middlemarch Women's Division is setting up a tea tent. I believe Saber has organized a bouncy castle for the youngsters too. We have also approached the local pub about setting up a beer garden, which would be available to those of age who are not playing rugby. Sid and I were very clear about the rules and told them this would be an experiment. Any misbehavior or hijinks would result in the closure of the beer garden, and they wouldn't receive a second invitation to participate."

"That is a good idea." Slightly mollified, Valerie glanced at the list again and checked off the item. "Prizes?"

"I've been banking the entrance fees. We're giving half back in prize money for the top three, plus the winning team receives a cup," Agnes said. "Our expenses have been minimal. The referees receive an honorarium, and we've had to pay for the trophy plus engraving. The scouts and Women's Division are giving the Feline council a portion of their takings."

"What about advertising?" Sid asked, now back in council-meeting mode.

"I spoke to London Allbright," Valerie said. "She is designing flyers for us to help spread the word. She said she'd donate the time and supplies in exchange for a mention of her virtual assistant business at the bottom of the flyer. I told her to go ahead."

"Where are we sending the flyers?" Ben asked, his feline-green gaze full of interest.

"Agnes and I are going shopping in Dunedin at the weekend. We'll take a handful and approach some of the shops at the mall," Valerie offered.

"I believe Lana and Duncan Sinclair are visiting this weekend," Sid said. "Lana is a good girl. She won't mind putting up a notice in her restaurant window. I'll ask Leo Mitchell about taking some for the vineyard."

"What about fancy dress?" Ben asked.

Valerie shoved her glasses up her nose. "Pardon?"

"Whenever I see the Sevens rugby on telly, the audience are dressed in costumes. We could offer a small prize for the best costume," Ben suggested. "I don't mind judging. I'm sure Kenneth would help me."

"I'll add that to the list." She tapped her pen on the page and made a final notation. "I think that's everything. All we need now is a fine day."

"I haven't heard any further rumblings about humans integrating into our community," Ben said. "Although they might flare up again when the werewolf arrives."

Sid accepted his notebook from Valerie and snapped it shut. "I don't care what anyone says. The werewolf we have now is a good lad. He kept his head when falsely accused of murder, and he volunteers to help with our projects. If the stepfather is of the same ilk, and all my inquiries bear this out, then the community will be the richer for his presence."

"When do London and Gerard leave for their holiday?" Agnes asked. "I was hoping to utilize London with more of the admin work for this rugby thing."

Ben snorted, his eyes gleaming with amusement. "Please. Middlemarch Sevens Rugby tournament. Get it right, Agnes."

Agnes rolled her eyes and turned her attention to Sid.

"Everyone is flying out this weekend," Sid said. "Henry, his stepfather, Leo and Isabella are going to Fiji for a three-day stay. London and Gerard are staying on for two weeks. I hear they're going island hopping."

"I thought they'd hurry the wedding," Ben commented. "It's been a few months since they met."

Sid shook his head. "Young Gerard told me they wanted Henry's stepfather at the wedding because the man was like a father to him too. They also waited on Sam and Lisa. Gerard said he couldn't get married without Sam and Henry. It's taken a while to organize everyone."

Agnes released a gusty sigh. "London will be away then. That's a pity. I like that girl. She deserves her happiness after everything she has experienced. She listens before she talks, not like my granddaughters."

The bell on the café door tinkled, and Kenneth pushed his way inside.

Sid straightened in his chair, concern flooding him. Kenneth's feature were flushed and his forehead gleamed with perspiration. More than was normal for the feline. One of the teenage after-school helpers stopped, her hands full of dirty dishes, to let him pass.

Ben frowned. "Kenneth looks terrible."

Kenneth spotted them and lurched in their direction, appearing none too steady on his feet.

Sid rose and pulled out a chair. Kenneth dropped into it, his breathing harsh, and the heat radiating off his body bore a sharp, sour scent. "You should have gone straight home. We would've understood. What did Gavin say?"

"Have elevated blood pressure. Told my son to pick me up here," Kenneth said. "Gavin had an emergency, and I had to wait longer than I'd planned. Walk here almost did me in. Don't know why." He gasped two harsh breaths. "Not far."

"Not serious?" Valerie whispered in an undertone.

"No. No, of course not," Kenneth said, slurring his speech. "Gavin has given me a diet sheet. He did tests, took a blood sample and started me on pills to treat the high blood pressure. Told me to rest, and he'd stop by and see me tomorrow. Will have test results then in case there is another underlying problem."

"I'll give you a ride home. Where is your fancy phone?" Ben held out his hand. "I'll ring your son for you."

Kenneth fumbled in his jacket, and even that seemed to zap his strength. Sid frowned, his instincts roaring on high alert. "Ring Gavin," he ordered. "Tell him Kenneth isn't doing well."

Ben stood and helped Kenneth remove the phone from his jacket inner pocket.

The café doorbell tinkled, and Felix Mitchell walked inside. He grinned at Tomasine, his mate, who was serving at the counter and started to go out the back.

"Felix, lad," Sid shouted.

The café went quiet and heads turned to stare. Somewhere out in the garden, a child started wailing.

Felix strode over to them, reminding Sid of his old friend Herbert in that moment. "What is it, Mr. Blackburn?"

"Kenneth is sick. We'll need help to get him to the car," Sid said.

Ben finished his call. "Gavin is on his way. Five minutes, he said."

A tremor slipped through Kenneth's big frame, and he clutched his chest. "Feel peculiar." He slumped and would've fallen if Felix hadn't grabbed him and hoisted him upright. Kenneth's harsh breathing ceased without warning.

"He's out," Felix said, and Sid was grateful for the younger feline's calm manner. "Check his pulse. I can't hear a heartbeat."

With a trembling hand, Sid reached out to check a pulse at Kenneth's neck. Young lad was right. He couldn't hear a heartbeat either. No pulse. Sid swallowed and a feline yowl of distress escaped him.

Valerie gave a harsh sob.

The doorbell tinkled. Gavin strode over to them, medical bag in hand. Charlie, one of the local cops, was with him.

"Crap." Gavin set down his bag and kneeled beside Kenneth. "What happened? He was ill, but not too bad when he left the surgery. I wasn't worried about him." He tested for a pulse and his frown intensified.

"He walked here." Ben's green eyes were full of fear.

"He clutched at his chest," Felix said.

Agnes clapped a hand over her heart, her green eyes echoing Sid's own unease. "Will he be all right?"

Gavin stood, his demeanor somber as he glanced at each of them with sorrow etched into his features. "I'm sorry. He's gone."

"Dead?" Sid whispered.

Agnes's eyes filled with tears. "Dead?"

"Yes, I'm so sorry," Gavin said. "I suspect it was his heart. I won't know for sure until I get him back to the surgery."

"What are we going to tell his family?" Valerie pulled off her glasses and wiped them free of tears with a paper napkin.

"I'll contact Laura," Charlie said. "She'll notify his family."

Felix called for Ramsey, the teenage shifter who was helping London in the kitchen. Numb at the suddenness of Kenneth's passing, Sid forced his trembling limbs to walk to the door. He held it open while Felix, Charlie, Ramsey and Gavin carried Kenneth from the café.

Tomasine Mitchell came to him and took his arm. "Come and sit with your friends. Emily keeps a bottle of whiskey out the back. I think you could do with a glass."

Sid allowed Felix's mate to guide him back to their table. His three friends had aged in the last five minutes, and he sank onto his chair, feeling every one of his years too.

Tomasine bustled over with a tray and four cups. "Don't tell anyone I've given you whiskey," she whispered. "I don't want to get into trouble."

"Thank you, lass," Sid said.

They waited until Tomasine left before picking up a cup each.

"What are we going to do without Kenneth?" Agnes asked, her voice full of anguish. "He's always been with us since we met at school."

Ben sighed, the sound heavy with pain. "We carry on. He'd hate to think we'd faltered because he wasn't here."

Valerie sniffed and wiped away a tear before it rolled down her cheek. "Fool man will haunt us if we don't do the right thing."

Sid barked out a hoarse laugh. "He'll probably haunt us anyway." He swallowed away the lump attempting to grow in his throat and lifted his cup. "Let's drink a toast to Kenneth. Go in peace, old friend."

"To Kenneth," the others chorused.

They sat in silence, each deep in their own thoughts.

Ben set his cup on the tabletop. "I'd better go. I promised my mate I wouldn't be late."

Valerie nodded. "I have a yearning to be with my family too. Are you ready to go, Agnes?"

"Yes." Agnes swallowed the last of her whiskey. "Sid?"

"I might sit a while longer." Sid waved off his friends and sipped more of his whiskey. Kenneth was gone. First Herbert and now Kenneth. He smiled faintly, recalling the mischief the six of them used to get up to when they were younger. At least Herbert wouldn't be alone now in that big savannah in the sky, and he took comfort from that fact.

He lifted his cup in salute. "Herbert, you look after Kenneth for us. Show him the ropes." Tears shrouded his sight until the entire café interior was a blur. "We haven't finished creating chaos here in Middlemarch, but soon. Soon, we'll join you for the next level of mischief." He swallowed. Once. Twice. "I miss you, old friend. You'd be so proud of your boys. So proud. They've grown into fine young men, and their mates are strong, independent women. Wouldn't surprise me if children come soon."

Sid smiled as he thought of children driving parents crazy with their antics. There would be love. He knew that. Herbert had done a good job with the Mitchell boys, and he and the other council members would leave the community in good shape to face the future.

One final toast. "Have fun up there, old friends. I'll see you soon." Sid drank the last of his whiskey, wiped his eyes and stood. He lifted his right hand in farewell to Tomasine and London and shuffled from the café to his farm vehicle. It had been a long day, and he wanted his family and his bed in that order. He needed a hug from his bonnie mate.

About Author

USA Today bestselling author Shelley Munro lives in Auckland, the City of Sails, with her husband and a cheeky Jack Russell/mystery breed dog.

Typical New Zealanders, Shelley and her husband left home for their big OE soon after they married (translation of New Zealand speak - big overseas experience). A twelve-month-long adventure lengthened to six years of roaming the world. Enduring memories include being almost sat on by a mountain gorilla in Rwanda, lazing on white sandy beaches in India, whale watching in Alaska, searching for leprechauns in Ireland, and dealing with ghosts in an English pub.

While travel is still a big attraction, these days Shelley is most likely found in front of her computer following another love - that of writing stories of contemporary and paranormal romance and adventure. Other interests include watching rugby (strictly for research purposes), cycling, playing croquet and the ukelele, and curling up with an enjoyable book.

Visit Shelley at her Website
www.shelleymunro.com

Join Shelley's Newsletter www.shelleymunro.com/newsletter

Visit Shelley's Facebook page
www.facebook.com/ShelleyMunroAuthor

Follow Shelley at Bookbub
www.bookbub.com/authors/shelley-munro

Also By Shelley

Paranormal

Middlemarch Shifters
My Scarlet Woman

My Younger Lover

My Peeping Tom

My Assassin

My Estranged Lover

My Feline Protector

My Determined Suitor

My Cat Burglar

My Stray Cat

My Second Chance

My Plan B

My Cat Nap

My Romantic Tangle

My Blue Lady

My Twin Trouble

My Precious Gift

Middlemarch Gathering
My Highland Mate
My Highland Fling

Middlemarch Capture
Snared by Saber
Favored by Felix
Lost with Leo
Spellbound with Sly
Journey with Joe
Star-Crossed with Scarlett

www.ingramcontent.com/pod-product-compliance
Lightning Source LLC
Chambersburg PA
CBHW052035240626
47153CB00006B/2085